THE ADVOCATE IN THE WILD

Boniface Ossai

Paperback Edition First Published in the United Kingdom
in 2017 by aSys Publishing

eBook Edition First Published in the United Kingdom
in 2017 by aSys Publishing

Second Edition Published in the United Kingdom
in 2021 by aSys Publishing

Cover: Adobe Stock

Illustrations: One Pixel (www.onepixel.com)

Disclaimer

This is a work of fiction. Names, characters, businesses, places,
events and incidents are either the products of the author's
imagination or used in a fictitious manner. Any resemblance to
actual persons, living or dead, or actual events
is purely coincidental.

ISBN: 978-1-913438-60-9
aSys Publishing

This book is dedicated in loving memory of my brother Felix Ossai. Felix will be deeply missed by the whole family.

This book wouldn't have been a success without the effort of my wife, Nkem, who worked tirelessly to ensure the success of this book, not to forget my children Ikechukwu
and Ifeanyichukwu.

Finally, a big thanks to my friend Mark Campbell for his immense contribution towards the success of this book.

CHAPTER

ONE

The Holiday

Professor Pratt Church is an animal rights advocate who's on his usual holidays to the Kenyan Wild Life Reserve. Interestingly, he went with his family this time. He'd his wife, Nora, his daughter, Eileen, and his son, Joe by his side, and the fun couldn't be any better. This family was having quite a nice time as they toured the grassland reserved for wildlife, in the tropics of Africa. The tour guide was on hand to transport them around as they move from one end of the forest to the other, enjoying the sight of wildlife in their natural habitat from a vantage position.

"I love seeing these Rhinos each time I come here," said Prof. Church.

"Mum, Dad, let's go over to the lions, we haven't spent enough time with the lions," said Eileen.

The Rhinos won Professor Church's admiration, and his heart sank because he was captivated by the Rhinos, and he suddenly turned to his wife, Nora. "Honey, isn't this beautiful? This is nature at work," he said. Nora nodded in affirmation, saying this is lovely, and no wonder her husband comes here every year, but without them most times.

Even though this trip was one among many and wasn't his first, the professor is always known to be carried away by the sight of these creatures doing their own thing in their natural habitat. His obsession overwhelms him and this obsession is unwittingly leading him down the garden path, and Nora knows about this and thought it wise to keep her husband on a tight leash.

Things suddenly got wacky and Nora got more than she bargained for immediately the professor opened his mouth next. "I feel like trading places with these Rhinos," the professor said jocularly. These utterances though not unexpected seem to set Nora on edge because she finds her husband's comment to be particularly lacking of wisdom and tried to put things back into perspective.

"What! Why would you say a thing like that?" she asked.

"Let me put it right, I'm jealous of these animals, and I love being around them at all times," said Prof. Church.

"You don't have to be jealous of animals, you're a human being, and I think you should control your obsession with these animals," said Nora.

This craving for the wild could unwittingly precipitate into a sickness of the heart because he might lose his mind, and it's now arguably obvious that Nora will never acquiesce any uncanny move that fans this craving, and she's now upfront about it.

Professor Church then steered the conversation away from his personal emotions to the welfare of these animals.

"Why shouldn't the preservation of these wonderful animals be everyone's priority?" the professor asked.

Nora and her husband are two peas in a pod but their differences always surface when it comes to talking about the amount of care given to wildlife in their natural habitat. "What makes you think they aren't protected? Somebody thought about protecting them, that's why we've this wild life reserve," she retorted.

"I want people to do more! I want to see these animals live forever and I want to help them do that," the professor exclaimed.

Nora burst into laughter as she listens to her husband's gaffe, it's like her attempt to slap down this line of conversation seemed not to have worked as he talks about his desires for the wildlife. "What makes you think you can help these animals live forever when yourself aren't even promised tomorrow?" asked Nora. The professor then used one of his hands to rub his head while holding a camera on the other, while Nora, in her limited mind, continues breaking the edges of her husband's obsession with the wild.

"Oh, you're right, it's just that I love to be around these animals at all times. I'll speak with one of these rangers to see the possibility of working as a volunteer here," he said.

"Aren't you taking this obsession too far, what about your job as a lecturer?" she asked. "Protecting these mammals is more important to me than protecting humans," he retorted.

The advocacy for the preservation of wildlife isn't something Nora intends to hold her husband's feet over the fire for, but saying he cares more for these animals than her and her children implies the cracks are now beginning to show and this got her all riled up. Sadly, this is just a peek into what's to come. "What about us, Joe, Eileen, and what about me, do you want to leave us and run off to some game reserve to work as a volunteer?" asked Nora.

Professor Church rubbed his head a second time and pulled his slightly grey beard. "Honey, you're right, my obsession for these mammals seem to be clouding my views," he said. Nora gave her husband a side-long glance as she thought to herself that this man is fast becoming a one-man three musketeers, with just an eye patch for three people.

"Dad, look over there," Joe pointed to some Giraffes. "Those are giraffes, let's go over to the giraffes," said Joe.

"Let's just take things one a time, we'll get there, and all your curiosity will be satisfied," said Prof. Church. As Prof Pratt Church and his family continued to enjoy their experience in the wildlife reserve, he met a known face from the past and there was a flicker of recognition, and that's Don Campbell, a forest ranger driving around the park. Don Campbell stopped his truck to exchange pleasantries with the professor and his family. "Hello Professor, how're you?" asked Don.

"I'm fine, Don, good to see you again and thank you for caring for these lovely mammals. I truly appreciate the job you're doing," said Prof. Church.

"Are these your wife and children?" asked Don.

"Of course, this is my wife Nora, my daughter Eileen, and my son Joe.

"Hello madam, good to see you. Your husband is a friend whose passion for the wild is known to many," said Don.

"Hello Don, how're you doing?" asked Nora.

"Nora was here with me five years ago," said the professor.

Don is used to the professor's visits to the park, but he's meeting Nora for the first time and judging Nora's passion for the wild, might not necessarily require her husband's obsession as a barometer for measurement.

"Does it mean she doesn't share your passion for the wild because I know you come around yearly and sometimes twice a year?" Don said.

"Err.., Nora shares my passion, but the intensity of our passion isn't the same," said Prof. Church.

"You're welcome professor, enjoy your stay," said Don.

Just as Don Campbell turned on the ignition of his truck to drive off, the Professor beckoned on him "Wait a minute, Don, is there room for volunteers?" he asked.

"Who wants to work as a volunteer?" asked Don.

"Me, I'm thinking of coming over to join you guys in protecting these wonderful animals," said Prof. Church.

This professor has an untamed passion for the wild, and sadly his appetite for the freedom the wild offers is everything but fascinating to his friends and family who thinks he's perhaps crazy. Nora immediately turned to her husband. "Honey, I think we just talked about this matter not long ago, and why're you still talking about this volunteering thing?" she asked.

"You're right, Nora. Don, please forget about it, I'm getting too carried away," said Prof. Church.

"Ok, enjoy your time in the park, professor," Don said and drives away.

Days later, while the spirit of holiday persists, the Professor was preparing to take his family on a visit to an old acquaintance who shares his passion for the wild. Unsurprisingly, the professor is making this visit interesting as he left them engrossed with deciphering what he has got wrapped under his sleeve, because he has a surprise for his family.

"Dad, where are you taking us?" asked Eileen.

"We're visiting Rudolph Pitt," said Prof. Church.

"That sounds strange; Mr Pratt is visiting Mr Pitt," said Joe in quite a jocular manner.

"Who's this Rudolph, and why the visit?" asked Nora.

"Rudolf is one of the Veterinary doctors working in the wild life reserve here in Kenya," said Prof. Church.

"Is there anything peculiar about him?" asked Eileen.

Prof Pratt Church kept the surprise up his sleeve and won't divulge any further clue. "It's all a surprise," he said.

It didn't take long before they arrived at Rudolph Pitt's apartment.

"Good to see you, Professor. Emilia told me she saw you and your family some days back?" said Rudolph.

"Meet my wife, Nora, my daughter, Eileen, and my son, Joe," said Prof. Church.

"You're welcome Nora, how's New York?" asked Rudolph.

"New York is fun, though there's more fun here," said Nora.

Rudolph Pitt seems to know why Pratt Church's family paid him a visit. Probably, Professor Church spoke to his friend, Rudolph, about it before leaving New York City. "I know why you're here, Professor," said Rudolph.

"Good you know why we're here, please take us to them," said Prof. Church.

Eileen seemed rattled by the fact that their host and her dad continued to speak in codes and this could spoil the fun for her. "Where's he taking us?" she asked. Interestingly, these two men aren't some kind of chauvinists doing their own thing, rather they're just men fervently committed to the preservation of wild life. Rudolph Pitt isn't speaking in codes after all, as he's quick to let the cat out of the bag, at least to keep the ambience friendly. "Your dad wants to introduce you to our cuddly baby lions," said Rudolph.

"You mean Lion cubs?" asked Joe.

"Of course, yes!" exclaimed Rudolph.

Eileen became excited and was eager to see these cuddly little big cats. "Where are they? I love to see them," she said.

Rudolf Pitt and his guests walked to the lion shelter behind the building, where he introduced them to these cuddly lion cubs. Unsurprisingly, Joe was the first to pick the cubs up as he carried them in his bosom.

"I like this one," said Joe.

"Be careful, so you don't get hurt," said Rudolph.

Funnily, Joe was quick to express his macho disposition as he quickly interjected. "These are baby lions, what's it to be careful of?" asked Joe.

"They could make you spend a month in the hospital, as small as they are," said Rudolph.

Eileen was also carrying one of the cubs. Unsurprisingly, she wants to do more than merely carrying the cubs in her bosom. "Can I feed her?" she asked.

"Of course yes, you can, but we use a feeding bottle to feed them with milk," he said.

After about an hour of nibbling and playing with the cubs, Eileen turned to Joe. "Joe, aren't you feeding yours?" she asked.

"I've had enough fun with these baby lions," said Joe.

"Should I get you something to drink? I've got drinks in the house," said Rudolph.

"A glass of Brandy will be fine," said Prof. Church.

After taking his friend's order, Rudolph turned to Nora "What about you Nora?" he asked.

"I don't mind a glass of red wine," she replied.

Professor Church and his family spent about two hours with Rudolph Pitt before returning to their lodge.

This holiday to Kenyan was quite exhilarating because it has in some ways knitted the bond in this family together, and after spending days enjoying all that the Kenya wildlife reserve has to offer, it's now time to return to the United States. Nora isn't particularly happy with her dawdling children because she's afraid they might miss their flight if they continue to hesitate. She decided to give them a little kick to hurry them up a bit, she then walked into Eileen's room and met her chatting on social media while nibbling on some nuts peculiar to Africa.

"Eileen, where's your brother? We're leaving in the next two hours," said Nora.

"Mum, I know, but it's Joe you should tell that to," said Eileen.

"Why should I be telling Joe and not you? I don't want any delay because you're used to spending so much time making up," said Nora. Passing the buck and sitting on the fence is Eileen's sensational approach to responsibility within the family and that's exactly what she just did as she passed the buck to her brother. Eileen insisted that she knew of their departure time, so they won't wait for her, she then hinted her mum that Joe is busy playing games on his phone, and he's the one she should be talking to. Nora then left Eileen and walked straight into Joe's room to hurry him up, but unsurprisingly, she found him rustling up some snacks and seated on the bed playing games on his phone. "Mum, I know we're leaving in two hours' time," he said.

"Then what are you still doing playing games on your phone?" she asked.

"Mum, it doesn't take time to get ready, it takes me two minutes only to wear my Jeans and shirt, and that's it," he said.

"The cab is already here, and I want you to move our luggage to the car, and that takes you more than two minutes," said Nora.

Moments later, they're all set and getting ready to depart, and ironically, all the others were by the cab ready to leave except Nora. Professor Church, Eileen and Joe were all by the cab now waiting for Nora. They waited for a while as Nora hesitated, but Eileen's whose patience grew thin then left to get her mum, and as she walked into her mum's room in protest. "We're all waiting for you," she said.

"Go back to the cab, I'm coming. I'll join you all in a minute," said Nora.

Interestingly, while the professor stood by the cab and waiting for his wife to join the pack, the professor saw some of the park Rangers leaving in a hurry. "Don, is anything the matter?" he asked.

"Yeah, we just got a message that one of the Rhinos has been attacked by poachers," said Don.

"Did they catch the poacher?" he asked.

"I don't think so, and that's what we're attempting to do. We'll be scanning the forest, to see if we can catch the perpetrators of this crime," said Don.

"Ok, I hope whoever is behind this is brought to book," said Prof. Church.

The news of this rhino's attack seemed to have touched some sore spot in the professor, and he watched as the rangers drove off, and it didn't take long before Nora joined her family members by the cab but noticed her husband's disposition was one to worry about. "Why're you looking so worried, is anything the matter?" asked Nora.

"A Rhino has just been attacked by poachers, and that saddens me greatly," said Prof. Church.

"Oh, that's bad! This is an ugly crime and I hope these poachers are caught." She then turned to her husband, honey, get in the cab, let's leave," said Nora. Nora doesn't have the talent of being a safe cracker to unravel the sloppy workings of her husband's heart, she watched helplessly as her husband sulked over this injured rhino. This time he isn't just sulking about the actions of poachers, and rather, he's taking step to do something about it.

"I can't continue with you until I'm certain this animal is safe," said Prof. Church.

"Honey, are you having a laugh or what? We're boarding within the next hour," said Nora. "Nora, I'm fully aware of our departure time, but I just can't run off with you and the kids while a Rhino is in a critical condition," the professor insists.

"Then allow the vets assigned to take care of these animals to do their job, where do you fit into all of this?" asked Nora. Sadly, Nora was irked by her husband's stubborn obsession with wildlife, and funnily, the professor isn't only talking the talk, but willing make himself available to work the work.

"They might need extra pair of hands in moving the Rhino to the place where she will be cared for," he said. Nora had rather not allow her husband stay back, she quickly interjected and stressed that the rangers are already there, she then urged him to allow the rangers to do their job. "We need to be on our way to the airport, let's not kill our time debating this," said Nora. Dereliction of duty is serendipitously something the professor finds to be quite riveting, and funnily, he isn't willing to pass the buck this time.

"Nora, you and the children can continue home, I'll reschedule my flight until this is sorted," said Prof. Church. Eileen wasn't particularly thrilled by her dad's excuses to stay behind as she watched her parents argue. She decided that convincing her dad to change course will require more than just hers mum's voice, and so, purposively decided to weigh in as she takes exception to her dad's decision.

"What do you mean we should go on without you, and why're you doing this, dad?" asked Eileen.

"I'm not doing anything, Eileen, an animal is down, and I think I should make myself useful," said Prof. Church.

"Why're you sounding as if you're captain America who wants to save the world and all the animals in it?" asked Joe.

"Eileen, please go with your mum, and I'll join you, maybe tomorrow or the day after," said Prof. Church.

"Dad, you're always like this, each time our fun becomes interesting, you definitely will come up with something to make the whole thing meaningless," said Joe.

"But you've had enough fun, joining you a day or two days later doesn't take away the fun you've had all these days," said Prof. Church.

Nora knew for sure that her husband isn't changing his position on this matter, particularly when his mind his made up, she was all teary-eyed as she dipped her hand into her bag and brought out her husband's travel document and handed it to the professor. "Take, that's your ticket and travel documents. You said tomorrow or a day after, I hope to see you then," said Nora. Even as the professor nervously awaits good news concerning the state of the Rhino in question, his daughter Eileen, decided to turn the heat on her mum for letting her dad off the hook easily.

"Mum, are you saying we should just return without dad?" asked Eileen.

"He has made his decision, and there's nothing we can do. Eileen, get in the car, and you Joe, get in, and let's go," said Nora.

"But mum...," Eileen interjected.

"Don't but... me, I want you in the car now," she stressed.

Eileen was hopping mad with her dad, yet she's handicapped because her mum has managed to shoot herself in the foot and had no choice but to get into the car since she wasn't able to win her dad. "Ok, bye dad," she said.

"Bye, honey, I'll join you guys as promised, thank you," said Prof. Church.

"Don't thank me! You're a very strange fellow," Nora said, as she entered the car and left to the airport.

Moments after his family left for the airport, the professor walked into the security unit within the park as he's eager to get his hands dirty. "Hello, I'm Professor Pratt Church," he said.

"Hello professor, I'm Greg Vincent, and I'm the supervisor," said Greg.

"I'm a wild life conservation advocate, a man who loves nature," said Prof. Church.

"I know who you're, professor, and your reputation precedes you. Though, we haven't had a one-on-one conversation but good to have you around," said Greg.

"Ok, that's good, please I'm supposed to return with my family to the United States, but I just heard the news of a Rhino being attacked by poachers," he said.

Greg Vincent was on hand to assuage the professor of his fears, and made him understand that another group of rangers will be joining the first team of respondents. "The animal is safe but injured, and we're sending another team to help in bringing the Rhino safely in for treatment," said Greg.

"Oh, thank goodness, and I'm happy the condition isn't critical, but can I join them, please?" asked Prof. Church.

James Kenyatta who was sat in the office, and also a security officer interjected and spoke to Greg in Swahili, a Kenyan language. "Be careful the way you let him into our operations before he starts saying negative things about how we work when he returns to his country," said James.

Greg Vincent turned to James in all fairness, and unwittingly dismissed any concerns of his, precipitated by the wrong assumption that he's giving the professor a blank cheque to poke his nose into their affairs. He then replied James in his usual Swahili language. "He's a man who loves the wild and loves nature as well, let's give him an opportunity to serve," said Greg. The professor stood there not knowing he's the subject of the conversation, he then innocently asked Greg what he thinks, and said he would love to join them."

"You can, they'll be here in a few minutes, and you'll join them," said Greg.

Minutes later, the professor and the team left the administrative department, as they drove into the wild and it didn't take long before they arrive at the scene of the crime, and interestingly, the rhino was in a stable condition. "Professor, you're here, I thought you were returning with your family to the United States?" asked Don.

"Of course yes, but I changed my mind when I heard of this sickening attack on the Rhino," said Prof. Church.

"Err.., that's good, though I realise you use every opportunity to express your love for the conservation of wild life," said Don.

"How's she?" asked Prof. Church.

"She's fine, just that she was hurt by the arrow the poachers shot at her," said Don.

"Did you succeed in catching the criminals responsible for this?" asked Prof. Church.

"No, they escaped, their intention was to kill the Rhino and cut off her horn, but they left when they noticed someone was approaching," said Don.

Prof Pratt Church watched as the doctors tended to the injured limb of the Rhino. "I'm here to give whatever help I can," he said.

An hour later the Rhino is on her feet.

"Is she ok?" asked Prof. Church.

"Yeah, she'll be fine, and her injury isn't a life threatening one," said Doctor Bruno, who's the lead Vet in the team.

This Rhino was the centre of attention as the emotional professor looked on as the Vet does his thing, and not long after the professor's team arrived the scene the rhino got back on its feet, and unsurprisingly, there's nothing left for the professor to do than to return to his hotel. Yet, the dream of being present and observe the Rhino return on her feet meant the professor has stunningly, realised his heart's desire. "Professor, you'll join your team back in the office, we're going on patrol, and will you still be around?" asked Don.

"I'll be around the rest of today, and I'll leave for the United States tomorrow," said Prof. Church.

As the professor turns to leave, Don commended him for his interest in helping them conserve the wildlife, saying his continued advocacy for the protection of wildlife around the world has been paying off. The professor considers the commendation as misplaced because he thinks he hasn't done enough to deserve a thank you, as he said his concern isn't just the wildlife within this reserve, rather he worries about other wildlife in forests that aren't protected.

"But you can't be everywhere professor! It's one step at a time," said Don.

"Yeah, you're right, just that I feel like I should be somewhere, protecting wildlife as well," said Prof. Church.

Don pressed on the professor, reminding him there's no need hibernating in the grassland of Africa, and volunteering, as he insists, the professor is an advocate, and the job he's doing has a wider reach than merely protecting a tiny section of the world's forest.

The professor was quite presumptuous as he pontificates on the subject, he was a bit bossy and quite opinionated. He didn't hesitate to pour out his heart, saying it doesn't look like his advocacy is going far enough, and if that continues to be the case then action should follow. Don on the other hand, is someone who doesn't believe in absolutes. "People are hearing you, and changing their ways on how they treat wild animals. You're impacting more people than you think, professor," said Don.

"Ok, Don, our vehicle is about to return to the office, thank you for the opportunity to help," said Prof. Church.

"Thank you, Professor," said Don.

After his conversation with Don, the professor entered the truck and minutes later the second rescue team returned and as the professor alighted from the vehicle, Greg Vincent was on hand waiting. "How did it go, professor?" asked Greg.

"I'm glad the injury wasn't life threatening; the Rhino is already on her feet and she'll be fine soon," said Prof. Church.

"How did you feel about being a part of the rescue team?" asked Greg.

"Oh, I feel so great, and I'm happy the animal is back on her feet, thank you for giving me the opportunity to give back," said Prof. Church.

Greg assumed a quite humbling posture as he insists he should be the one thanking the professor because his advocacy has greatly reduced the activities of poachers.

It's sad to say that the professor has been plagued by the needling thought that he isn't doing enough to protect the wild. This sadly, has kept him perceptually anxious that wildlife is exposed to the dangers of creepy poachers lurking in the shadows of the grassland. Greg actually did a great job assuaging the professor of his worries, and it did got to him.

"Are you sure I'm making such an impact? Because I don't seem to feel it," asked Prof. Church.

"You are, just that you want to see the results all at once," said Greg.

"Ok, I think I should be going, thank you," said Prof. Church.

CHAPTER
TWO

The Kenyan Drama

Now that the Rhino is back on its feet, there isn't anything keeping the professor behind and dawdling around in the Kenya wildlife reserve. The next day Professor Pratt Church had to return to his family, and it's now time to head for the airport. Unsurprisingly, while he was in a cab heading for the airport, he spotted a man using a Baboon for a road-show. "Stop now! Driver, I say stop now," said Prof. Church. Interestedly, the cab driver suddenly slowed down in the middle of the speed lane, thinking there's immense danger ahead. Sadly, this cab driver is experiencing the professor's gritty side on the fast lane.

"Is anything the matter, I'm in the fast lane, and why're you asking me to stop abruptly?" asked the Cab driver.

"I don't care what lane you're in, just stop the car now," the professor retorted. The driver is now in a bind, and professor's feisty protest sounds vaguely like a threat, but this isn't directed at the cab driver but to Mr. Ringo, as they call him.

"Ok, I'm already stopping but aren't you going to the airport?" asked the Cab driver.

"I need to sort this mess out right away, but can't you see that!" exclaimed Prof. Church. Sadly, the cab driver looked around but found nothing he could lay his finger on that can best be described to be strangely out of the blue, that would warrant such jumpiness from his enlightened passenger. The professor was quick to throw his toys out of the pram, and disappointingly, he was quite childish at it.

"See what! I don't understand what you're talking about. I've looked around and can't see anything that warrants this seriousness," said the cab driver.

The driver slowed down and stopped eventually. "Please, reverse your car, can't you see that Baboon being abused?" asked Prof. Church. It didn't take long before the cab driver realised what the professor was alluding to, and unwittingly, the cab driver burst into laughter and trivialised the whole repartee. "Oh my God! You're talking about the baboon. With your reaction, I expected to see something more serious going wrong," said the cab driver.

"Isn't that a criminal act enough for you to worry? Give me a few minutes, I'll be back," the professor retorted. Juxtaposing the professor's facial disposition, the cab driver suggests the professor's action doesn't fit the situation on ground.

"I don't think that's a good idea," said the Cab driver.

The professor stepped out of the cab, and hurtled along as he intends to address this glaring abuse of a baboon in the streets of Nairobi head on, against the wisdom of his cab driver. He then walked straight to James Kampar, the owner of the show.

"What do you think you're doing?" the professor queried.

"I don't understand, what are you talking about?" asked Kampar.

"You're abusing the Baboon, and that's a criminal offence," said the professor.

"How come it's a criminal offence to use my Baboon for my show? This is my show, and my Baboon is happy, and that's why they call me Mr. Ringo," said Kampar.

"This foolishness has to stop!" exclaimed Prof. Church.

The exchange between Professor Church and Mr. Ringo became heated and went on unabated, yet seem not to yield any result. The cab driver was worried sick that this could precipitate into a fighting match as they went back and forth trying to prove their point, and funnily, the professor decided it's time to finally free the baboon from its captors. Just as the professor went ahead to forcefully unchain the Baboon, a scuffle between the professor and Mr Ringo ensued.

"I don't care what you think, and I'll beat you up if you don't show some respect," said Kampar.

Things quickly precipitated into a scene and James Kampar didn't take the professor's interference well, because he considers the professor's accusations as utter nonsense, and fortunately, while the brouhaha continued, the professor felt fortunate as a police patrol van passing by came to the scene. Professor Church was quick on his feet to approach the police officer, as he told them this man is breaking the law, and he wants them to arrest him.

"What has he done, and what law has he broken?" asked the Police Officer.

"He's abusing the rights of this Baboon, and it's against the law," said Prof. Church.

In a bizarre move, the police officer who's expected to put James Kampar in cuffs, wants to know what law the professor claimed was broken. "Do you know that what's illegal where you come from might not be illegal here?" said the Police officer.

"I don't think so, officer, but he's breaking the law, this can't happen in the United States," said Prof. Church.

"Are you trying to teach me my job or what?" asked the Police officer.

The professor continued pacing up and down, and sadly, the police officer finds the professor's restiveness to be vaguely unpleasant. He was quite tacky in his tone and effort to calm the irate professor who was busy flouncing around was futile, and this left the police officer quite irritated. The professor then turned the focus away from James Kampar to the dawdling police officer.

"I'm letting you know what you should do, just do it and stop being lazy," said Prof. Church.

"You'll have to control yourself if you don't want me to arrest you, and I suppose you know I'm aware that people domesticate animals in the name of pets in the United States," said the Police Officer.

"But we don't abuse these animals, we keep them as pets and treat them as family members, we eat together and even share a bed with them," said Prof. Church.

This Police Officer seemed not ready to take lectures from this foreigner, it's like he had an axe to grind and asked Professor Church if those who keep pythons as pets eat with them and treat them as family members.

"Officer, this man, Mr Ringo or whatever he calls himself should be in handcuffs by now, and I don't know what you're waiting for?" said Prof. Church. Unsurprisingly, the Police Officer finds this feisty professor insufferable, and seemed to have had enough of the professor's kerfuffle.

"Gentleman, if you don't leave now, I'll charge you with public misconduct," said the Police officer.

This is wrong, and I'll take it up with the authorities," said Prof. Church, as he flounced off and returned to the cab, then continued to the airport. Oops, that didn't go well, the cab driver thought to himself, and yet kept quiet so as not to inflame the already angry professor any further.

Somehow, some bystanders who find the drama to be of interest filmed the drama between Mr Ringo and Professor Church and posted it on YouTube. Somehow, the press serendipitously obtained a copy of the video, and it was aired on the news, and titled: the Kenyan Baboon drama.

Eileen was the first to see the news of the Kenyan drama involving her dad, and rushed to the kitchen. "Mum come quickly they're showing dad on the television, dad is in the news," said Eileen.

Nora rushed to the living room following Eileen from behind and Joe equally followed. "Oh, that's really your dad, what has he done this time to take up the headlines!" exclaimed Nora.

"He was fighting with the owner of a Baboon because he felt the Baboon was being abused," said Eileen.

By the time they all assembled at the living room, the news concerning the professor was almost over, and all they got was just a peek, but that didn't stop Joe who quickly brought out his phone and began searching. "They said the video of the drama between dad and the owner of the show is on You Tube, and that's what I'm searching," said Joe.

"Your dad is taking this animal-rights thing too far," said Nora.

In a twinkle of an eye Joe found something. "Mum this is it," said Joe, he then played the video repeatedly as they watched the drama.

"I just don't understand why your dad is behaving like this. First, he wants to help a Rhino, now he's saving a Baboon, who knows where he's now and what animal he'll be saving as we speak?" asked Nora.

Eileen had blamed her mum all along from the very moment she handed the professor's travel documents to him to enable him stay back, she thinks her mum's posturing wasn't well choreographed and now that failure is laid bare before their eyes.

"Mum I told you it wasn't a good idea to leave dad behind, but you didn't listen," said Eileen.

"Mum, I suggest you give him a call, let's know where he's so we'll be sure we aren't returning to Kenya in search of him," said Joe.

Nora was quite pensive as she reflects on the content of the Kenyan drama YouTube video, she quickly picked up her phone and dialled her husband's phone continually, but sadly, the line failed to connect. "The line isn't connecting, he should be on his way home," she said.

"But mum, that incident happened just two hours before his departure time, and are you sure he'll be able to make it?" asked Eileen.

"That drama didn't last more than thirty minutes, so I'm certain he will make it," said Nora.

It's now glaringly obvious that the gesture of rescuing a baboon wasn't well received by the professor's family, because they were all cagey watching their dad create a scene in the streets of Nairobi.

"This shouldn't be a surprise to us, we all know that when it comes to animals, dad is always upfront and acts as Captain America who wants to save all the animals on planet earth," said Eileen.

Joe interjected in his attempt to give a piece of his mind, "One thing I know for sure," he then turned around and looked at his mum, then paused for a moment. "I know, mum wouldn't want me to say it," said Joe.

Sadly, Nora wasn't up for any clunky joke and her disposition changed immediately, as she fixed her gaze at Joe without batting an eyelid because she took an exception to Joe's comment. "If you know I wouldn't want you to say whatever you want to say, then don't say it," said Nora.

"I told you, mum, you don't always like us speaking our minds and saying the truth," said Joe.

"What's it you want to say?" Eileen asked Joe, she then turned to her mum in a show of passive support for Joe. "Mum, let him say what he wants to say," said Eileen.

"All I'd wanted to say is that it's arguably obvious that dad loves animals more than us," he said.

Nora got all riled up by Joe's remark, because she finds it itchy in her ears, even though she knew in her heart that her son is right. Things suddenly became icy within the home as Nora insists on her eccentric parental style where children are seen but not heard, and insists it's better for her to live in denial than to give fuel to her son's assertion. "Joe, I've warned you never to say a thing like that in my hearing, don't push me, ok!" Nora retorted.

"Ok, sorry mum," said Joe.

While in the plane, Professor Pratt Church happened to run into Dr Alice McDonald, a climate change advocate. Dr. Alice was already seated when Professor Church walked in and was trying to locate his seat. "Oh, Professor Church how're you doing?" she asked.

"Dr. Alice, good to see you, it's been quite a while," he said.

"When was the last time we saw each other?" she asked jocularly.

"That must be the last G8 summit when we were pushing the climate change agenda," said Prof. Church.

While the pair exchanged pleasantries the professor serendipitously realised his seat is right next to Dr. Alice's and without dawdling any further he made himself comfortable as he took his seat. They continued chatting away, and catching up on their achievements on global agendas.

"Then I'm lucky to have you cross my path today, and this coincidence will be to my advantage," said Dr. Alice.

"Then you've got me, is there anything happening?" asked Prof. Church.

"We're holding a workshop on climate change and the conservation of nature, and I'll want you to take a session during the workshop," she said.

"Where's it taking place?" he asked.

"Oh, we're holding the workshop in Washington DC," she said.

"Ok, I'll go through my Itinerary and get back to you," said Prof. Church.

"Please Professor, I wouldn't want a no for an answer," she pleads.

"Don't worry, I'm certain the answer won't be a no!" he exclaimed. While the conversation was going on the hostess interrupted, as she wheels refreshment along the aisle of the plane.

"Hello, what can I offer you?" asked the hostess.

Professor Pratt pointed to a menu in the hostess' trolley. "That meal contains beef, doesn't it?" he asked.

"Yes, it does," said the hostess.

"Then I want that, and possibly with some red wine in my glass," said Prof. Church.

"Do you have white meat, like chicken? That's what I want," said Dr. Alice.

The hostess served the pair and then moved on to the seat in front of them, allowing the professor and her animal rights friend to continue their conversation.

"Professor, I'm surprised you still eat meat," said Dr. Alice.

"Why're you surprised at my choice of meal! And what should I be eating then?" he asked.

"Sorry, I thought you're a vegetarian," she said.

"Why would you think that? The last time we met at the G8 summit, we shared a table together, and I had beef in my meal," he said.

"That was many years ago, then your interest in the conservation of wildlife hadn't peaked to this point," she said.

"I get it, there's this general belief that most wild life conservation advocates should be vegetarian," said Prof. Church.

"Of course, yes, from my observation, I've just realised it isn't always so, advocacy is about humane treatment of animals," said Dr. Alice.

The pair chatted all through their flight until they arrived New York City, and it didn't take long after their arrival at the airport that Professor Church alighted from the cab in front of his house. Funnily, the professor tried using his key to gain access to his apartment but sadly, it was bolted from inside, he then decided to knock, before Nora came to open the door. "Hey honey, you're back," said Nora.

"Yeah, I'm back, and it's good to be home," said Prof. Church.

"Were you able to reschedule your flight?" she asked.

Nora followed her husband from behind as she asked him about his trip, but the professor is more inclined to settle in than take questions, as he makes himself comfortable on the sofa.

"No, I couldn't, by the time we were through with the Rhino; the opportunity to reschedule was over," he replied.

"I thought as much, and that's an extra cost," said Nora.

"Yes, it is, but it was worth it," said Prof. Church.

"How did it go with the Rhino?" asked Nora.

"Err.., thank goodness, she was slightly injured but was back on her feet after receiving medical attention," said Prof. Church.

Unsurprisingly, in her usual display of stoicism and disposition of keeping things under wraps, Nora asked her husband too many questions about his flight, and obviously left the Kenyan baboon drama out, and this isn't because she forgot, but her failure to discuss the obvious.

"Did they catch the poachers responsible for the Rhino's injury?" asked Nora.

"No, they escaped as they realised rangers were approaching the scene, and that was why the poachers didn't succeed with the Rhino," said Prof. Church.

While Nora intends to leave something out, there are those who aren't keen to keep certain conversation under wraps, and as the professor and Nora continued their conversation, Eileen and Joe walked into the living room, and without the platitudes of exchanging pleasantries. "Dad, what's it with the Baboon?" asked Eileen.

"What Baboon are you talking about?" asked Prof. Church.

"The drama between you and the owner of a Baboon was aired on the television during the news here in the United States," said Nora.

"What! That happened in Kenya and not here in the United States, and how did they get the video of the scene?" the professor asked.

"Dad, it was uploaded on YouTube, and over a half million people have viewed it." The professor was surprise at how soon news travel, and perceived his children are making a mockery of the drama, as Joe played the footage for his dad to see for himself. "Look at this, dad," said Joe.

In a face-saving mission, the professor quickly turned the conversation around and had no qualms telling his family that it's good the scene was aired in the news as it will enlighten more people about what it means to abuse animals in the name of domestication. Now that the professor took the bait, Nora didn't hesitate in awfulizing her husband's indiscretion.

"But..., don't you think you're going about this the wrong way? Causing a scene like this one is an embarrassment to your family," said Nora.

Having his foot in his mouth isn't something new for an animal rights advocate itching to precipitate international conversation on animal rights, but it's like the professor will need a lot of rabbit foot to make the ugliness of this one go away. "Don't you think your action was awful? My friends who watched it were calling me and making a jest of me," said Joe.

"Dad, people didn't see it the way you think, they see it as an American professor causing a scene that's an embarrassment to the country," said Eileen.

"But why should the news report it differently?" asked Prof. Church.

"Honey, you 're a professor, there are more dignified ways of handling such matters and not the way you went about it, I even tried to call you to be sure you aren't missing your flight," said Nora.

The professor had to find a way to bring an end to this conversation because he perceived that his family enjoyed feasting on topics of this nature, and he's no longer comfortable with the feeding frenzy, particularly one in which his obsession for animals seem to make a fool out of him. "I've heard enough. Eileen, get me a glass of cold water," said Prof. Church.

"Ok dad," she said.

Now that the Professor's holiday to Kenyan has ended in a rather bizarre note, it's now time to return to his work as a university lecturer. While in the university campus the next day, he met Professor Stone Walker, a fellow lecturer who's also a close friend and sometimes a confidant.

"Hello, Pratt, how was your family holiday?" asked Prof Walker.

"Err.., the holiday couldn't have been any better because it was fun-filled and interesting, just that I couldn't make it to the university yesterday," said Prof. Church.

Professor Stone Walker became jocular, and said he doesn't think it was as much fun as he just told him, and Professor Church finds this to be hysterical. "What a conclusion! You didn't travel with us, so what makes you suggest a thing like that?" asked Prof. Church. Unsurprisingly, Professor Stone Walker didn't just draw his conclusion in a whim, and he's funnily among those privileged to watch his friend's surreal Kenyan brouhaha and finds it distasteful. Professor Walker was particularly unimpressed that a professor of Pratt's calibre should condescend as low as engaging in street scuffle.

"I'm not suggesting, the video on YouTube suggests you were chasing owners of domesticated animals around in Kenya," replied Prof. Walker. "But that isn't what the video said, you're making a mockery out of the video," said Prof. Church.

"Then what's it with the video? At least you deserve to be heard," said Prof. Walker. Conversations between these two friends have the tendency of reflecting the cracks in their philosophies about life, yet their friendship never gets sour because nothing is taken to heart. Professor Church retorted that he only tried to stop the man from abusing the Baboon, and sadly, he stuck to his guns insisting that using the Baboon to entertain people is a form of abuse. "Your poorly choreographed drama has ignited a national reaction, with many deriding your action in Kenya," said Prof Walker.

Professor Church wasn't quite so defensive of his actions, neither is he on the offensive, as he stood on the fence expressing surprise at the national furore over his attempt to stop a man from abusing a Baboon. Yet, Professor Walker continued to toe his earlier assertion as he presses home the awfulness of the drama, insisting that the society decried his friend's action in Kenya.

Unsurprisingly, Professor Church isn't particularly bothered about what others think, provided his action precipitates international action on animal conservation. "My actions will only open doors for discussions that'll give room for international action," said Prof. Church. "Are you implying your acts of brigandary will shape thematic intellectual discussions on wildlife conservation?" asked Prof Walker.

"Of course, yes, but why the cantankerous conclusions?" asked Prof. Church.

"I considered you to be a balanced character, except you want to play to the gallery. Stop being a new kind of joke, Pratt," Prof Walker said and laughed.

Professor Walker felt the need to impress on his friend who isn't keen to listen to what close associates felt about his colossal misdemeanour. Sadly, his tough talks seem not to make any in-roads into Pratt's mindset because Pratt was quick to shirk these concerns irrespective of how it impacts on his impeccable academic career.

The army of critics within his close circle seem not to make this error of judgement any easier for the Professor, and awfulizing his action is all he gets from friends who he thought should support him. He suddenly became irritated and asked Professor Walker if he just laughed to scoff and belittle his actions.

"Of course not, I laughed because I considered your actions a charade," said Prof Walker.

Sadly, Professor Church finds his friend's attack overbearing, and in a sudden turn of events decided to own up to his lack of judgement in the Kenyan drama. Even in his admission of error of judgement, Pratt insists he hates people with unscrupulous and sinister intentions towards wildlife.

"Such issues should be handled with the Kenyan authorities and not by engaging in street scuffles," said Prof. Walker.

"You're right; maybe I didn't handle the whole thing very well, but I don't need to be unnerved," said Prof. Church.

"The vice chancellor wants to have words with you," said Prof. Walker.

"Ok, I think it's best I see him after my lectures," said Prof. Church.

Professor Pratt Church hurried to deliver his lecture before attending to the call of the university's Vice Chancellor. Funnily, Professor Church entered the class and realised all the students were on YouTube playing the video of the altercation between him and the Baboon owner in Kenya. The professor then walked to the front of the class and wrote the topic for the day on the board, and yet didn't get the attention of his students as they were still consumed with his Kenyan stunt on YouTube. "Today we're looking at the impact of climate change on the Arctic," said Prof. Church.

While the professor remained in the front of the class waiting to gain their attention, suddenly, John Calvin, the cheeky one, raised his hand. "Sir, sorry, but we were all expecting you to address the Baboon incident in Kenya," he said.

"Ok, but what've my actions in Kenya got to do with class work?" asked Prof. Church. Some of the cheeky students in the class burst into laughter, in a subtle mockery of the professor's action. "Janet raised her hand up and stood up. "Professor, you're our lecturer and news making the rounds is that our professor is crazy, so we all want to know why you did that, so we can defend our professor, even before our parents," she said.

"But what makes you students think you should be the ones defending my actions? And I can see that you're all on YouTube watching the Kenyan drama," the professor said.

"Professor, what really happened? We all want to know," asked Calvin

It's now glaringly obvious to the professor that the students aren't willing to mind their business, and the day's lecture won't sink in while this elephant is still in the room, the professor then decided to address the obvious.

"Ok, we'll put today's topic aside and talk about the Kenyan Baboon drama as the news headlines described it," said Prof. Church.

"Is it wrong to domesticate animals?" asked David.

"Domesticating an animal is one thing, and using the animal for activities that could be against the animal's will, is another," the professor said.

"How do you know, using the Baboon for show is against her will, even when the baboon is well catered for, as Mr. Ringo stated in the video on YouTube?" asked Janet.

"A lot of animals don't like being paraded in that manner, which makes Mr. Ringo's actions wrong," said Prof. Church.

"Professor, you should've handled things differently, I suppose, considering your level of exposure and education," said David.

"Sincerely, I was carried away, I acted on impulse as opposed to reason, and if given another opportunity I would handle such a matter differently," the professor said.

After taking out time to satisfy his students' curiosity, the class became calmer, and then the professor moved on to the topic for the day. Immediately after lectures the Professor went straight to answer to the Vice-Chancellor's call. Sadly, the Vice Chancellor was telling-off the landscaping engineer for the slow pace of work, and Professor Church had to step aside and wait while the Vice Chancellor had conversation with Billy Guy.

Professor Church walked in immediately Billy guy finished having a conversation with the Vice Chancellor and stood right opposite him. "Professor, you sent for me?" he said.

"Of course, I did, are you just resuming work? Because I said you should see me immediately you arrive," asked Prof Scowl.

"No, I resumed this morning and was told you wanted to see me, but I had to postpone my appointment with you until after my lectures," replied Prof. Church.

"Pratt, what was that?" asked Prof Scowl.

"What are you talking about, Professor? I don't seem to be following," said Prof. Church.

"The Kenyan drama, what was that all about and why would you engage in a public show of shame?" asked Prof. Scowl.

Professor Church laughed, as he attempts to make light of this drama that have touched the nerves of those associated to him, he then became silent momentarily like a man who have just lost track of time. "But when does trying to stop people abusing an animal become a show of shame as you've just put it?" he asked. Professor Church seemed to forget he isn't just some guy in the street. He's a respected academia whom the world holds on high esteem and expects some level of decorum from. Interestingly, the Vice Chancellor isn't letting him off easily, he then prodded him with further questions.

"When did you become a Professor who forgets civility and decency, and condescends to an animalistic level?" asked Prof Scowl.

Realising the invitation by the Vice Chancellor was to give him the short end of the stick, Professor Church wasn't particularly happy with the tough talk coming from his boss, but he'd no choice but to take it on the chin. It's like his boss was keen to wipe off the cheeky grin on his face.

"Why this furore over an attempt to stop a man from abusing a Baboon?" asked Prof. Church.

"Aren't you being hubristic?" asked Prof. Scowl.

"Hubris, no, not at all," he replied.

"Pratt, your action does not only reveal a lot of absurdities, but a case of brazen crass and monumental fanaticism," said Prof. Scowl.

For all it's worth, the welcome from holiday he's supposed to get from his boss, is now a matter of tough talking, and this animal right advocate thinks his boss is taking the proverbial in the manner he's going about this. Even as he tries to wriggle himself out of this fiasco by claiming the victim, the Vice Chancellor doesn't seem willing to let him off easily without tightening the screws on this animal right professor a little longer.

"Where's all this scorn coming from?" said Prof. Church.

"I'm not pouring scorn on you, and it seems to me it'll be an arduous task convincing you that I'm being sincere," Prof Scowl retorted.

"I know you're an animal conservation advocate, but you should as well remember that you're first an ambassador of this university, and we can't afford the name of our university being in the headlines over issues of mockery," said Prof Scowl.

"Are you saying advocating for the conservation of wildlife is wrong or what?" asked Prof. Church.

"You've always advocated the conservation of wild life, and I've never in any way stopped you, rather I've supported you," said Prof Scowl.

The tensed conversation seemed to be thawing as these two professors relieve themselves by getting their concerns off their chests, and frayed nerves are now becoming calmer as the tone of their conversation suddenly becomes a bit cordial.

"Then, why're you blowing hot and cold, I really don't get you?" asked Prof. Church.

"Are you telling me the way you were fighting in the streets of Nairobi over a Baboon is the right thing to do?" Prof Scowl queried further. "Actually, I should've handled the matter differently," he replied. "If you had handled the matter differently, maybe you would've gotten a better outcome, compared to that in which the police were threatening to arrest you over your conduct," said Prof. Scowl.

"Though, I acted on impulse, but next time I'll handle things better," said Prof. Church.

Interestingly, people exchange pleasantries before going into the crux of the matter, Professor Scowl decided to do things the other way round this time, as he chose to hit the nail on the head before exchanging pleasantries with Professor Church.

"Good, how was your family holiday? How're Nora and the kids, did they return with you because I didn't see them in that Kenyan drama video?" asked Prof. Scowl.

"The holiday was fun, just that Nora and the kids returned a day before me," he replied.

"I gave a circular to your Dean, take a look at it and get back to me," said Prof. Scowl.

"Ok, I'll do that," he replied with a smile, then left.

CHAPTER
THREE
The Advocacy

The Workshop in Washington DC

Dr Alice: Ladies and gentlemen, fellow advocates, for the past three days we've been doing nothing other than discussing climate change and the conservation of wildlife. We've looked into how the activities of man have impacted on nature and how we can help salvage the situation to ensure the continued existence of us humans.

Washington DC knows you're here, and this workshop has been described as a big success, but before we formally draw the curtain on this workshop, I'll like to invite Professor Pratt Church to give us some words of encouragement.

Prof. Church: Ladies and gentlemen and every other person out there, I want to bring to your knowledge that climate change isn't rhetoric. We need to manage our environment and our activities that impact on nature to ensure our continued survival. We need to manage our plastic waste, and recent research has discovered about five trillion pieces of plastics in our oceans. We also need to ensure that the conservation of wildlife is our priority because they all have a role they play in balancing the works of nature.

Recently we had news of a dead Whale off the coast of Norway with so much plastic waste in its stomach.

For you my fellow advocates, I know it hasn't been easy, while our efforts towards the conservation of nature and wildlife have been met with fractious antagonism, I must also confess that a morale depleting reaction from world powers makes the fight against poachers more difficult.

We must continue to talk because our commitment and zeal towards the conservation of wildlife must remain unwavering. For those of you who believe in climate change, please continue to work with us, but for those of you who see climate change as a mere rhetoric, please change your mentality and work with us to help balance nature. Thank you.

The Washington DC workshop was a big success and weeks after the workshop, Prof. Church walked into the Vice Chancellor's office. "Hello Professor," said Prof. Church.

"Hello Pratt, how're you doing?" asked Prof Scowl.

"I'm fine Professor, I know we don't see eye to eye on a lot of things, but there's something I want to inform you about," said Prof. Church. The Vice Chancellor stopped taking notes and fixed his gaze on Professor Church as he attempt to discuss the matter at hand.

"I hope the matter you're bringing up isn't one of those things we don't see eye to eye on?" asked Prof Scowl.

"I wouldn't know because we haven't talked on this subject before. I want to compete in the game of archery in the next sports competition," said Prof. Church.

Professor Scowl grimaced, and looked down into the file on his desk, to at least give himself a break, even as he fiddles with his pen. He then raised his head to address Professor Church's request. "How old are you, Pratt?" asked Prof Scowl.

"I'm fifty-eight, is anything the matter?" asked Prof. Church.

"Why would it be you indicating interests in the university games that are meant for students?" asked Prof. Scowl.

Professor Church seemed to be needled by the fact that his conversation with his boss seems to always go south of late. So, he quickly interjected and said he's well aware that the university games are meant for students, and that's not where his interest lies. Sadly, Professor Church's facial disposition suggests he's being unnecessarily tackled by his boss without the privilege of being heard, and funnily, Professor Scowl got the message, yet Professor Church still has a lot of explaining to do.

"Then, where and what tournament do you intend to compete in?" asked Prof. Scowl.

"I'm talking about the national sports festival," he replied.

"Of all the sports on earth, why archery and why not other sports?" asked Prof Scowl. The Vice chancellor couldn't get his head around why this rustic animal right professor suddenly found love in the tracks in the name of sport. Funny enough, Professor Church is young and wild at heart despite being perceived differently.

"I grew up in South Africa, and I used to join my dad for hunting, that was where I developed the skills, and I'm good at it, you know," said Prof. Church.

A white American professor with attachment to Africa makes this professor to be a rather strange fellow, and everything about him is odd, and this includes his taste in sport.

"Then let's call that a perfect coincidence," said Prof. Church.

Professor Scowl chuckled as he promised to be of assistance to Professor Church since this is possibly the one thing they could see eye-to-eye on.

"Thank you," Prof. Church said as he left the office.

Later that evening, Professor Church walked into the house from work and met his family watching the television, and finds it exciting to break the news of his indication of interest in the national sport festival. "Honey, welcome," said Nora.

"Honey, guess what?" asked Prof. Church.

"Hmm, you're going for another workshop," she said.

"No, who else can guess?" the professor asked.

"I can, dad," said Eileen.

"Ok Eileen, try," he said.

"We're going on another holiday to Kenya," said Eileen.

"That would've been nice though, but you missed it," said Prof. Church.

"Dad, what's it, then?" asked Joe.

The professor decided to break the guess since his family members aren't particularly thrilled with his guessing game.

"I'm taking part in the national sports festival," he said.

"As a sports official, or what?" asked Nora.

"As a competitor," the professor said and then smiled.

"Wow, wow, dad is now out for another joke, and I can't be part of this," said Joe, who's always on a different path with his dad, as he walks away. Interestingly, Eileen and Nora stayed back after Joe stood up and walked away. Joe is unfortunately an arrogant person walking about, shoulder high, with a chip the size of New York on his shoulder. For all it's worth, Joe is someone who unwittingly owns his own truth, and that makes him quite an unbearable person, and this guy is damaged goods, sort of.

"Dad, don't disappoint us, we don't want any more shame," said Eileen.

"Who's talking about shame here, this conversation is over," said Nora.

"Don't worry, I'll win, and you'll all be proud of me," said Prof. Church.

It's been seven months since his return from Kenya, Professor Pratt Church was leafing through the pages of wildlife news, and was shocked to be faced with the sad news that poachers have killed the very Rhino he stayed back to rescue in Kenya seven months ago. This sad news got to him, and made him quite emotional that he'd to cancel the rest of his lectures for the day, and left the University. It didn't take long before the professor walked through the door into the house from work, and sadly, his wife is quick to decipher what his facial expression meant. "Honey, why is your face like that? You look so depressed," he said.

"Good you noticed I'm looking so off, and that's because I'm actually unhappy," he said.

"Is there any problem in school, are the students giving you problems?" she asked.

"No, but this is a dastardly act, and it's horrible, Nora, I'm sick to my stomach," he retorted. Sadly, Nora watched helplessly at the idiotic grim on her husband's face as he displayed hissy fit with screams of blue murder, his expression screams, murder, murder. She was lost as to what the problem with her husband was, as he has said nothing despite the furious outburst expressing his disappointment.

"What's it, honey? You're only expressing your frustration, but you haven't said what the problem is," said Nora.

"I just read from a wildlife magazine that poachers have killed a Rhino in the Kenyan wild life reserve," said Prof. Church.

"Oh my God! That's bad, but your countenance won't solve this ugly crime, your advocacy is what will do the magic, and it's already doing that," said Nora.

"Just that the news mentioned one striking detail about the dead Rhino and that's what makes me get more upset," said Prof. Church.

The death of this particular Rhino actually yanked the professors' psychological chain, and Nora's sweet talking might not do the trick of soothing the professor's emotional trauma.

Nora listened with keen interest trying to figure out what the striking detail that got her husband all riled up was. It didn't take long before he laid it bare before her that the news emphasized that the dead Rhino was attacked by poachers some months back, in which his hind foot was injured.

Nora quickly worked out the puzzle in her head, and it didn't take time before she asked her husband if he's suggesting that it's the same Rhino he stayed back to save in Kenya when they went on holiday months back that just got killed.

"Yes, that's what I think it is," said Prof. Church.

"This means your attempt to save the Rhino was in vain, and why're these poachers doing this?" asked Nora.

"I don't think they've enough hands to help them protect these animals," he said.

With her husband feeling so exasperated, this news is fast turning into a wild wind, and to slow things down a bit, Nora had to urge her husband not to rush into the conclusion that it's the same Rhino that just died. At least, such a conclusion will be a hasty one. Instead of going back and forth over the specificity of the dead Rhino in question, the professor decided to give Don Campbell a call at least to put this triviality to rest.

"Hello Professor, is that you?" he asked.

"Of course, it's me, Don. How're you?" asked Prof. Church.

"I'm fine, professor, how're your wife, Nora, and your kids?" asked Don.

"They're all doing great, and I'm calling you to make an enquiry," said Prof. Church.

"What's the enquiry? You can go ahead, Professor," said Don.

He then went on to say, he just read the news of a Rhino killed by poachers, and proceeded to ask if this is true. Don is well briefed on the happenings on ground, and said yes, it is, it happened the day before yesterday, that it was quite a sad experience.

Nora stood up as she observed keenly and following the conversation between Don and her despairing husband, and funnily, her husband's facial wrinkles increased by the second implying that the news isn't a good one.

"Err.., it's true, but the description of the Rhino fits the one I joined you guys to save during my last trip," said Prof. Church.

"Yeah, it's the same Rhino, and it's sad to say that poachers remain our biggest problem," said Don.

"What about the perpetrators of these sickening acts, were you able to apprehend them?" asked Prof. Church.

This is a classic case of an advocate sucked in by his intention to confront poachers' in their manoeuvres, and this brazen gesture of good will might be a sting in the tail as he points fingers of accusation at the forest rangers doing their best to keep wildlife safe.

This isn't the story of a jealous lover who burnt the family Bunny in a pot, this is an animal rights advocate that's very protective of the wild.

"Yes, we caught them, they're in the custody of the police and will face justice," said Don.

"But why aren't you proactive as opposed to being reactive in the manner you do your job?" asked Prof. Church.

This allusion got Don spooked, and interestingly, the professor had to pass the buck to the rangers who he thinks should get off their butt and stop lazing around. Suggesting they have been unable to protect the forest that was left in their care. No matter how subtle the professor makes his accusation, Don got the message, and finds it rather unpleasant and itchy. He felt like his friendship with this professor opened the doors for undue criticism.

"What are you saying, professor, are you telling me we don't know our job or what?" asked Don.

"That isn't what I meant, and I'm sorry if you reasoned it differently, all I'm saying is that you should do things differently," said Prof. Church.

Don tried not to let the professor's accusation and assertions get to him, but took time to enlighten the professor on the arduous tasks of being a ranger. He reminded the professor that watching over animals isn't an easy task, stressing that animals aren't immobile objects because you can see a Rhino here right now, and the next hour she's seven kilometres away.

"Then you'll need more hands, and I think that'll help," said Prof. Church.

"What do you mean; I don't seem to get you?" said Don.

"I'm thinking of resigning my job and coming over," said Prof. Church. It didn't take long before this conversation takes a new turn as Nora grimaced at the professor's comment because she finds it quite itchy, and she immediately frowned at her husband who seemed unperturbed by his wife's facial disposition.

"What difference do you think you alone can make in the forest? I don't think resigning your job is a good idea either," said Don.

"But we all can't just sit on our hands and do nothing while all these animals are being killed," said Prof. Church. Interestingly, Don Campbell laughed at the Professor's move to resign his job as some form of hogwash, and his subtle effort to persuade the professor to change course doesn't seem to yield any fruitful result.

"I know advocacy remains the best approach, as opposed to running around with the animals. At least, from statistics here and even the one you have with you, poaching have drastically reduced," said Don.

"Maybe I'll have to combine both, and I think that'll give me a better result," said Prof. Church.

My husband is going psycho Nora thinks in her mind, and for all it's worth, Nora sure knows that this neat little life of hers seems to be on the verge of being picked apart piece by piece with perfect excuse that has just presented itself, that enables her husband to pursue his volunteering interest. She now thinks her husband is turning into a cuckoo of some sort, and how does a professor who's reputed for advocacy suddenly become a night watchman in the forest. The thoughts in her heart raced faster than a formula one car, as she tried to process her husband's last comment.

"You mean you want to combine both advocacy and physical protection of the animals?" asked Don.

"Yes, I think that's the best way to go about this," said Prof. Church.

"Then you're welcome; just write to the authority in charge of the wildlife," said Don.

Just as this phone conversation comes to an end, Nora didn't hesitate to state her position on the matter after her husband's shocking interest has added a new twist to the mix. She's now red-eyed and beginning to talk tough.

"Honey, you wouldn't do a thing like that, and what's it with you?" she asked.

"Someone needs to do the right thing, and I just can't sit here while animals are being butchered by poachers," said Prof. Church.

"What about your National Sports Festival competition, are you leaving that behind as well?" asked Nora.

"Taking part in the National Festival is of no significance when compared to wildlife conservation," said Prof. Church.

"I suggest you take a second look at your decision, how can you leave us and even resign your job just because you want to live with animals?" said Nora.

"I'm resigning my employment next week, and I'll be travelling immediately to Kenya where I feel I'll be much needed," said Prof. Church.

Eileen lurked in the shadows while her mum and dad debated the issue on hand, she hesitated for a while but her patience grew thing and then she broke her silence immediately and walked into the conversation. "What did dad just say?" she asked.

Nora became passive with Eileen as she replied her daughter saying she heard her dad correctly, that he's resigning his job to assist with animal safety in Kenya. Eileen screamed her lungs out. "Dad, what's it with you! Why're you so odd and conceited?" she said. Sadly, respect for her dad is now relegated to the bin, but her mum who takes exception with her daughter's comment finds Eileen to be highly disrespectful, and she's having none of it. "Keep quiet, Eileen, you don't have to talk to your dad in such a rude manner," said Nora.

Woefully, voices were raised and that brought Joe to the living room, and in his usual fashion he walked majestically into the living room, only to get enmeshed in the rumbling drama. "Oh my God; what's it, Eileen? I heard your voice, and it's loud," said Joe.

"Dad is resigning his job to spend time with some animals, and mum is saying I should keep quiet," said Eileen.

"What? But he just indicated interest in the National Sports Festival," said Joe.

"Err.., that's now in the dustbin," she replied.

"Mum, why're you stopping her from talking, dad needed to be told the truth, and why's he always looking for a reason to run off?" asked Joe.

"Eileen, why're you and your brother sounding like this? The step I'm taking is something I expected you to be proud of me for," said Prof. Church.

Professor Church is now faced with an army of resistance within his home, and funnily, his interest is glaringly in conflict with those of his household, and things could get fiery.

"What's it to be proud of, dad? My friends always tell me my dad is a psychiatric case, even though I fight with them over their utterances," she retorted.

Nora's cage was rattled as the conversation she started degenerated into name calling, and she immediately have to choose side between her children's poor choice of words and her adventurous husband. For all it's worth, she isn't pandering to her husband rather she's making sure that caution hasn't been thrown to the wind. "Never use such description for your dad, I'm not having it," said Nora.

"Mum, it isn't me, it's what my friends are saying, and that's all," said Eileen.

"It doesn't matter, and I just don't want you echoing what your friends have said into your dad's ear," said Nora.

Now that lines are drawn and each family member have taken side, Joe and Eileen now seemed to direct their anger at Nora for obfuscating the truth, and unsurprisingly, she's now backed into the corner which will advertently mean Nora have a lot of explaining to do. "Mum, what is it with you, and why're you covering evil? Dad's action is evil and wicked, he's abandoning us?" said Eileen.

"Don't worry, your dad will rethink his decision, and everything will be fine," said Nora.

"Mum, you don't know dad, he won't, when it comes to animals he gets carried away," said Joe.

"You kids are becoming unreasonable, this session now is over," said Prof. Church.

"We aren't! Dad, you've to sort this out," said Eileen.

Joe's position on the matter is that this is a lost case, particularly now that his mum has taken sides with her dad and falsely hoping that all will be fine. "Suit yourself, dad, I don't care," said Joe as he walks away.

A week later, Professor Pratt Church was hurrying to the Vice Chancellor's office, but he interestingly stumbled into his friend, Professor Stone Walker. His friend engaged him for a while, and sadly, as he dips his hand into his pocket and unbeknownst to him a receipt slip fell out of his pocket.

"Professor, why're you in a hurry? A slip has just fallen out of your pocket," said Prof Walker who then pointed to a receipt on the floor.

"Oh, thank you professor, I'm rushing to the Vice Chancellor's office and I learnt he'll be leaving for a meeting," said Prof. Church.

His affirmation to go the whole hog to keep the wild free from poachers might arguably be a tall order, and that could be the beginning of his undoing.

"Err.., 'he chuckles' "Is that why you're in such a hurry? Then you don't have to be in a hurry because the meeting has been postponed until tomorrow," said Prof. Walker.

"That's good then, and at least I'll have enough time with him to discuss my resignation," said Prof. Church.

The news of Professor Pratt's resignation came as a big shock to his friend whom he met and chatted with hours earlier. Professor Walker's instinct was that his good friend is moving to a different university to pursue his career. This news isn't one that Professor Walker can just shrug off without making a comment to that effect.

"What, resignation?" asked Prof Walker.

"Yeah, I'm resigning with immediate effect," said Prof. Church.

"To which university, if I may ask?" asked Prof Walker.

"I'm moving to Kenya, and I want to join them in protecting wildlife from the activities of poachers," Prof. Church said, with enthusiasm. Sad to say that Professor Church's comments and enthusiasm came as a stinker to his friend, who least expect that his friend will resign from the comfort of the academic environment to take up the graveyard shift in the grassland of Africa, amidst wildlife. The smiles in Professor Walker's face suddenly dissipated and quickly metamorphosed into a wacky look.

"Don't be silly, Professor, you mean you want to be a Ranger? This choice of yours is quite a startling one," said Prof Walker.

"Why're you mortified by my choice, you should know that protecting the wildlife is the right thing to do," said Prof. Church. In a subtle and vague defense of his moves, Professor Church presupposes his friend understands him, and the opposition to his decision to relocate to Kenya amazes him.

"Why're you all over the place? The other time, you wanted to take part in the National Sports Festival and this time you're becoming a Ranger," said Prof. Walker.

After trying laboriously to dissuade Professor Church and failing, Professor Walker then took a swipe at him, yet he kept a straight face and looked away as if nothing happened. Professor Church still remained exited and unperturbed as he reminded Professor Walker that taking a swipe at him might seem petty but it doesn't matter. He then informed Professor Walker that he might've been all over the place in the past, but this time, he has opted to be in just one place, and that's in the wild.

"Are you sure you aren't making a theatre out of yourself, and why is it the right thing to do?" asked Prof Walker. This is a professor who earns a living defending what he believes in, and this time he's willing to do that again and again. "Poachers are killing these animals, and I think we need more hands helping out in the preservation of this wildlife," said Prof. Church.

Professor Walker insists advocacy is the best way to go, reminding his friend he has the voice and the authority that'll make people listen to him. He then urged him to let those who have the shooting skills do the job of a Ranger.

Professor Church wasn't too keen to continue as he was itching to walk away, he then took a step forward but stopped, and walked back. Sadly he felt particularly drained by the too many opposition from his nagging family and friends.

"You're becoming a sensationalist, and all I want to do, is just to ensure the survival of wildlife," said Prof. Church.

"I've a bad feeling about this, and I don't think your family will be in support of this either," said Prof. Walker.

Professor Church had to confess that Nora and the kids don't actually like the idea, but he just can't sit down and do nothing because his family felt otherwise. In hind sight, it's all making sense to Professor Walker that his friend's talk is stilted and this obsession with the wild is now a crapshoot that has grown beyond bound, and sadly, they never saw this coming.

"This decision could affect your marriage, even your kids will be hurt by your choice," said Prof. Walker.

"I'm putting the animals first, and that's why you see this clash of interests," said Prof. Church.

"You're responsible for your family so they should come first, and not the wildlife," said Prof. Walker. While these two friends had their conversation, Professor Walker saw that his friend his bent on running off to the wild, and he thought of a way to put a stud in his way, and the only way to get Professor Church to call off this move will be through his wife Nora. Sadly, see no evil, and allow no evil is just a cliché that meant nothing because his wife Nora no longer has an iron clad hold on him.

"I've to go to the vice chancellor, maybe we'll talk about this later," said Prof. Church.

"Ok pass my regards to Nora, tell her I'll come over to the house next week to see you guys before your departure," said Prof Walker.

Professor Church smiled and then chuckled as if his smile was a parting gift to his friend. "That's if I'm still in the United States," he said.

Immediately after their laborious conversation, Professor Church didn't hesitate as he walked into Professor Scowl's office reflecting some unrestrained enthusiasm. "Good morning professor," said Prof. Church.

"Good morning Pratt, how're you doing?" asked Prof. Scowl.

"I'm fine, and I am here to tender my resignation," he said.

"What! Why the sudden decision to resign and which university are you moving to?" asked Prof Scowl. The Vice Chancellor's misgivings in this matter is that he wouldn't want his university to suffer brain drain from exodus of his best and renown professors leaving to other universities. The first thought that ran through the Vice Chancellor's mind was that he may have been too hard on Pratt, and maybe, leaving the university might be Pratt's own way of kicking off, but he has no idea Professor Church has something else up his sleeve.

"I'm not moving to any University, I'm just resigning to volunteer in the Kenyan wildlife reserve," said Prof. Church.

This is nothing but semantics the Vice Chancellor thought to himself as he suddenly turned his eyes away from Professor Church, and after moment of thought processing he realised he isn't dreaming. Professors resigning their jobs and moving on to other universities is something the Vice Chancellor is used to, but he isn't used to his professors resigning to take up the job of a ranger in the grassland. "Your comments just sent chills down my spine," said Prof. Scowl.

"Why the chill feelings?" asked Prof. Church.

"Your action is what can only be expected from a pre-pubescent teenager," said Prof Scowl.

"You seem to be taking this too far," said Prof. Church.

The naivety of Professor Church wasn't just a kick in the teeth for his family but a stinker to those who cared about him, and sadly, he isn't perturbed by his stomach churning decision.

"The dissonance accompanying your startling choice of retiring into the wild could result in a foreseeable disaster," said Prof. Scowl.

"And why this abysmal prediction, Professor Scowl?" he asked.

Professor Scowl finds the news of this resignation to be quite depressing, particularly because he thinks running around with wildlife means being eaten by a wild animal. Interestingly, the rights of these animals are being trampled upon so despicably and it's time for someone to do something about it. Yet, Prof Scowl finds this choice appalling, and described Professor Church as an ineffectual intellectual.

"This is quite strange, did you think this through before taking this decision, and what about Nora and the kids, what did they think about this?" asked Prof. Scowl.

"They weren't ok with the decision, but I feel it is something I've to do, a practical step at least," said Prof. Church.

Thinking that this decision to run off into the wild was impatiently taken in the heat of a rash decision, the Vice Chancellor was quite forgiving, and thoughtfully bestowing a second chance to his animal right professor.

"Pratt, I'll advise you to keep the resignation letter with you, in case you change your mind," said Prof. Scowl.

"I don't think so, I should be in Kenya a few days from now, please take it," Prof. Church insists.

"Pratt, I don't think you're doing the right thing, you're a professor and you've a lot to offer to the world, but why would you prefer running around with animals?" asked Prof Scowl.

"I'm sorry Professor, the decision has been made, and my receipt for payment in lieu of notice of resignation is attached to my letter," said Prof. Church.

"Since I can't stop you, the best I can do is to wish you well," said the Vice Chancellor as he takes the letter from him.

"Ok, thank you, Professor," said Prof. Church.

Immediately after handing his letter in, Professor Church stretched out his hand for a hand shake for a proper goodbye, and he then turned to leave, but unsurprisingly, the Vice Chancellor felt it was needful to give his friend a parting word.

"Pratt, I suppose you know that one day the world could liken you to an animal, considering your intensifying obsession for the wild," he said.

"That wouldn't be bad, and maybe I'm actually wild at heart, but why are you so mean spirited towards animals?" asked Prof. Church.

The professor cared less about the Vice Chancellor's banter, and as far as he's concerned, so be it if he chooses not to accept his decision to resign, he thought in his heart. The Vice Chancellor didn't blink as he fixed his gaze at him, and unknowingly holding his fist so tight that his facial disposition expressed the animosity in his heart.

"What makes you think I'm mean spirited," asked Prof. Scowl.

"Your fist! I suppose," said Prof. Church.

"Don't dwell on your childlike wonderment," said Prof. Scowl.

"No, this has got nothing to do with being childlike, just take a look at your fist," Prof. Church said, then pointed to the Vice Chancellor's clinched fist.

"Ah! Sometimes your actions make me clench my fist so hard, until my fingers make my hand bleed," said Prof Scowl.

"Funnily, Professor Church shifted the focus of the discourse away from himself to the Vice chancellors' state of mind and made him understand that the anger he just exhibited through his clinched fist calls for an avalanche of questions. Unsurprisingly, Professor Scowl insists that it's blindingly obvious that Professor Church has lost his way. "Don't talk about me in this manner, soon you'll be addressing me as your guest as I'm no longer your staff, and I beg to take my leave," said Prof. Church.

"Err.., have a safe trip, and say hello to the Rhinos," said Prof. Scowl.

CHAPTER

FOUR

The New Normal

It was just two days ago he resigned from his job as a university lecturer without the knowledge of his wife and children. Nora was in the bedroom with her husband trying to make him jettison the idea of running off to the wild. Oops, too little too late, because too much water has gone under the bridge, and she's now left on the back foot and all she could do at this point is play catch-up.

"Honey, I suppose you're rethinking your decision to travel to Kenya," said Nora.

"But we've concluded on this, why're you revisiting it?" asked Prof. Church.

"Why not! We're a family, and do you want to run off and shatter everything we've built all our lives?" asked Nora. Professor Church isn't willing to play ball at the point, as far as he's concerned, playing ball implies coasting the grassland of Africa in the interest of the wild.

"No one is running off, I'm going to Kenya to help protect wild-life," said Prof. Church.

Nora was red-eyed at her husband as she insists that the decision to resign his job and retire into the wild isn't for him alone to make, and as a family, they have to reason together. It's important to reason together as a family, and Nora thinks, taking the responsibility of who makes the decision away from her husband will help check the excesses precipitated by the lunacy of the human mind.

"Honey, the idea of reasoning together is now a bit too late," said Prof. Church.

"Why're you talking like that, what's it?" asked Nora.

"I just resigned my job with the university two days ago," said Prof. Church.

"What!" Incensed by her husband's insensitivity and lack of empathy for his family, she slapped her husband so hard that he saw stars. He took the pain from the slap to the chin, while still trying to calm things down, but without bending backward. "What do you take us for? This is a family, not a playground where you just wake up and take an arbitrary decision such as this," said Nora.

"Calm down, Nora. You're beginning to take this too personal," said Prof. Church.

"Your insensitivity affects us directly, why then do you expect me to keep quiet? The kids are right about you," said Nora. Sad to say that the kerfuffle between the pair was one-sided, as Nora's anger escalated by the minute with a raised voice, and sadly, her husband who was on the receiving end was doing all he could to calm things down.

"I hate it when you respond to issues in a dogmatic and biased tone," said Prof. Church.

"Your views are clumsy, and your position in this matter is also clumsy," said Nora.

"Why're you fuming over this matter?" asked Prof. Church.

Nora continued fuming because she just realised her husband has become irrational, and lost all sense of time, but the professor is now the one claiming to be the victim, as he insists Nora is bent on thwarting all of his interests. Funnily, Nora isn't giving up simply because she finds his choices startling, rather she's only trying to help him shape them into what the society finds acceptable.

"You heard all the kids said about you, at least they expressed their minds in your presence even though I tried to shut them up," said Nora.

"Nora, please I've to do this, and I'll need your support," said Prof. Church.

She serendipitously calmed down and said her husband have resigned already, hence she would've suggested that if he's so keen to assist with the protection of the wild, he should only be joining them during his holidays. "That won't be enough; I want to give much more than that," said Prof. Church.

All of Nora's suggestions supposedly fell on deaf ears because her husband wants to go the whole hog, by jumping right into the deep end of this adventure. Sadly, this man is like a bull and the danger in the wild draws him closer, and it's sad to say that she's beginning to give in to her husband's persistent twists and turns. "Honey, just go away! Your children were right about you, and I'm so disappointed in you," said Nora, who then walked out of the bedroom angered.

"Where're you going? We need to conclude this because I'll be leaving for Kenya the day after tomorrow," he said.

There was quiet in the home that day and the day after, and sadly, there was no warmth between the pair as the ambience in the home was cold, and then sour, yet two days after breaking the news of his resignation, it's now time to set off to Kenya.

Professor Church walked into the living room where Nora was already seated, he had his luggage by his side, Nora immediately looked away as there isn't any need dipping feathers in the flutter any further. After all, his mind is made up and all is now set for this trip to commence. In a brisk, there was a crackling noise that gave them quite a scare, and funnily, there was Joe's hamster crawling out from under the sofa. It didn't take long before they recover from the nerve wrecking moment with a sudden laughter, yet the bristling tension between the couple remained. "Nora, where are the kids?" asked Prof. Church.

"They should be in their rooms," said Nora.

"Ok, let me inform them I'm leaving," said Prof. Church. He left his luggage in the living room and walked into Eileen's room first. "Eileen, I'm leaving," he said.

Eileen stood up from her bed and walked towards her dad. "Dad, I must confess I'm not happy with you," said Eileen.

"Don't worry, I have you in my mind always," said Prof. Church.

Unsurprisingly, Eileen was quick to ask her dad if it's her or the Rhinos and elephants that he has in mind at all times, but the professor shrugged off the banter and was quick to push back as he looked straight into his daughters' eyes to remind her that the fact that he shows interest in those animals doesn't take away the love he has for her.

"Ok, let me continue to hope so, what about your stuff, is it all ready?" she asked.

"Yes, everything is ready, and I love you," he said and then kissed her forehead.

Eileen gave her dad a hug. "I love you too dad, stay safe," she said.

After saying a proper goodbye to Eileen Professor Church then walked into Joe's room to say goodbye to him but met him playing computer games.

"Joe, I'm leaving," said Prof. Church.

Joe didn't blink an eyelid neither did he look to his dad's side, he just focused on his game as if there wasn't anyone around, because he's convinced that his dad's adventure got nothing to do with him. The professor stood by for a while expecting to hear is son wish him a goodbye, but all he said eventually was that he isn't stopping him from leaving. This family's past was what binds them together, and that bond is now under threat.

"Joe, you're taking this too far, you know I love you and will always support you," said Prof. Church.

"Goodbye, dad, you're free to go, and I just need some space," said Joe.

Professor Church has no option than to leave Joe's room "Ok, I have to leave now," the professor said and then turned around and left, he then walked straight into the living room and picked up his bags. Funnily, Nora doesn't want her husband to leave under unfriendly terms. She then offered to accompany her husband to the airport, to at least clear every air of animosity. Nora grabbed her car keys and gave her husband a lift and thirty minutes later they arrived the airport.

"Thank you, please look after my children, and I'll always call you to inform you of everything," said Prof. Church.

Nora got out of the car, they hugged and kissed. "I love you, and stay safe," said Nora.

"I love you too, and I'll stay safe," he said, and then chuckled.

By evening of the same day Professor Pratt Church arrived in Kenya and headed straight to the wildlife reserve where he intends to offer his services as a ranger. On arrival, Professor Church went straight to Austin Impale, the head of the Kenyan wildlife reserve. "Hello professor, it has been quite a while, are you here on holiday?" asked Austin.

"Hello Austin, if I'm here for a holiday it would've been good, but I'm here for something more," Prof. Church said with a smile even as he pontificate on the subject.

"Oh, then what can I do for you, professor?" asked Austin.

The professor was quite upfront and all smiles as he didn't hesitate to tell Austin he's here to submit an application letter to volunteer in the wildlife reserve.

"I don't get you, professor, what're you volunteering for?" asked Austin.

Austin's question put Professor Church on a back foot, and the professor is now forced to make his intentions a bit clearer, and had to convince Austin Impale that he realised poachers are on rampage killing wildlife so he has decided to give his support in the protection of these animals. Interestingly, Austin Impale finds it surprising to see this renowned animal rights advocate moving away from his advocacy role into becoming a Ranger.

"It doesn't matter, provided I stay around these animals and protect them," said Prof. Church.

"Professor, being in the wild requires special skills, which I think you lack," said Austin.

The professor became highly incensed because Austin Impale wasn't upfront at accepting his offer to give extra support in their fight against poachers, he then urged Austin to stop being vague in his response with regards the skill of becoming a ranger. "Firstly, you must understand the behaviour of these wild animals, and you must be good with your gun," said Austin.

"What do I need a gun around the animals for? I should be protecting, not shooting them," said Prof. Church.

Austin Impale stated the obvious to free the professor from his naivety and told him rangers use tranquilisers but also use guns where necessary.

"I can shoot; if that's the skill you're seeking," said Prof. Church.

"The most desired skill is that of understanding the behaviour of these wild animals," said Austin.

"What are you implying?" asked Prof. Church.

Sadly for the professor, Austin gave it straight to the professor that he doesn't think he has a job for him in the wildlife reserve, and as a way of letting the professor off politely, Austin told him he has exhausted the space for new intake. Funnily, the professor knows it when someone gives him the run-around, and after all, he has been around the block a couple of times.

"What do you mean? I'm not asking you for a paid job, I want to work as a volunteer, and I expected you to see it as a thing of honour," said Prof. Church.

"I understand you, professor, but we've strict policies on numbers of people working in the park," said Austin.

Professor Church stood in front of Austin Impale looking helpless and pitiful as his effort to volunteer wasn't successful. More painful is that he just resigned his job for this purpose, and any attempt to deny him the opportunity of doing this will be a nerve wrecking blow that hurts really bad. Even as the professor stood statue-still in the mist of this disappointing response, Austin Impale didn't hesitate to remind the professor that he should've ensured the vacancy was there before he resigned.

"Should I have applied and get an approval from you before resigning my job?" asked Prof. Church.

"Of course yes! That's how things are done everywhere in the world," said Austin.

"But I didn't think that would've been necessary," said Prof. Church.

"Why! Is it because this is Africa where you think you'll lord your ideas over us or bulldoze your way through?" asked Austin.

"You've to stop putting words in my mouth, and I never said the words you're crediting to me," said Prof. Church.

"I'm sorry about that, but we sincerely do not have a place for you," said Austin.

The professor suddenly became emotionally drained, and this rejection really did give him a big emotional blow because he isn't used to being given the middle finger in the most cruel and casual of ways. His posture as a musketeer who wants to go on two dates with just one dance has left him looking like a man chasing the rainbow. "Ok then, I know what to do," said the professor. An hour after his conversation with Austin, the emotionally distraught Professor Pratt Church called Nora to express his disappointment. But moments before the phone from her husband came in, Nora walked into the living room where the dining table was left in absolute mess. "Who used the dining table and left it like this?" she asked.

"Err.., mum, that should be Joe," said Eileen.

"Where's he?" She walked into Joe's room. "Joe, I want that dining table cleared right now, and why must you leave it in such a messy state?" she asked.

"Mum, I'll be there in ten minutes time," said Joe.

Nora isn't having it, so she insists on getting the job done right away, Joe then stood up and walked to the dining. Coincidentally, she asked her children if their dad called, but they said he didn't, then Nora brought out her phone and decided to give her husband a ring.

"Honey, how was your trip, and how did it go?" asked Nora.

The Professor didn't hesitate to inform his wife about his disappointment with the authorities in charge of the wildlife reserve, but Nora was quick to tone things down, as she asks her professor husband why he's so upset on phone.

"They said there isn't any vacancy for me, that the places have been taken," said Prof. Church.

"What places are they talking about, and did you let them understand that all you wanted is to work as a volunteer?" asked Nora.

"Yes, I did, but the guy just doesn't want to listen," said Prof. Church.

While the professor broods over his disappointing encounter with Austin, Nora didn't hesitate to remind her husband that he really didn't think this whole adventure through before resigning his job and setting off to Kenya.

"I told the guy I resigned my job for this, but he just won't listen," said Prof. Church.

"What are you thinking of doing now?" asked Nora.

The professor's doggedness didn't abate as he was upfront in saying his coming to Kenya mustn't be in vain and further insists he must look for something to do. Nora was lost as to what her husband meant, but was quick to remind her husband who isn't willing to throw in the towel so soon that the option of returning home is still open particularly now that the rubber has hit the road.

"No, Nora! I'm not returning home, I must see this through, and Austin Impale cannot prevent me from expressing my passion for wildlife," said Prof. Church.

Troubled by her husband's quagmire, Nora was quick to offer to speak to Austin Impale, and maybe her sweet talking might pave the way for her husband. Sadly, Professor Church doesn't think his wife's involvement would be necessary because he has something else in mind. "I'll find somewhere to fit in provided I stay close to these animals," said Prof. Church.

"Honey, I'm worried about you. Things could deteriorate further and are you really sure about this?" asked Nora.

The professor insists he knows what he's doing and urged Nora to stay out, as he assures his wife he has things under control and all will be fine. It's obvious he has painted an image of himself that endures and turning that around will be quite an arduous task for Nora.

"Ok, stay safe, I'll call you later to know how you're doing" said Nora.

Sadly, Nora wept immediately she ended the phone call with her husband, and Eileen who was around while the pair had their conversation was quick to lend her support to help in the situation.

"Mum, what's it, and why're you crying?" asked Eileen.

"No, I'm fine," said Nora.

"Is anything wrong with dad? We know you were talking to him," said Eileen.

Nora was obviously still living in denial, as she insists to Eileen that her dad is fine and made a passing remark of her dad being refused the opportunity to work in the wildlife reserve as a volunteer. Funnily, this news was well received by Joe who was lurking in the shadows. Joe was quite elated because this refusal implies that his dad should be on his way home, and somehow providence is on their side.

"Joe, keep quiet, I wouldn't want to hear you say a thing like that, you're aware there are utterances you know I wouldn't like; don't say them in my presence," said Nora.

As it's always the case, Eileen was quick to come to Joe's defence, making her case to her mum that Joe has said nothing wrong and insisting that if their dad didn't get the job he went for then what's he still doing in Kenya. Eileen avoided ruffling feathers with her mum, yet decided it's better to hit the nail on the head requesting that her dad should come home. This whole thing is now a carbuncle and Nora has to go softly, softly.

"I understand you, but your dad has refused to return home," said Nora.

"So, how's that Joe's fault?" asked Eileen.

Troubled by the too many twists and turns precipitated by her husband's adventurous move to Africa, Nora admittedly accepted that it's neither Joe's nor Eileen's fault. It's hers because she did nothing when her husband's obsession for wildlife started, and now it'll be difficult to curb such obsession, particularly now that too much water has passed under the bridge.

"What do we do now?" asked Eileen.

"I don't really know what to do about this, and this whole thing is taking me by surprise," said Nora.

Eileen picked up the phone and decided to speak to her dad, hoping that her charm will prevail on her dad, and make the old man change course, Nora however hesitated for a while yet allowed Eileen to get on with it. "Ok, but you've to be civil in your conversation," said Nora. Unsurprisingly, Eileen promised Nora she'll be civil on the phone. She then dialled the phone, and funnily, Professor Church saw the call and muttered because he thought that it was Nora that was calling back.

"Why is Nora calling me back? Hello, Nora," he said.

"Hello dad, it isn't mum, it's me, Eileen," she replied.

Sadly, Professor Church isn't keen to speak any longer on the phone, he just wants to be left alone so he can get on with it, but dismissing his pestering daughter might result in more trouble for him as opposed to listening to her, so he thought to himself that it's better to be calm and engaging. "Eileen, how're you?" asked Prof. Church.

"I'm fine, dad, and what about you, are you ok?" asked Eileen.

"Yes, I'm fine, I just had a little hitch, but I'll be fine," said Prof. Church.

"Mum said they refused to give you the job you went for, why don't you come back home then?" asked Eileen.

"I just can't run back home and forget about my reason for being here in the first place," said Prof. Church.

Eileen didn't hesitate to express her thoughts with her dad as she asked him what then will he be doing over there, and reminded him that since he has a family that loves him the best thing is to return to them. "That shouldn't be to the detriment of the wildlife," said Prof. Church.

"What's going on, dad, and why're you doing this?" asked Eileen.

"Doing what, Eileen?" he asked.

"Why do you prefer to remain in a state of limbo, and walking around in the streets of Kenya, instead of being with us, your children?" Eileen queried further.

"That isn't true, Eileen. I've to go, and we'll talk about this later," he said.

This conversation took a new turn with the professor's sudden interest to end the conversation even when Eileen still has more persuading to do. She pressed on her dad to hold on for just one more minute, but time is now a luxury he can't afford, particularly when that time means he's being nagged to death.

"What's it, and why're you looking as if you just saw a ghost?" asked Joe.

"Dad just cut the phone on me, and that's rude," said Eileen.

"I told you, dad is a joke, but you all didn't believe me," said Joe.

"This discussion is over, and I don't want to hear any of it again," said Nora.

Later the same day, just as Professor Church tries negotiating his way out of his depressing situation, he saw Don Campbell returning from patrol, and then rushed to him.

"Hello, Don," said the professor.

"Professor, have you just arrived?" asked Don.

"No, I arrived a few hours earlier, and how're you doing?" asked Prof. Church.

"I'm fine professor, have you met them in the office to discuss your volunteering interest?" asked Don.

The Professor didn't hesitate to inform Don Campbell that he was already with Austin Impale who refused to consider him for the role, and that he just left his office after a disappointment conversation.

"Err.., that's not good, but you can return to the United States and continue with your advocacy," Don advised.

"I don't think so, because I've resigned my job," said the professor.

"Err.., that's a pity, and what are you going to do next?" asked Don.

"I don't know, but I'm thinking of something," said Prof. Church.

Don Campbell pressed on the professor as he's keen to know what plan he has got up his sleeve next as this adventure takes a weird turn. The professor's hesitation shows he's in a fix and Don, who isn't a fan of bursting bureaucracy suggested to the professor to consider returning to the United State, and perhaps speak to the university authority to give him back his job. Funnily, the professor has other things in mind, as he told Don Campbell he's thinking of guarding the forest on his own. "What do you think?" asked Prof. Church.

"That sounds weird, how're you going to do that?" asked Don.

"It's easy, I'll just look for a large expanse of the forest and continue protecting the wildlife in it," said Prof. Church.

Now that the professor gave Don a sneak peak of his next move as he told him his intention to obtain a license to secure a patch of the forest. Don held back laughter, as he subtly burst the professor's bubble, and told him the Kenyan government doesn't give individuals the right to protect the forest on their own. He didn't hesitate to let the professor know that such proposal won't fly off the ground, because he won't get such license from the Kenyan government.

"I just can't go back," said Prof. Church.

"Professor, why do you sound as if you're trapped or something?" asked Don.

"I just can't go back, I want to be around these animals, at least watch them run around and ensure they're protected," said Prof. Church. Don Campbell was open mouthed at the adventurous move of his professor friend, as he made the professor realise that this is quite out of the blue. The professor on the other hand, was quite unperturbed by Don's concerns as he didn't hesitate to tell Don Campbell not to worry, that he possibly might need a new pair of gloves going forward because he has got things under control.

"You have to be careful, Professor. It's quite risky for an inexperienced foreigner wandering alone in the forest," said Don.

"Is there any difference when a foreigner or a native wander in the forest?" asked Prof. Church.

Don Campbell reminded the professor that if a native is killed in the forest, it becomes a community matter, but if he a foreigner dies in the forest it becomes an international issue. Funnily, Professor Church interjected while Don was still speaking, placing emphasis that the international outcry over his misfortune in the forests of Africa will be louder particularly where the mishap befalls a renowned professor of his repute.

"Yeah, you're right," said Don.

Now that the idea of setting something up in the forests of Kenya has failed, the professor thought to himself and suggested to Don Campbell that he might go to Zimbabwe and get an area of their forest he'll occupy. Don Campbell is now stretched thin by the professor's crazy thoughts, and he now needs to make a run, but has no choice other than to okay the professor's move. He had no choice but to tell him that it isn't a bad idea, and at least Zimbabwe has a lot of wildlife.

"I'll take off tomorrow, and maybe you should join me for drinks this evening at the motel," said Prof. Church.

"Oh, that's a kind gesture, and I'll come over later tonight," said Don.

The next day, Nora was quick to give Professor Walker a phone call as she rallies around for help.

"Hello Nora, how're you doing?" asked Prof Walker.

"Walker, I'm not doing great at all, where were you when your friend decided on this quest, adventure or what do I call it?" asked Nora.

Professor Walker was quite upfront with Nora, and said he intended to ask her the same question she just put to him, but since Nora asked the question first, he chuckled and muttered that it's a shame that they were both rattled by Pratt's retirement choice. Nora couldn't help it but laughed at Professor Walkers' choice of word, for calling her husband's adventure a retirement choice. "You already have a name for it, Walker?" asked Nora.

"What else do I call this, Nora?" he asked.

"Did he tell you about this? He must have discussed it with you?" asked Nora.

"He didn't, I only knew about it on his way to the Vice Chancellor's office, with his resignation letter already in his hand," said Prof. Walker.

Nora isn't letting Professor Walker off the hook, as she's convinced that her husband's friend knew all along about this plan to retire into the wild, and never bothered to try talking him out of this crazy adventure. She laid the blame at Professor Walker's feet for not trying enough even when he knew about this in the last minute. "I tried, Nora, but Pratt was as stubborn as a mule, and cared less about whatever I had to say," said Prof Walker.

"The decision came up suddenly out of the blue, over the death of a murdered Rhino," said Nora.

Professor Walker wasn't convinced that the death of a rhino should be enough to provoke a reaction like this from his friend. He finds Professor Church's excuse to retire into the wild to be beyond reason and common sense as he just can't get his head around what the death of a single Rhino got to do with a renowned professor resigning his job and running off into the wild. He's convinced the death of the rhino was a mere smoke screen, sort of, that allowed the professor pursue his inner desire. "I'm bewildered by this," said Nora.

"I'm having trouble getting my head around why Pratt suddenly became rustic," said Prof. Walker.

Nora took it on the chin, as she took the blame for her husband's failings, and she blamed herself for not taking the tell-tale signs seriously. She never saw this coming, because she thought that what her husband has for these animals was love, and sadly, she now realised it's beyond love and can perhaps be described as obsession and he's now consumed by it.

"Is he still in town, or he has gone to Kenya?" asked Prof. Walker.

"He left three days ago, and I don't understand the stories he's telling me," said Nora.

"Then how're you and the children coping?" asked Prof. Walker.

Nora's trouble isn't with her children whom she could muscle with her parental skill, and her husband is now her major concern even though her children are distraught about their father's decision. Professor Walker was eager to help in whatever way he could, understanding that the matter at hand is a sensitive one. Nora began to sob, she now needs all the help she can get to make her husband return to her, she then asked Professor Walker to call him, and monitor his situation.

"It's ok, Nora, we'll see what we can do to get your husband back for you," said Prof Walker.

"Thank you, Walker, your call is a big relief," said Nora.

Professor Walker then urged Nora to just keep faith, and promising her everything will be fine again. Immediately after his phone conversation with Nora, Professor Stone Walker called Professor Pratt Church to keep tabs on him, even though keeping tabs on his movement is the least Professor Church expects in his present circumstance.

"Hello Walker, how're you doing?" asked Prof. Church.

"Professor, where are you? I just finished speaking with Nora now, and I don't think everything is alright," said Prof. Walker.

Professor Church was quick to push back at Professor Walker's assertion that Nora isn't fine, he told Professor Walker that he spoke to his wife a day before and his family is fine from his conversation with them. Unsurprisingly, the push back from Professor Church didn't deter his fried from telling him as it is.

"Are they fine as per health or as per emotion, how do you arrive at your conclusion?" asked Prof. Walker.

"Walker, I know this whole thing has been difficult for me and my family, please let's not make it any more difficult," said Prof. Church.

Professor Walker went on to ask his friend how they could locate him in case the need to reach him in Kenya arises. Sadly, Professor Church was hesitant to divulge his location because he doesn't want any negative publicity from the media, stressing that he has had enough of their negative reporting.

"This isn't about the media, but about family and friends knowing where you're situated?" said Prof. Walker.

"I'm in Kenya, but will be crossing to Zimbabwe in days to come," said Prof. Church.

Professor Walker avoided every corrupt flattery as he scoffed at his friend's worry for the negative reporting by the media while unperturbed with the emotional trauma he has put his family through. Bent on moving his adventure from Kenya to Zimbabwe the animal rights advocate continued being defensive. Professor Walker was also quick to remind his friend that with this his preferred choice of running around in the wild, he hopes that Professor Church won't be left holding the hat.

"Are you insinuating I could end up dancing in the wind?" asked Prof. Church.

"Of course yes, my eyes are rheumy when I think of the egregious harm you could suffer," said Prof. Walker.

"Don't worry, Walker; I have it all under control," said Prof. Church.

Professor Walker made his friend understand that since it has become difficult to stop him from this quest, he should at least do the honourable thing of keeping them abreast with where he is and what he's doing on a regular basis.

"Ok, I get you, and how's Gloria?" asked Prof. Church.

"Oh, my wife Gloria is fine, but she still remains startled over your choice," said Prof. Walker.

"I understand how she feels, just try to assuage her fears about me," said Prof. Church.

"I've been doing that, may be that was why she hasn't lost her mind yet," he replied.

After the tough talking between the pair, Professor Pratt asked to be allowed to end the phone conversation, but also thanked his friend for his interest in the welfare of his family. Professor Walker didn't leave without a parting rebuke as he told him he hopes he's aware his actions are unbecoming for a professor, and interestingly, Professor Pratt took the rebuke on the chin.

"That's because I'm wild at heart," said Prof. Church.

Professor Church arrived in Zimbabwe two days later and while in the city of Harare, the professor visited the zoo where he met Komati one of the zoo attendants.

"Hello, Pratt Church is my name, I'm a professor of animal science, and you're an attendant here in the zoo, aren't you?" he asked.

"Good morning professor, my name is Komati, have you come to enjoy the sight of our zoo animals?" asked Komati.

"Actually, no, but something close to that," said Prof. Church.

"Professor, sorry I don't seem to be following," said Komati.

Prof Pratt Church took Komati aside and told him he isn't here just to enjoy the sight of the animals in the zoo, rather he's here to spend some time in the wild with the animals. Komati unwittingly reminded the professor that if he intends to spend some time in the wild with the animals then he shouldn't be in the zoo.

"That's why I'm here, because I'll need your help to be able to do that," said Prof. Church.

"Ok, how will I be of help, and where do I fit into all this?" Komati asked.

Professor Church informed Komati that he'll need someone who has good knowledge of the forest to be his assistant, but Komati asked if what the professor wants is someone who'll be walking around the forest with him.

"Of course yes, I'll pay him for his services," said Prof. Church.

Komati promised to help the professor get someone who'll help him but didn't hesitate to remind the professor as succinctly as possible that a mission of this nature is dangerous. Professor Church who remained unruffled by Komati's caution quickly interjected and said that he's quite aware that wild animals are dangerous. After making his intentions known and promises made, Komati had to leave the professor because he'd to go and feed the lions, as it's their feeding time.

"What about what we were discussing?" asked Prof. Church.

"I'll get you someone by evening, how do I meet you?" asked Komati.

"I'm lodged at the Brown Oak Motel, do you know where it is?" asked Prof. Church.

Komati is home grown and knows the terrain quite well, he didn't hesitate to inform the professor he knows where the lodge is located, and that it's right opposite the drama square, and interestingly the pair set up an appointment for the evening of the same day, as Komati promised to come over to the professor's lodge.

"Ok, that'll be good; maybe we'll spend some time for drinks together," said Prof. Church.

"Ok, just expect me," Komati said, then left and went to the lion's cage.

When evening came, Professor Church was sitting in the bar when Komati and his friend walked in, they exchanged pleasantries, and Komati then introduced his friend Jonas Baum to the professor. They went on to shake hands as they were formally introduced.

"Good to see you, Jonas. Komati said you're good with the forests and wildlife," said Prof. Church.

"Yes professor, my dad is a renowned hunter, and I'm a hunter myself," said Jonas.

"Good to hear that," said Professor Church. The professor then raised his hand to catch the attention of the barman, and called the barman over, who later came to their side to take their orders. "Hello sir, you called for me?" asked the Bar man.

Professor Church told the barman that he did call him, and pointed to Komati and Jonas, then asked the barman to ask his guests what they cared to drink. It didn't take long before their orders were brought.

"Thank you, Professor," said Jonas.

"Never mind," the professor replied. They chatted generally, and at some point in their conversation the professor turned to Jonas and asked him when he'll be available to start working for him as his forest guard. Interestingly, Jonas was on hand for an immediate start but he told the professor it all depends on him. "I'm ready, I don't mind starting tomorrow if you don't mind," said Prof. Church.

Jonas decided to steer the conversation away from the starting time, into other important nitty-gritty of dealing with wildlife, as he asked the professor about which wildlife survival skills he has. Unsurprisingly, instead of telling Jonas what wildlife survival skills he has, Professor Church steered the conversation into specificity and asked Jonas whether it's the skills to protect the animals or the skills to protect himself from the animals that he seeks.

"You'll need both of these skills in the wild," said Jonas.

"I'm a good archer, presently I consider myself one of the best in archery in the entire United States," said Prof. Church.

Jonas was quick to inform the professor that his skill in archery might not be suitable in this circumstance, he then went further to assure the professor he'll cover for him and told him not to worry. Interestingly, while Jonas and the professor trashed out the terms of their contract, Komati turned to the Professor and asked if Jonas matches the description of what he wanted.

"Knowledge of the wild is written all over Jonas," said Prof. Church.

"That's good then, and I'm happy you're ok with the choice I've made for you," said Komati.

"Jonas, don't worry I'll pay for your services and you'll enjoy working with me," said Prof. Church.

"Ok professor, I look forward to working with you," said Jonas. They chatted and chatted about the wild and after about an hour together Komati and Jonas left.

Not long after the professor retired to his room, Nora's phone call came in, and she was surprised to learn that her husband is now in Zimbabwe. She didn't hide her despair as she asked how he expected her to reconcile how a visit to Kenya ended up in Zimbabwe.

"There's nothing to reconcile; since I couldn't get the opportunity I was looking for in Kenya, I decided to travel to Zimbabwe," said Prof. Church.

"What actually are you planning on doing there in Zimbabwe, is there any opportunity to volunteer in a wildlife reserve or something?" asked Nora.

The Professor is in no mood to obfuscate his moves any longer, after all he has found a good pair of hands in Jonas, he then told his wife that he intends to look for a patch of the forest and occupy. At least, a place of freedom where he'll enjoy some closeness with wildlife in their natural habitat. The professor's comment unwittingly shines a new light into his intention and now the truth is beginning to emerge, and for Nora, this isn't about the protecting of wildlife, rather it's just about closeness with wildlife and nothing more.

"Yes, that's it, exactly," said Prof. Church.

"So, this isn't about protecting the wildlife, after all. It's about running around with them," said Nora.

Prof. Church was quick to hit the nail on the head as he made it clear to his wife that protecting the wildlife, running around with them, and being close to wildlife are all one and the same thing to him. Now that the professor has his position stated in no uncertain terms, Nora flashed back to memory lane, as she drew her husband's attention to when he said he wanted to trade places with the Rhinos. "I thought it was a slip of the tongue but now it's all making sense to me," said Nora.

"Nora, you might call it crazy, but this is my fantasy, and I'm working hard to realise it," said Prof. Church.

"Ok, just make sure you don't get yourself killed while running around with wildlife," said Nora. She immediately drops the phone and sobbed after giving her husband a piece of her mind.

"Hello Nora, Nora," said Prof. Church, but there wasn't any response.

Not long after the heated phone conversation, Joe walked in only to see his mum crying her eyes out. He didn't hesitate asked to his mum why she's crying, and sensing that the only the only reason her mum will be alone by this time of the night and crying was if it involves his dad, he then asked to know if his mum spoke with their dad.

"Does it matter?" asked Nora.

Joe didn't hold back in his bid to let his mum know that his hunch tells him she must have been speaking with his dad, and he then reminded her he has suggested they let him be because all he does is to make the family unhappy. Sadly, Nora isn't bulging as she just can't get her head around why she should let her husband be, and after all, he's her husband. "I don't understand what's going on with him," said Nora.

"What else can you do, since he has chosen to remain in Kenya?" asked Joe.

Nora had no choice but to break the news of the professor's new location to Joe, and told him his dad is no longer in Kenya, and that he's now in Zimbabwe looking for a part of the forest he'll govern. "What? This man must be a joke! He's already in

Zimbabwe wanting to take charge of a part of the forest, mum, I already told you about dad," said Joe.

"I'm glad you didn't share in this his crazy fantasy as he calls it," said Nora.

Joe couldn't bear the news of his dad turning into a drifter in the wild, he immediately screamed his sister's name. "Eileen, Eileen I've news for you," said Joe.

Eileen walked into the living room. "What is it, Joe, and mum, why are you crying?" asked Eileen. "Your dad is now in Zimbabwe looking for a part of the forest to govern," he said.

Eileen was taken aback by this news and immediately turned to her mum and asked if actually her dad is in Zimbabwe as they speak. Sadly, her mum remained mum on the matter and Eileen asked again to know if it's true. Nora hesitated, but seeing that her mum had been sobbing, Eileen perceived it's true and told her mum she thinks it's true because that must be the only reason she has been crying.

"He just finished speaking with mum, he wants to govern animals, I told you he's tired of living with humans," said Joe.

Sadly, Joe's comment must have touched a nerve that got Nora's cage rattled, and she isn't having it. "Joe! If you repeat that, I'll be mad with you, you must watch your comments," said Nora.

Eileen was quick to come to Joe's defence as her mum's anger seemed misplaced, she reminded her mum that it isn't about Joe, rather it's about their dad who precipitated their present crisis. Eileen's investigative antenna took the best of her as she then asked her mum one last time if it's true that her dad is currently in Zimbabwe and if so, what's he doing there.

"I don't know, all I know is that he wants to be running around with animals in the forest," said Nora.

"Why's dad doing this! If they refuse him the opportunity to volunteer in Kenya, why doesn't he just come back home?" asked Eileen.

"I'll speak to Professor Walker to see if he can convince him to return home," said Nora.

Joe turned to Eileen and urged her to put the call across to their dad, and let him know their mum is crying, that his insensitivity is tiring her out. Interestingly, Eileen objected to making the phone call to her dad because their last conversation wasn't successful because her dad ended the phone call even when she was still speaking.

"Maybe I should do the calling then," said Joe.

"That'll be just fine, at least he might hear you out since both of you don't see eye to eye on a lot of issues," said Eileen.

Fearing that her husband could resort to avoiding their phone calls and drift further if they trouble him so much, Nora instructed her children not to pester their dad with further phone calls to prevent the situation getting more complicated than it already is.

"Ok, I get it," said Joe.

Two days later, while his family continues to brood over the fact that he has gone AWOL, the professor is busy walking the grassland of Africa and enjoying the wild freedom he only ever imagined, but this time, he's doing it with Jonas, his forest guide. They were walking the forest freely, and the professor then stopped and stretched out his hands with his eyes closed as a way of expressing the freedom he's now enjoying. After a moment of wild semantics, the professor and Jonas then spent some time walking in the wild, prospecting for a spot to pitch a tent, and moments later Jonas pointed to a particular spot. "Professor, let's pitch our tent over there," said Jonas.

"Jonas, why're you choosing this spot for our tent?" asked Prof. Church.

Jonas Baum told the professor that based on his experience of the forest, the spot he has just picked is a vantage position, and they'll be able to see what's going on in the forest from there. The professor interjected and asked Jonas if he could see poachers from there.

"Yes, why not, you can see poachers and even wild animals as they move around," said Jonas.

It didn't take long before they began trying to pitch their tent, the professor then told Jonas to hold his end of the tent firmly, while he pulls his own end. The professor's joy was nothing but palpable because he was quite ecstatic, acting like someone floating on cloud nine, and Jonas couldn't help himself but ask the professor why he's looking so excited.

"Jonas, this is a dream come true, and this is the best day of the rest of my life," said Prof. Church.

"Professor, what about your wife and kids?" asked Jonas.

Professor Church told Jonas that his wife and kids are fine, and he wished they'd joined him in this adventure of life in the wild, but stopped short of mentioning their objection to his adventures. Jonas smiled and asked if the professor's family has the same passion for the wild as he does. "Actually, they don't, their passion isn't the same as mine," said Prof. Church. Minutes later, the tent is ready and standing, but before the pair settled into their tent, Jonas reminded the professor to be aware that they must be armed at all times.

"My guns are here, and I'll need some arrows. Though, I hope you aren't implying we'll use the guns to shoot animals?" asked Prof. Church.

Jonas has to enlighten his companion who knows what's at stake but chose to remain illusory about the obvious. He then reminded him that where necessary, the gun will be his last hope of survival, he may have to use it either to scare or to kill an animal when his life is on the edge. The professor's disposition changed immediately he was told he might have to shoot an animal to save himself. He quickly interjected and told Jonas he doesn't think it'll come to the point where he will have to use his weapons to save himself, and if at all, it comes to that, then his weapons are meant to kill poachers and not for the animals he came to spend time with.

"You aren't licensed to kill poachers, you can only arrest them, and if you kill anyone you'll be imprisoned for that," said Jonas.

The professor wasn't joking about his intention to keep the animals safe from poachers, as he insisted he doesn't mind going to prison provided these animals are safe. Jonas thought the professor is just playing to the gallery, but even at that, he was quick to remind the professor that his plans to protect the animals will be defeated if he's in prison. The need to put things into proper perspective is now necessary for Jonas, so he and his employer will be on the same page.

"You're right Jonas; I need to manage my excitement," said Prof. Church.

"I'll get some arrows for you, since you're good with arrows," said Jonas.

It didn't take long before Professor Church began pestering Jonas to give him a tour of the forest even as Jonas was still giving the professor the code of conduct for living in the wild. Jonas was quite upfront for the tour of the forest, but his condition for this tour to happen will be that the professor is armed with his gun. While their conversation persists, the professor's phone rang almost immediately.

"It's Nora," said Prof. Church.

"Who's Nora?" asked Jonas.

"My wife," said Prof. Church.

The professor then picked up the phone to attend to his wife. "Hello, honey, how're you doing and where are you now?" asked Nora.

"For your first question, Nora, I'm fine, and for your second, I'm in the forest pitching my tent," said Prof. Church. "Oh, what forest are you in, and I hope the forest you pitched your tent isn't infested with all these dangerous animals?" asked Nora.

Professor Pratt took exception with Nora's qualification of the animals as dangerous, he then quickly cautioned his wife, reminding her that none of these animals are dangerous, and it's all her perception. "Ok, whatever you call it," said Nora.

"How are the children?" asked Prof. Church.

Nora told her husband that her children are doing great, just that they miss their dad, but her worries about her husband's ability to cope in the wild was quashed when the professor choice of words suggests he has a company to help him cope.

"We have to cope in whatever way people who live in the jungle do," said Prof. Church.

"What do you mean 'we', do you have company?" asked Nora.

"Yes, I'm here with Jonas, and he's my guide and my assistant," said Prof. Church.

"Are you sure you're ok? Because you don't sound ok to me," said Nora.

Professor Church hesitated, but Nora went further to remind her husband that from his tone, he sounded hungry and weak. The professor steered the conversation away from his being poorly and began asking about Eileen, and after telling her husband their daughter is fine, Nora took exception to her husband's inquiry as she accused him of not showing interest in their son because he never asked about him in most of their conversations.

"Yes, does it mean you don't care about him? I noticed you hardly mention him in your conversations," said Nora.

"Sorry, my bad, how's he?" asked Prof. Church.

"He's fine," said Nora.

The professor finds this conversation a bit spooky, and tries to wriggle himself out of his wife's grip "Nora, I've to go, we'll talk some other time," said Prof. Church.

"Ok, stay safe," said Nora.

CHAPTER

FIVE

The first tour

It didn't take long after his conversation with Nora, that Jonas introduced the professor to the forest as he gives the professor his first tour of the forest. They started off the party with a stroll in the grassland, and their tour suddenly picked up pace at some point in the forest as the professor pointed to some elephant's dung.

"This is from elephants isn't it?" asked Prof. Church.

"Of course yes, you're right, why then are you acting as if you knew nothing about the forest?" asked Jonas.

"Professor Church owned up to the fact that it doesn't mean he knew nothing, and the little he knows about animals was as a result of holidays at the wildlife reserve in Kenya. Jonas then concurred with the professor that he does have some idea about animals. While the pair continued their tour, they strayed into the deeper end of the forest, and things got steamy. At some point, the professor pointed to a water body at distance, and asked if that's a stream or a river.

"That's a stream," said Jonas.

"Then let's go over there because that could be our source of water," said Prof. Church.

Interestingly, Jonas has other things in mind, and quickly reminded the professor that he has to be very prepared if he must visit the water body. "Prepared for what?" asked Prof. Church.

Jonas hesitated as he considered the risk associated with the professor's request. He then advised the professor that hunters are weary of the wild animals that do come to the stream to drink, and big cats also lay in ambush to prey on the animals that usually comes to the stream to drink water. "Then that's what I'm looking for because poachers could lay in wait around the river as well, so that's the kind of place I'll love to be," said Prof. Church. This got weirder as Jonas's advice seems not to resonate with the tone-deaf professor, who's now bewitched by his newfound freedom in the wild.

"As I said earlier, that's the most dangerous place in the forest, because that's where danger lurks, and death is sometimes imminent," said Jonas.

Professor Church pressed Jonas to take him to the stream, and Jonas eventually caved in, but as they walked towards the stream Jonas gave the professor one last word of caution, asking him to be careful and watchful.

"I get you, we need to be careful," said Prof. Church.

Sadly, few meters away from the stream Jonas suddenly stopped and pointing to hoof prints on the ground, he then asked the professor if he knew what animal made those prints. Professor Church took a keen look at the prints with all seriousness, and said he can't really tell, but Jonas told the professor that the prints are from Rhinos. "Is it possible to see these Rhinos around here?" asked Prof. Church.

"If you can see their hoof prints then they're around as we speak, which means we've to be careful," said Jonas.

The professor was quite excited that his tour of the forest is paying off after hearing there's a possibility that these rhinos are round because the prints are fresh. His disposition lightened up, after all, he would love to see himself roam freely alongside these Rhinos in their natural habitat, but Jonas then told the professor that what he's wishing for is nothing but blood and guts. He then urged him to be ready to run for his life the moment he encounters one. "You mean they'll chase us?" asked Prof. Church.

Jonas told the professor that rhinos will not only chase him, they'll possibly kill him, and Jonas stopped suddenly for the second time. "Why did you stop abruptly, is anything the matter?" asked Prof. Church.

"Let's go back to the tent, I've a bad feeling about this tour, we can continue another day," said Jonas.

Sadly, the professor isn't ready to return to the tent after reaching the stream, as he pushed back at Jonas's advice, he then pressed on, as he walked with apparent impunity. He reminded Jonas that being a part of the experience in the jungle is the primary reason why he undertook this expedition, and now that he's a few meters away from where the party is, he just can't tuck his tail and cower away.

Interestingly, jungle living is like a mixing bowl that accommodates everything, and anything is expected. Jonas unblinkingly reminded the professor that these animals aren't his friends, and they've got no idea he's here to play with them. Since he unwittingly didn't pay heed to his earlier caution, Jonas had no choice at this point but to prepare the professor's mind, as he sternly told him to be rest assured that the rhinos will attack to kill, the moment they encounter him.

"At least we haven't seen any of them yet, who knows if poachers are in ambush waiting to kill them as well," said Prof. Church.

They took few steps closer as they approach the stream, and Jonas began pointing to the ground. "Can you see these prints all over here, they're from big cats," said Jonas.

"Yeah, I can see them, but they aren't fresh," said Prof. Church.

"Yes, they aren't fresh, but you can't predict big cats that much, sometimes they leave deceptive prints, that print is from a lion, this one belongs to a leopard and that print by the rock belongs to a cheetah," said Jonas.

"Oh, that's spectacular, and you're really good at what you do," said Prof. Church.

As they drew closer to the stream they stumbled on some gazelle that were also coming to drink water, and Jonas quickly told the professor to wait as he brought out his bow and arrow, but changed his mind and quickly pointed his gun at the gazelles.

"What are you doing? Don't shoot," said Prof. Church.

"Why? That's for food, we'll need one of them for lunch," said Jonas.

"I said, don't! I didn't come here to kill them," said Prof. Church.

Jonas brought down his gun, and looked on as his possible meal walked away free, he then turned to the professor. "How do you expect us to survive in this forest without some protein," asked Jonas.

"I'm here to spend quality time with these animals and watch them grow," said Prof. Church.

Jonas interjected. "You have only mentioned your intentions but haven't answered my questions." Professor Church is always armed with answers to questions, as he told Jonas not to worry, after all, they'll have to improvise.

"But I'm not a vegetarian, and I don't intend to change my diet anytime soon," said Jonas. They eventually arrive at the stream, and the professor dropped his gun as he scooped water and drank from the stream, he felt refreshed, and didn't hesitate to say the water is clean and fresh, and he needed to drink some more.

"Drink from the other end, its cleaner," said Jonas.

"Have you been to this stream before?" asked Prof. Church.

"Yes, I've been here a lot of times, but we're always careful with any water body," said Jonas.

The professor asked Jonas if his being careful is because of the possible presence of the big cats he talked about; Jonas concurred and reminded the professor that at least he just saw their prints all over which implies they have been around. Professor Church wasn't quite impressed with Jonas's sensational assertions and accused him of demonising these animals. Unsurprisingly, the professor emphatically told Jonas that he sees these big cats as understanding creatures that won't attack a person unless they feel threatened. The professor suddenly changed tack and lapped to drink water, but Jonas quickly admonished him and asked him not to lap, but suggested to him to scoop water with his hands and drink instead.

"No, I want to have a feel of how these animals feel when they drink water in this manner," said Prof. Church.

"There are plenty of fish in this water, but no one dares to fish here," said Jonas.

While the pair was busy going back and forth, the professor's wild fantasy grew as he imagined himself fishing in this stream, but first took the step of asking Jonas if he has fished in this particular stream in the past. Jonas on the other hand, gave an unexpected rhetorical response as he turned the question around and asked the professor if he could fish in the presence of a big cat. Reminding him he can't stand here and fish when a lion or other cats are also here.

Professor Church laughed hysterically at Jonas's pettiness as he told Jonas he must be a sensationalist, in the manner with which he builds in so much emotion into his stories. Jonas walked some steps along the edge of the stream and sadly, his countenance changed suddenly. "Err.., oh my God!" he exclaimed.

"What's it, Jonas, and why're you sounding as if you just saw a ghost falling off a tree?" asked Prof. Church.

"These prints belong to big cats, they're fresh, and there are two cats," said Jonas.

"Which of the big cats are you talking about?" asked Prof. Church.

Jonas began speaking in whispers, as he told the professor that these prints belong to leopards, and in all possibility, he believe they're around and watching them as they speak. Professor Church looked around and saw nothing. "But I don't think there's any big cat around, and why should we be afraid?" he asked.

"We just chased the gazelles they came here for, and now we're their target," said Jonas.

The professor was hesitant as he cautioned Jonas to stop putting fear in him, yet asked Jonas what he suggests they should do next. Without further ado, Jonas proposed they tuck their tails and do the obvious. "Let's walk quietly out of here, today could be our lucky day," said Jonas.

"Ok," said the professor. Sadly, as they turned to leave, the leopards were already onto them and Jonas screamed immediately.

"Professor, run, they're coming?" said Jonas.

Professor Church suddenly looked back and realised the animals were already behind them. "Oh, you're right, Jonas!" he exclaimed.

Jonas brought out his gun to shoot, and urged the professor to get his gun and shoot if he can, but things soon precipitated into a drama. The sudden dramatic situation got weirder, because even as he ran for his life, the professor constrained himself from using his gun to protect himself as he told Jonas he wouldn't do that because he isn't here to hurt these animals.

Jonas was more alert and younger, and as such was able to run ahead of the professor, the leopards caught up with the professor who was behind and began attacking him. Jonas hesitated because the professor insisted they aren't here to kill these animals. Eventually, Jonas realised he'd no choice but to shoot to save the professor's life. At first, he fired warning shots into the air which scared the leopards, but they seemed very hungry and didn't let go. Jonas then decided to take aim at one of the leopard's legs and fired, injuring one of the leopard's hind limbs; then the leopards abandoned the professor and ran away.

Jonas ran to the professor, who had blood gushing from his head. "Professor, are you ok? Oh my God you're badly injured by these leopards," asked Jonas.

Sadly, the professor was responding in a faint voice. "You were right, after all. I don't think I'll make it, will I?" asked Prof. Church.

"I'm taking you out of here, to a place you can be treated," said Jonas.

Unfortunately, these two leopards have dealt a great deal of injuries on the Professor, and as at the time Jonas picked him up, he unwittingly told Jonas he's beginning to lose consciousness, and it's like he's dying.

"I'll need to bind your body parts up to reduce the bleeding," said Jonas.

"These animals have ripped my body apart, I feel flesh from my legs, my shoulder, my head and my hands falling off," said Prof. Church.

Sadly, the professor's First Aid kit is a few kilometres away in the tent, Jonas quickly improvised and removed the Professor's shirt and ripped it apart so he can use it in place of a bandage. He started with the professor's legs and urged him not to scream, but before he starts, Jonas immediately picked his gun and fired warning shots into the air.

"Why did you do that?" asked Prof. Church.

"What are you talking about?" asked Jonas.

"The gun you fired," said Prof. Church.

Jonas told the professor that it was necessary to scare any big cat coming in this direction, since they stroll to the stream regularly to drink water, so they don't get taken unawares. The professor reacted to the pain as Jonas bound his wounds.

"Easy, easy, it's painful," said Prof. Church.

"I know, but you have to be strong, at least, let's stop the bleeding," said Jonas.

"Do you think I'll be able to walk?" asked Prof. Church.

Jonas assured the professor that he will be able to walk now, but when the pain sets in, he might not walk for many days to come, the professor interjected by telling Jonas he wished he'd listened to him.

"Going to the stream or river for any hunter is an arduous task; because you've to be alert, in your heart and with your arms," said Jonas.

"Where do we go from here?" asked Prof. Church.

"I'm taking you to the hospital," said Jonas.

"I don't want you to take me to the hospital," said Prof. Church.

Jonas was thrown into confusion as the professor refused to go to hospital, he just can't get his head around why a dying man would insist on not going to the hospital for treatment. Jonas's despair increased because the professor is growing weaker by the minute and even at that, he's still refusing the hospital and he doesn't want this man to die here in the forest. The professor reiterated his weariness for the media as he doesn't want the media to talk about this. Professor Church wasn't pretending to be beloved by the press, as his previous baboon experience in Kenya turned out to be one of mockery, and it hurts. He then urged Jonas to take him somewhere else, natural healing or whatever, he doesn't mind.

"But I don't want to get into trouble if this goes wrong," said Jonas.

Even as the Professor's hand bleeds, he dipped his left hand into his pocket and brought out a piece of paper and a pen and then scribbled "Nora, I asked Jonas not to take me to the hospital after the attack" and then signed it. "Take it," said Prof. Church.

"What's this you're giving me?" asked Jonas, as he took it and read the content.

"If anything happens to me just give that to my wife, you'll be exonerated," said Prof. Church.

Jonas quickly put the piece of paper in his pocket and decided to take the professor to his dad, who he thinks might be helpful in times as this. It didn't take long before Jonas finished with the first aid and it's now time to get going, but the professor groans in pain just as Jonas attempted lifting him up.

"Gently, hmm," said Prof. Church.

After going through the hurdles of moving a grown man out of the forest, Jonas and the professor eventually arrive his father's house, and Jonas screamed out to his dad as he carried the professor into his father's compound. "Dad, mum, is dad home?" asked Jonas.

Bolo Baum, Jonas's Dad, rushed out of the house. "What's it, Jonas? Isn't this the American you talked about?" asked Bolo.

"Of course yes. Dad, he was attacked by leopards," said Jonas.

Bolo Baum didn't hesitate to lay the blame of this attack on his son, who he thinks should know more, particularly when leopards are lurking in the forest, he scolded Jonas for not doing a good job of guiding his principal properly. Jonas tried explaining to his dad that he told the professor about the impending danger, but he made light of everything and didn't listen, but with a dying man in their hands, the attention quickly shifted to the dying professor who have already lost a lot of blood.

"Why don't you take him to the hospital, and why're you bringing him here?" asked Bolo.

"He said he doesn't want the hospital, and he suggested I take him for a natural treatment," said Jonas.

Worried that this whole adventure could quickly turn into quicksand or a carbuncle of some sort, Bolo was quite upfront and didn't hesitate to remind his son that this man isn't a fellow native. He stressed that the man is an American, and if anything happens to him here, it will become a different story and he doesn't want any problems with the Zimbabwean police.

"Dad, don't worry, just help him, he gave me a note which states, it isn't my fault if anything happens to him," said Jonas.

Bolo called his wife, Esther, and asked her to please get hot water ready, telling her the professor is badly injured. Esther rushed to the scene but as she turned to leave she noticed the professor is becoming unconscious, and told her husband that it seems the professor has lost a lot of blood. Bolo then hurried his wife to get the hot water ready to see if there's anything they could do to save the man's life.

Professor Church spoke in a faint voice "Are you Jonas's dad?" he asked.

"Yes, I'm, and my name is Bolo, what's your name?" asked Bolo.

"My name is Pratt, Pratt Church. I'm a university professor, please save me," he said.

"Don't worry, I'll save you, stop talking, you're losing strength," said Bolo.

"Ok, I'll stop talking," said Prof. Church.

Bolo was quite touched by the plea of this dying man, he then rushed to the garden at his back yard and plucked some leaves. He immediately asked Jonas to unbind the professor's wounds and clean the wounds so he could apply herbs on them. Sadly, the sight of the wound isn't good for the fickle mind and Jonas reminded his dad that the professor is badly injured.

"Just unbind the wounds," said Bolo. Jonas then unbinds the wounds to display the extent of the injuries. "Err.., hmm, he's badly injured and his flesh was ripped off," said Bolo.

"Awe, he's badly injured!" Esther exclaimed, after she saw the injuries and her tummy churned, and then turned to Jonas. "Why didn't you protect him from the leopards?" asked Esther.

"I did protect him, and that's why he's alive now," said Jonas.

Esther left, and returned carrying a bowl of hot water. "The hot water is ready." She took a second look at the professor. "He is now unconscious, what do we do?" asked Esther.

"He's still breathing, he's just in a deep sleep," Bolo replied. Bolo has now finished with preparing the concoction, and then turned to Jonas, and reminded him to make sure he holds the professor down because he'll wake up forcefully immediately the hot water gets into his wounds.

"Yes dad, I know, I'll have to hold him down," said Jonas.

Bolo now asked his wife Esther to send the kids away because the next hour is going to be very raw, and he doesn't want the kids to be part of such an experience. It didn't take long before Esther sent all the kids away.

"Esther, please add some disinfectant to the hot water," said Bolo.

Bolo used the hot water on the wounds, and immediately the hot water got to the wounds, Professor Church got the message in his brain and jumped out from his slumber and screamed. "Hold him down Jonas, his wounds need to be thoroughly cleaned," said Bolo.

Professor Church screamed but his voice was too faint. "Stop, please stop, it hurts, please stop," he said.

"Sorry, sorry, you have to be strong, be a man, be a man," said Bolo, as he continued administering the hot water to the wounds.

"Ouch, ouch, hmm, this hurts so bad, please stop," said Prof. Church.

After cleaning the wounds, Bolo Baum washed and squeezed the leaves he plucked from the garden, he then continued with his usual traditional semantics as he applied the herb. Funnily, by the time Bolo Baum was through, the professor had fallen into a deep sleep.

"Thank you, dad," said Jonas.

Now that the professor is stable, it's now time to take stock. "That was a close call, Jonas. You almost lost the man you were meant to protect," said Bolo. "We'll have to let him sleep, and see how he's doing when he wakes up," said Esther.

"Mum, is there any food in the house, I'm hungry? asked Jonas.

"Go into the kitchen and you'll find something to eat," said Esther.

Interestingly, now that Jonas is at home and the professor's condition is stable, Jonas needed to eat something but guessing if his favourite meal will serendipitously be in the kitchen. His mum who sensed what Jonas was all about burst into laughter, telling Jonas today is his lucky day, and that she made his favourite and it's there in the kitchen.

Bolo spent all day monitoring the professor and by morning of the next day Bolo Baum walked into the hut where the professor was staying and asked Jonas how the professor was doing. Jonas was quick to tell his dad he thinks the professor is ok, though he hasn't opened his eyes today and he's just in some kind of deep sleep.

"He hasn't eaten anything since yesterday, he should be hungry by now, and we'll have to wake him up," said Bolo.

"What food will he eat? You know our type of food is quite different from theirs," said Jonas.

Bolo interjected and said there is rice in the house, that everywhere in the world people eat rice, Bolo then bent down to feel the Professor's temperature. He immediately exclaimed saying the professor is burning with fever. Surprised, Jonas was in shock as he told his dad that the professor's temperature was normal about two hours ago. Bolo wasn't quite convinced his son did a good job watching over the professor, as he asked Jonas what if he'd left the professor with him and went to the farm, what would the situation have been like.

"His temperature was ok two hours ago, and I've been by him since I woke up," said Jonas.

"Stay with him, I'm coming," said Bolo.

Bolo then rushed into the garden and put together a variety of leaves different from the ones of the previous day, and brought them to the compound. Jonas collected the leaves from his dad but then asked him what the leaves are for as he has no idea of what to do with them.

"Get your mum to boil them; she knows how I want them," said Bolo.

"Mum just left for the market," said Jonas.

"But I saw her about an hour ago, when did she leave?" asked Bolo.

Sadly, Jonas's mum left to the market about forty-five minutes ago, and that's possibly when Bolo went into the garden. In the absence of his wife Bolo would have to get this sorted himself, as he asked Jonas to get a clay pot, wash these leaves and put them inside.

"Should I just wash the leaves and put them in the pot, or they should go into the pot in a particular order?" asked Jonas.

Bolo asked Jonas to place the stems at the bottom of the clay pot, and the rest of the leaves can go in irrespective of which one goes in first, except the broad leaves which should be placed on top and used as cover for the pot.

"Should I cook them after washing and placing them in the pot?" asked Jonas.

"Yes, just boil them, that's all, and when that's done let me know," said Bolo.

An hour later, the medicine was ready, and Bolo Baum was on hand to administer the medicine to the Professor who went back to sleep almost immediately. Jonas was hoping this herb will do the magic better than the one administered the previous day, but Bolo gave a cautious response. Yet, he assured his son that this herb will obviously help to bring the professor's temperature under control, but urged Jonas to get some food ready so the professor can eat something immediately he wakes up.

"Will he be able to eat? He doesn't seem to be himself," said Jonas.

"He'll be very hungry by the time he wakes up, and as such he'll need food," said Bolo.

"Ok, let me hurry and get rice ready," said Jonas.

Bolo instructed his son keep a close eye on the professor to watch his temperature, and he also urged Jonas to alert him immediately the professor wakes up. As Bolo turns to leave Jonas thanked him and apologised for getting him involved in this poorly concocted contract, but also acknowledging that he has prevented his dad from going to the farm.

"You're my son, your troubles are mine, every day has its own trouble, and the worry of any man is his ability to stem the troubles that come with each day," said Bolo. By evening of the same day, the professor woke up and looked around but didn't recollect how he got to his present location. "What am I doing here?" asked Prof. Church.

Jonas answered in excitement. "You're in my house, good to have you back," said Jonas.

"How long was I gone?" asked Prof. Church.

Jonas understands that the professor has lost track of time, and told him he has been in slumber for close to twenty-four hours, and he's happy that the professor's fever has subsided. The professor tried getting up from the bed but the pain was immense. "Hmm, ouch, this is so painful," said Prof. Church.

"Take it easy professor, you're badly injured and won't be able to stand on your own, let me help you stand," said Jonas.

"I only remember you bringing me into this compound, and that's the last thing I remember," said Prof. Church.

"You blacked out the moment we arrived here," said Jonas.

"I know the flesh in most parts of my body was ripped out by those leopards. What did you do to me?" asked Prof. Church.

"I don't get your question?" asked Jonas.

The professor rephrased his earlier comment and told Jonas he meant to ask him what treatment he gave to him with respect to his injuries. Interestingly, Jonas quickly told the professor that it wasn't him who saved the day, it was actually his dad who did the job of saving his life.

"Does he live here?" asked Prof. Church.

"This is his house, you spoke with him when I brought you in," said Jonas.

Professor Church smiled as Jonas reminded him he did had a chat with his dad before becoming unconscious, but sadly, the professor said he didn't remember having such conversation, and asked Jonas if his dad is in. "Yes, let me get him, and he actually told me to get his attention the moment you wake up," said Jonas. He then left to get his dad, and moments later Bolo was by the professor's side.

"Oh, professor you're back, how're you feeling now?" asked Bolo.

"I feel so much pain, and I'm feeling dizzy," said Prof. Church.

Bolo assumed the position of the big man in the house, as he told the professor the pain is to be expected considering the severity of his injuries. Bolo felt it's time to discuss the obvious with the professor, as he advised him he still need to go to the hospital because his condition is still critical even though he's stable for now.

"You must have done a lot of work on me. I suppose, I was almost dead when your son brought me here," said Prof. Church.

"I blamed my son for allowing you to put yourself in such a danger," said Bolo.

Professor Church quickly absolved Jonas of the blame as he told Bolo that this isn't Jonas's fault, he made it clear that Jonas actually warned him, but he was obstinate and considered the animals friendly. Bolo was taken aback by the professor's admission and then asked him why he disobeyed his guide. Bolo did a good job as he laid bare the contrast between the professor's thought and the possible thinking of the animals, as he reminded the professor that these animals have to kill to feed, and when they saw him they consider him a possible meal, maybe not as an enemy, but as a meal.

"But I do see people playing around with some big cats," said Prof. Church.

"These are special cases where people form a bond with the animals from when they're suckling," said Bolo.

The professor thanked Bolo for everything he and his family has done for him, and also apologised for putting Bolo's family under great stress within the last twenty-four hours.

"I know you must be very hungry," said Bolo, who then turned to Jonas and asked him to get the professor something to eat.

"Ok dad," said Jonas. He left his dad and the professor behind and walked inside the house to get the rice he'd prepared for the professor.

The professor then smiled, and said he now has a taste of how preys suffer in the hands of these big cats. Moments later, Jonas returned with a plate of rice. "You've to eat," said Jonas.

"Oh, thank you, but I'll need to wash my mouth, how do I do that? I can neither stand nor walk," said Prof. Church.

Jonas quickly brought water and a bowl and asked the professor to gargle his mouth with warm water and salt and then empty it in the bowl. The professor tried opening his mouth, but he couldn't due to the extensive injury on his head and face resulting in a swollen face. The gargle isn't working, and he then gave it a second try and succeeded. "Err.., I can't; let me just see if I can eat a little," said Prof. Church.

"My son told me you have a wife and children, I advise you to return to them immediately so they can give you the best care," said Bolo.

Sadly, the professor was weary of the media because he finds the media insufferable, and he also doesn't want his family knowing about this his oops moment. He stopped short of coming out straight with what his fears are, and rather the professor told Bolo that his situation is still critical and as such will prefer getting treatment around here. "Then we'll have to take you to the hospital this evening?" said Bolo. Professor Church then turned to Jonas and inquired about his mum. "What about your mum, I haven't seen her?" asked Prof. Church.

"She went to the market this morning, and should soon be back," said Jonas.

Now that that the professor has given his consent to Bolo concerning visiting the hospital, Professor Pratt Church was taken to the hospital later that evening, and the medical director of the hospital was on hand to attend to the ailing professor. Sad to say, that the professor wasn't fully conscious as he kept going in and out of consciousness, and Bolo has to speak to the doctor on his behalf.

"I'm Doctor Samuel Shekuh, what's wrong with him and why's he burning with fever?" asked Dr. Shekuh.

"He was attacked by two leopards, and his situation was far worse than this when they brought him yesterday," said Bolo.

Sadly, Doctor Shekuh was quite unhappy that a man in such a bad shape was brought in for treatment a day after he was attacked by big cats. Bolo insisted that the professor wanted natural treatment, but now that he has regained consciousness, he'd to convince him to come to the hospital, and for all it's worth, Bolo's excuse didn't in anyway make the situation any palatable.

"He doesn't seem to be fully conscious, and he's going in and out of consciousness," said Dr. Shekuh.

"But you saw him speaking with us when we came here?" said Bolo.

"I knew he was conscious when you brought him, what I'm implying is that his situation is critical," Dr. Shekuh.

Bolo urged the doctor to start treatment immediately, but the doctor inquired about the professor's family. Bolo didn't hesitate to give the little details he know about this professor, as he told the doctor that the professor has a wife, and children, but also told the doctor that the professor insisted they stay out of this.

"Which means you're standing in their place?" asked Dr. Shekuh.

"Of course, yes, but I want you to make sure he's alright, just do everything you can to get him on his feet," said Bolo.

Doctor Shekuh walked up to Nurse Theresa and asked her to take the professor's vitals and then administer drip immediately to the professor. "Is it the man that was brought in minutes back?" asked Nurse Theresa.

"Of course, yes, who else is in bed ten?" asked Dr. Shekuh.

The nurse administered the drip almost immediately and an hour later while Bolo Baum and his son were at the professor's bedside, the doctor walked in and told Bolo that the hospitals' accounts department just informed him Bolo just made some deposit towards the professor's treatment to facilitate things.

"Yes, please you've to commence treatment," said Bolo.

"That's why I'm here, I'm starting treatment immediately," said Dr. Shekuh.

Bolo assured the doctor that his balance will be ready as soon as the treatment continues. Funnily, Bolo just received his pension payment, and he couldn't help but to expend a portion of it on this rustic professor. Doctor Shekuh told Bolo that the professor is badly injured, and will need stitches, and will also need to go for a scan to be sure his brain isn't affected because the attack on his head was quite severe. The news of a possible impact of the accident on the professor's brain seemed a bit too much for Bolo, particularly for a foreigner he knew little or nothing about. More so, whether the bill is something he alone could cough out.

"You mean his brain could be affected?" asked Bolo.

"The MRI scan will reveal that, but for now let's start with the stitching," said Dr. Shekuh.

Two hours later, Doctor Shekuh was done with the stitching of the professor's injuries, and assured Bolo that the professor's brain scan results will be out the next day, which will determine the extent of his injuries and how well to approach to his treatment.

"Does he need to eat something?" asked Bolo.

"He's on a drip, and he'll be fine for now. I'm trying to stabilise him further," said Dr Shekuh.

The possibility of having a bleed in the brain is now a scare that kept Bolo troubled. "But you're sure he'll be fine?" asked Bolo.

"Yes, let's be positive," said Dr. Shekuh.

That night Nora had a dream, and in that dream it was Saturday, Nora and the professor were preparing to go for an early morning jog, but this time their dog Billy was joining them for the early morning jog.

"Ok, what direction do we go?" asked Prof. Church.

Before they set off for their jog, the couple argued over what direction they should go, but the professor prevailed. "Let's go right since we've been going left. Let's do things differently today," he said.

As the couple jogged along the street, Professor Church suddenly took a turn into a bushy lane away from their usual jogging route which is a street in a neighbourhood. Nora was quite uncomfortable with her husband's decision to take a new route. She hesitated in joining in this bushy path as she pressed on her husband that this isn't their usual route and refused to join him.

"Let's explore something new, life is about experience," said Prof. Church.

"What's new in this bushy path? This is a dead end," said Nora.

"Why don't you explore with me for once and stop bickering?" said Prof. Church.

"Ok, let's go but I don't like this, and I hate it when you come up with odd surprises," said Nora.

The professor then told Nora that it's odd, but he likes the fun, and after about ten minutes in this bushy path Billy began to bark. Sadly, Billy's reaction spooked Nora, and she began wondering what the problem with Billy was.

"What's happening, and why is Billy barking?" she asked.

"Most times Billy barks over nothing, and I've gotten used to that," said the professor.

"Billy is stopping and refusing to continue jogging with us, and I think something is wrong somewhere," said Nora.

Professor Church urged Nora to forget about Billy's tantrums and suggested they continue with their jog and Billy will find his own way home. Nora hesitated and suggested that they call-off the morning exercise and return home, insisting that something must be definitely wrong to precipitate Billy's reaction. The professor remained as stubborn as a mule, as he insists on having his own way.

"Then I've to continue, without you," said Prof. Church.

"Stop, where are you going, and why won't you listen for once?" asked Nora.

She then stopped and watched as her husband continued jogging, and fifty meters away from where Nora stopped, two leopards came out of the bush and attacked the professor, dragging him away into the bush. Watching from a distance, Nora cried. "Honey, honey, no, no, she wept as she dialled 911 and informed the emergency services that her husband has been attacked by leopards and he would need help.

While all this drama was going on, Nora suddenly woke up from her sleep, and from what was quite a terrifying dream.

"Oh, oh, it's all a dream, thank goodness this is all a dream," said Nora. She got up from her bed and walked to the living room as it was exactly 6.15am. She was quite scared, and her disposition reflects her state of mind, but Eileen who was already awake and preparing to go to school asked her mum what the problem was, and if she's Ok.

"Yes, I'm ok, and why're you asking?" asked Nora.

"The expression on your face says otherwise, and I don't think you're ok," said Eileen.

"Actually, I just woke up from a terrible nightmare and its mind boggling," said Nora.

Eileen asked her mum what the dream was about, and she told her it's about her dad.

"It's about your dad, we were jogging, and two leopards came out from the bush and attacked him," said Nora.

"Mum, you know your dreams do come true; let's call to be sure dad is ok," said Eileen.

"I'll do just that, he was quite as stubborn in the dream as he's in real life," said Nora.

Joe who's never too far away when issues of this nature pops up, walked into the living room and inquired to know what it is about his dad this time.

Worried, Eileen told Joe that their mum had a dream about their dad being attacked by leopards, and she said the whole thing looked so real. Interestingly, Joe shared Eileen's view and insisted that if their mum had a dream then it should be taken seriously, and he actually grew weary about his mum's dreams because they usually comes to pass.

"Mum wants to call dad to find out how he's doing," said Eileen.

"Eileen, aren't you going to school?" asked Nora.

Eileen finds her mum's dream to be scary enough to make every other matter less important, and she wants it sorted out before leaving the house for school. She isn't leaving the house for any-thing as her despair grew particularly when it's her mum that had the dream. Funnily, Joe has something else in mind, and laid the blame squarely on his mum's feet.

"Maybe mum should stop dreaming, that'll help to keep our minds at rest," said Joe.

Eileen finds Joe's comment to be mere gibberish and asked him to stop being cheeky because people can't decide for themselves whether to dream or not, and to say the least, what dream they choose to have.

Joe seemed bent on steering the conversation away from serendip-ity and suggested that his mum seek treatment to help stop her from dreaming. Eileen interjected immediately, reminding Joe that he can't stop a person from dreaming, and the only time people get treatment to stop them from dreaming is when the dream is caused by a condition, or maybe the person is hallucinating.

Sadly, Nora didn't appreciate her children talking about her as if she wasn't present, and she was particularly irked by Joe's suggestion. "Are you out of your mind, Joe! Is it me you're recommending treatment for?" asked Nora.

"I'm sorry, mum, but you know each time you dream it comes to pass," said Joe.

Nora decided that calling her husband to be sure he's fine is the best way forward, and decided to give her husband a phone call right away. Her husband's phone rang but there wasn't any response from the other end.

Two hours later, Professor Pratt Church woke up for the first time since he was brought to the hospital the previous day. "Oh, how long have I been out?" asked Prof. Church.

"Since yesterday evening, you were burning with fever and fell asleep the moment we arrived here," said Bolo.

"What happened, and what did they do to me?" asked Prof. Church. Bolo Baum told the professor that the doctor stitched his wounds up, and his scan result is expected. Though, he went on to hint him that the doctor said the professor will need skin grafting because of the nature of the scars that will result from his injuries.

"What about the bills?" asked Prof. Church.

"I've made some deposit, you sure can't make a deposit when you are asleep," said Bolo.

The professor was taken aback by the action of this selfless family, and he couldn't help himself but said he's stunned by the kindness and generosity of this family towards him, saying he's truly grateful. Bolo on the other hand, asked the professor if he remembers what he said to him the moment his son brought him into his compound and before he became unconscious. The professor was surprised at Bolo's comment because he really didn't recollect saying anything to Bolo. "You said, 'please, save me', and that's what I'm doing," said Bolo.

"Err.., I said that? Then thank you for making it happen," said Prof. Church.

"Thank you for making what happen?" asked Bolo.

"For making it happen that I'm still alive," said Prof. Church.

Bolo told the professor his phone rang while he was still asleep, but they didn't respond because they don't know who it was, he now handed the phone to the professor. The professor collected the phone and checked to see who the caller was. "Err.., it's Nora, my wife, and I don't want her to know about this," said Prof. Church.

"Ok, let's pray for your quick recovery. I know you can't hide this forever, and even the scars will speak for themselves," said Bolo.

Bolo gave the professor some touchy piece of advice as he reminded him that some battles are never won, that even if he's able to keep this accident under wraps from his family, he can't do the same with the scars. Professor Church couldn't hold back his thoughts about Bolo that a lot of people expect a hunter to be local and uneducated, but he's rattled by Bolo's level of enlightenment and exposure. Bolo interjected as he quickly informed the professor that he was a senior civil servant who found love in hunting, but he's retired from the service.

"That explains it," said Prof. Church.

Though, the professor would rather not take his wife's phone call, but Nora's phone call came in just as the professor and Bolo had their conversation. This time he reluctantly picked the phone call to stop it from ringing and causing nuisance. "Hello Honey, are you ok?" asked Nora.

"I'm fine Nora, how're you doing?" asked Prof. Church.

Not long into their conversation Nora realised her husband seem off and possibly isn't fine, as she quickly pointed out to the professor he isn't sounding well, and she then asked him why his voice was so faint and cracked. In his bid to cover his tracks the professor quickly asked his wife to excuse his voice, because he'd a cough, and said he's beginning to feel better by the day.

"I had this strange dream last night, in fact, I was terrified, and I said I should call you to be sure you are ok," said Nora. The professor unwittingly exclaimed and then began to cough as he wanted to laugh. "Are you ok? My hunch tells me you aren't fine," said Nora.

Even though the odds are pretty much against him, the professor insisted he's fine, and pushed back at Nora's assertion as he argued that if he isn't fine he wouldn't be on the phone with her. Interestingly, he was also keen to know what Nora's dream was about.

CHAPTER

SIX

Welcome to the media

Tina Mbolelu is a news reporter whose mum was admitted to a ward in the same hospital where Professor Church was also admitted, she walked into the doctor's office "Doctor Shekuh, good afternoon," she said.

"Tina, how're you?" asked Dr. Shekuh.

"I'm fine doctor, I was meant to be in the field giving a correspondence report, but I'd to come and see how my mum is doing," said Tina.

Doctor Shekuh's reply to Tina was that her mum is doing great, but asked if she has seen her mum before coming to see him. Sadly, Tina has seen her mum and her visit to the doctor's office isn't for mere exchange of pleasantries but to register her protest as to why her mum was moved from bed ten to bed nine in the ward. "We use bed ten for critical cases, and your mum has improved greatly, that was why we moved her," said Dr. Shekuh.

"Are you sure you didn't move her because you want to give priority attention to the white man, the American," said Tina.

Tina's accusation touched a nerve, but the doctor was subtle in his response as he took it on the chin and painstakingly disabused

Tina's mind. Doctor Shekuh then urged Tina not to suggest a thing like that because he considers all his patients to be priority patients and Tina's mum isn't an exception.

Nurse Theresa walked into the doctor's office while Tina and Doctor Shekuh were still speaking and the nurse immediately interjected, as she told the doctor that the scan result for the patient in bed ten is ready.

Doctor Shekuh quickly stretched out his hand and collected the scan result from the nurse, as he asked to take a look at the scan result. Sadly, the nurse went on to talk about the result of the scan even when Tina was still in the doctor's office. "From this result, Professor Pratt Church will need a brain surgery," said the nurse.

That name 'Professor Pratt Church' clicked in Tina's memory, and as a journalist she vividly remembered the professor who made fame for chasing a baboon owner in Africa "Did you say Professor Pratt Church?" asked Tina.

Sadly, the nurse unwittingly continued providing Tina with too much information about Professor Church. "Yeah, the man attacked by two leopards in the forest," said Nurse Theresa.

Realising that Tina is a journalist, Doctor Shekuh used his eyes to signal the nurse to put a sock in it. He then asked Tina to excuse them and asked her to wait at the hospital's reception, or wait by her mum's bed side. Nurse Theresa immediately realised her blunder and apologised, saying she actually didn't remember that Tina is a journalist.

"But this patient will need brain surgery," said Nurse Theresa.

"Let's see how ready he's to follow through with the procedure," said Dr. Shekuh.

Tina Mbolelu caught the name of Professor Pratt Church the moment it was mentioned and later went into ward ten to see Professor Pratt Church who made headlines in the past over the

Kenyan Baboon drama. Interestingly, the Professor was awake when Tina walked in. "Hello professor," said Tina.

"Hello madam, but I don't think we've met before," said Prof. Church.

"Err.., I'm Tina Mbolelu, and I know you're Professor Pratt Church," she said.

The professor concurred he is, and it didn't take long after Tina began her manoeuvre with the professor that Nurse Theresa walked in holding the scan result. The nurse wasn't quite up for a manoeuvring journalist, and didn't hesitate to remind Tina she isn't supposed to be there, and then she asked Tina to leave.

"I'm sorry, nurse," said Tina, who later left.

Nurse Theresa turned to the professor. "I hope you didn't tell her about yourself?" she asked. "Who's she? She looks friendly and I seem to like her warm disposition," said Prof. Church.

"That's her mum in the room next to yours, and she's a journalist, that was why I don't want you divulging any information about yourself to her," said Nurse Theresa.

Professor was sure to tell the nurse of his perception of Tina as he jocularly told her Tina seems to know him more than he knew her. Nurse Theresa burst the professor's bubble as he went on gushing about how friendly Tina was, the nurse reminded the professor that journalists are known for their flattery and for snooping around when it comes to getting information to make headlines.

"Is that the scan result?" asked Bolo.

The nurse told the professor that the doctor will be here soon to speak with him about the result of the scan. Though, the professor became inquisitive as he asked the nurse to know what the result of the scan looks like and wants to know if it's positive.

"Sorry professor, the doctor is in the best position to give you the details of the scan result," said Nurse Theresa.

Doctor Shekuh walked in as the conversation was on going and told the professor that his scan result is ready, and he's sorry the result isn't too good.

"Oh, no, doctor, how bad is it?" asked Prof. Church.

Sadly, the doctor broke the news to the professor that the scan result shows traces of blood in his brain.

"Meaning?" asked Prof. Church.

"Meaning you're bleeding in your brain, and that's why you're feeling so dizzy and always going in and out of consciousness," said Dr. Shekuh.

"What does this mean for me?" asked Prof. Church.

"You'll need to go in for surgery, and we've to do that as soon as possible.

"What about the cost, this must be an expensive procedure?" asked Prof. Church.

"Sure, it's expensive," said Dr. Shekuh.

Professor Church quickly asked the doctor about the possible side effects that could result from the surgery, and the doctor didn't hesitate to list out the odds of this surgery to include stroke, memory loss, and possibly a disoriented brain function.

The professor grimaced then his face dropped, as the odds of this surgery seemed stacked against him, he then told the doctor to give him some time to think things through. "I'll leave you to think about it, but we'll continue to care for you until you reach a decision," the doctor said.

Moments later the doctor left after his brief chat with the professor leaving the professor to think through his next move. Now that the rubber has hit the road, Bolo Baum didn't hesitate to urge the professor to inform his family about this new development. He did a good job dissuading the professor from masquerading himself as a man who has things under control because this might not work at this point as it's now beyond what can be kept under wraps.

"Let me weigh my options, I know for sure I won't die immediately," said Prof. Church.

Bolo then advised the professor to make the wisest of decisions even as he weighs his options because this might come to bite, the professor then turned to Jonas and inquired about his bag because his debit card is inside his wallet. "I've your wallet here with me, but your bags are still in the jungle," said Jonas. Professor Church collected the wallet from Jonas and thanked him.

"Let me go home, Professor. I've arranged with the hospital, and they'll get you something to eat," said Bolo.

"Thank you very much; I truly appreciate your kindness towards me," said Prof. Church.

Bolo Baum stood up to leave, and then turned to Jonas, and asked him to stay and assist the professor. By the morning of the next day "The Crowers" which is a Zimbabwean television station where Tina Mbolelu work reported the news of Professor Pratt Church being attacked by two leopards and the news was immediately reported by United States television stations and other western media.

Unsurprisingly, Eileen who usually wakes up first to prepare for lectures at the university woke up by 5.30am and turned on the television only to see the news about her dad. "Mum, mum, you said it," said Eileen. She screamed and cried and interestingly, Joe was the first respondent as he dashed into the living room in shock.

"What's it, and why are you screaming?" asked Joe.

It didn't take long before Nora rushed out of her room in shock, and joined her children in the living room "What's it, are you out of your mind?" asked Nora.

"Dad has been attacked by leopards," she cried.

"Where did you get that from, is it because I narrated my dream to you?" asked Nora.

"It's everywhere in the news, I suppose all the news channels have it," said Eileen.

"You can't be serious" said Nora. Joe quickly picked up the remote to search for the news of the leopards' attack as the channel on the screen has just finished airing the news by the time they arrived. He flipped through the channels and found some channels still airing the news.

"There it is, mum," said Eileen.

"Why has your dad chosen to do this to me? I called him and asked him about this, but he kept it from me," Nora cried.

"I said it that mum shouldn't dream; now her dream has come true," said Joe.

"From the news, this has happened even before mum dreamt about it," said Eileen.

"Why is this happening to me? I don't deserve this," Nora cried because she thinks this is too bitter a pill to swallow.

Eileen became highly exasperated as she anxiously asked her mum what their next move should be in the mist of their confusion.

"Let's call dad, maybe it's time dad and I talk, we've been avoiding each other, and things have gone from bad to worse," said Joe. Eileen finds Joe's comment to be distasteful as he seemed to have poured gasoline into the flaming furnace.

"What are you saying? You sound as if you're dad's boss," said Eileen.

"As men, we bottle-up our emotions and don't talk, you and mum have spoken with dad expressing your emotions and it doesn't seem to have worked, so let me speak with him with my emotions intact," said Joe.

Sadly, Nora doesn't want her children rattling their dad's cage any further, particularly now that the situation was quite inflammable, she immediately instructed Joe and Eileen not to call their dad until she permits them to do so.

"Mum, why? Stop sounding as if our dad is your personal property, he's ours as well," said Eileen.

Nora interjected and informed her children that this isn't about whose property their dad is, she then urged them to just look through the window and see for themselves, those waiting to take advantage of their difficulties for profitable purposes. Eileen rushed to the window to verify if the press were actually there and waiting for them to come out. Unsurprisingly, their front house now hosts an encampment of journalists.

"Your dad is as stubborn as a mule, and he doesn't even understand the hell he's putting his family through," said Nora. Joe in his usual dramatic move walks to the door as he intends to address the press so they can leave, but Nora was quick on her feet as she quickly pulled Joe back and shut the door, and instructed her children to stay indoors until she has a conversation with Professor Stone Walker.

"But the press can't just remain in the front of our house, we need to do something about them," said Eileen. Nora was quite upfront as she reminded her children to be calm since the press won't burst into their house, particularly now that their dad needs brain surgery, and the press want to sell their papers irrespective of their pain.

Nora immediately picked her phone and put a call across to Professor Stone Walker. "Hello Nora, how're you doing?" said Prof. Walker.

"We're fine but rattled, and did you see the news?" asked Nora.

"Yes, I was taken aback by the news and was about to call you, but your call came in first," said Prof. Walker.

Nora continued sobbing and asking why her husband would do a thing like this to his family, saying he doesn't even care. Professor Walker unwittingly remained silent on his end of the phone as he allowed Nora some time to vent and pour out her emotions and when she finished venting, he told her he's troubled about Professor Church's condition.

"I called him after the attack," said Nora.

"You did? And what did he say?" asked Prof. Walker.

"I had a feeling he was sick, but he insisted he was fine, even though I could hear it in his faint and cracked voice," said Nora.

Professor Walker wasn't particularly impressed by his friend's insistence that he's fine even in his present state, only for his family to receive the news from media reports that he will need brain surgery.

"Do you know, the annoying thing about this was that I told him of my dream where he was attacked by two leopards, and yet he maintained he's fine and alright," said Nora. Professor Walker laughed after Nora finished narrating her dream, he then asked Nora if she did actually dream about this particular attack, and Nora concurred saying she told her husband about it just to warn him, not knowing the attack had already happened.

"You're truly gifted; and your husband does talk about your ability to discern danger as it approaches," said Prof. Walker.

"Of what use is the gift if I can't keep my family safe with it," said Nora.

"I know, but what do you suggest we do?" asked Prof. Walker.

"This whole thing is because of his interest in remaining in the wild," said Nora. Professor Walker then suggested to Nora that the best way out of this predicament was to find a way to lure Pratt out of the wild. The problem has become multifaceted and the

Church's family debacle isn't a secret anymore, but dispersing the press that's camped in the front of her house is now her priority.

"Have you called him since you learnt of the attack from the news?" asked Prof. Walker.

"No, I haven't, I felt I should call you first so we can think of a way out," she said. Nora's emotions got the best of her as she continued to sob, and all Professor Walker could do was to urge her to be strong in times like this, at least, for Eileen and Joe.

"What did I do to deserve this? Why am I on the news for the wrong and pathetic reason such as this?" asked Nora. "Remember, bad things do happen to good people as well," said Prof Walker.

"I know, Walker. What do you suggest we do now?" asked Nora.

Instead of spending all day kicking herself in the foot, Professor Walker suggested to Nora that it would best they both travel to Zimbabwe immediately. Professor Walker sensed that his friend might not want to come back with them and also advised Nora that it's best to involve the foreign office or the embassy. Funnily, Nora doesn't think informing the foreign office is a wise use of her time because she believes the embassy staff must have heard of the news and the foreign office is aware of the news.

"Their knowledge of the news isn't enough but pushing them to act should be more appropriate," said Prof. Walker.

"Ok, you can contact them, but it's just 6.15am and we should contact them after the office opens," said Nora.

"You're right, but I suggest you call him and let him know the whole thing is out in the open, and I'll do the same," said Prof. Walker.

"Ok, I'll give him a call immediately," said Nora.

Interestingly, Eileen was waiting to hear the outcome of her mum's conversation with Professor Walker. "Mum, what did he say?" she asked.

"He's contacting the foreign office and the embassy, but he suggested I call your dad to let him know it's already in the news," said Nora.

Nora then gave her husband a ring for some straight talk, but the moment the professor picked up the phone from his end and answered with a faint voice. "Hello Nora, and why're you calling me this early?" asked Prof. Church.

"Why've you decided to punish us, and what have we done to deserve this?" she asked.

Professor Church was still under the illusion that the leopard attack was still under wraps and pretended he has no knowledge of what Nora was talking about, as he told her he isn't following. Sadly, his jaw dropped as Nora told him the news of the attack is all in the news, she gave her husband some parting banter as she reminded him that the professor involved in the Kenyan Baboon drama, is now in the news again.

"What's it about me that's making the headlines?" asked Prof. Church.

"Stop being naive, you were attacked by two leopards, and you'll need brain surgery, but I asked you about this yesterday, and you denied everything flat out and said you were fine," said Nora.

Sad to say, that the professor's worst fears have just happened, as he exclaimed over the phone and saying, this is what he has been avoiding. He knew for sure that his wife is a reasonably intelligent woman, who doesn't talk gibberish, and this time Nora wasn't particularly interested in the professor's fears as she proceeded to hitting the nail on the head. She then asked her husband if the news is true, and if his condition is as critical as it's described in the media.

"Partially true, but how did this news get to the media?" asked Prof. Church.

Nora slapped down her husband's question as she reminded him he put himself in the headlines for the wrong reasons, she then urged him to worry about how he'll undergo a successful brain surgery and stop worrying about how the news got to the media.

"How're the kids taking this?" asked Prof. Church.

"They are mortified and sick to their stomachs just as I'm," said Nora.

The professor's attempt to manage the headlines precipitated by this attack seemed to have been a mess as things snowballed out of his control, yet he's still under the impression that he could manage this whole drama going forward. He then asked Nora not to worry about him that he will take care of himself. Unsurprisingly, Nora wasn't having any more of the professor's dim-witted adventures, as she told her husband she will be in Zimbabwe the next day, and she's coming over with Professor Walker.

"I don't need all this because I'm returning to the wild the moment I am back on my feet," said Prof. Church.

"I don't know what you're talking about," said Prof. Church.

Nora angrily ended the phone call abruptly as her husband began blabbing about returning to the wild once he's back on his feet, but a phone call from Professor Walker came almost immediately.

"Professor, how're you doing?" asked Prof. Walker.

"I'm fine Walker, Nora just told me about the headlines," said Prof. Church.

"Has she called you already?" asked Prof Walker.

"Of course, yes, we just finished talking few minutes back," said Prof. Church.

Professor Walker began with banter as he reminded Professor Church that he thought he once said that he has got this whole thing about living in the wild under control, and sadly, things have now gone terribly, terribly wrong.

"Under control, what do you mean?" asked Prof. Church.

"Most of the time you sound as if you have all the wildlife under your control," said Prof Walker.

"I fantasise about being around wildlife, and I'm going right back to the wild the moment I'm back on my feet. Though, I never saw this attack coming," said Prof. Church. Professor Church remained illusory, forgetting that the narrative has overtaken him, and he's no longer the one writing this script.

In a chilling rebuke, Professor Walker quickly remanded his friend that he didn't call to discuss his return to the wild and won't get bogged down by such conversation, he then went further to ask him how he's feeling.

"I'm sick, that's the truth, and from what Nora just told me, all of the details are out there, so you know already," said Prof. Church.

"You have to make sure you get the best care, I'll speak with Nora, and we'll be in Zimbabwe tomorrow," said Prof. Church.

Professor Church finds this visit to be an unnecessary inconvenience yet wasn't keen to ruffle feathers with his wife and friend whose support he considered unsolicited.

Professor Pratt continued playing hide and seek with the reality facing him, as he insists he doesn't think it will be necessary for his wife and friend to come over to Zimbabwe. He blatantly told Nora he can take care of himself.

"See you tomorrow, Professor," said Prof. Walker.

Professor Pratt Church is now on the back foot, as he turned to Jonas Baum to inquire of how the press got hold of his medical record. Jonas seemed lost as he asked the professor what record he's talking about.

"Did you or your dad tell anybody about the attack or about the brain surgery?" asked Prof. Church.

Jonas didn't hesitate to speak up for his dad as he told the professor outrightly that he knows his dad too well, and he wouldn't do a thing like that.

"I know your dad; he' isn't the kind of man that would do a thing like that," said Prof. Church.

"Then who did?" asked Jonas.

The professor replied Jonas saying he has no idea about who did, and then turned his attention to the staff of the hospital, as he tried to unravel the person behind the leak. He then asked Jonas to get him the doctor, and minutes later Nurse Theresa was by the professor's bed side. "Professor, you asked to see the doctor?" she asked.

"Yes, I want to see the doctor," said Prof. Church.

"The doctor is in theatre but is there anything I can do for you?" asked Nurse Theresa.

The professor told the nurse that details of his medical record are all in the news and making the headlines, and demanded an explanation from this hospital over the source of the leak because this can't be the handwork of the ghost of Christmas past.

"Actually, we saw the news this morning, and the doctor was equally furious about it, but he went into theatre to attend to some emergency," said Nurse Theresa.

The professor finds it absurd that while he remained in the dark concerning the news about him making global headline, everyone including the hospital staff have seen the news of the attack making the headlines. He expressed his reservation concerning the leak and demanded to know how it happened. Sadly, the nurse's attempt to absolve the hospital of any blame was carefully choreographed as she quickly pointed her finger of blame at Tina Mbolelu, as the possible mole behind the leak.

"Who is this Tina Mbolelu, and how did she get hold of my medical record?" asked Prof. Church.

"You remember the Journalist that was here yesterday, and I told you her mum is in the room next to yours?" asked Nurse Theresa.

"Yes, I remembered quite well, but I can't remember giving her my medical details," said Prof. Church.

Nurse Theresa told the professor she's certain that this journalist is behind this ugly act, but that didn't do it for the professor as he was keen to know why Tina Mbolelu would do a thing like that. He was quite lost for words as he tries getting his head around why the journalist will do a thing like this knowing how damaging it would be to him.

The moment I saw her yesterday, snooping and sneaking around, I knew she's up to no good," she said. The professor isn't willing to take this betrayal lying down, he then suggested that it'll be better if Tina is made to understand how damaging her stunts are to him.

"I'll call her right away," said Nurse Theresa.

The professor sensed some kind of conspiracy between the nurse and the journalist because he was quick to ask the nurse if she knowingly passed his details to the journalist. He then asked how come she's in possession of Tina's phone number. "Why would you think I'll engage in such a nerve wrecking stunt, I intend to get her phone number from her mum's file; she's her next of kin," said Nurse Theresa.

"Ok, sorry about that, I'm just rattled by this surprise," said Prof. Church.

Minutes later the furious nurse stepped outside and put a phone call across to Tina Mbolelu and sadly, the nurse didn't allow time for any exchange of pleasantries, as she went straight to the point.

"Tina, this is Nurse Theresa of the Wonder World Clinics," said Nurse Theresa.

"Hello nurse how're you doing, and is my mum ok?" asked Tina.

The nurse didn't hesitate to subtly remind Tina her mum is ok, and she doesn't have to worry about her. She then immediately asked her why she did what she did, but the journalist at the middle of this unfolding drama remained evasive because she seem out of touch with the impact of the reality of her journalistic stunt, as she quickly asked the nurse.

"Do what! What did I do?" asked Tina.

"You came to our clinic sneaking and snooping around our patients, did you know the trouble you've just caused us by telling the world about Professor Pratt Church's medical details?" asked Nurse Theresa.

"For the record, I didn't sneak, I did not snoop, and I didn't go into your patient's file," said Tina.

"Then how best can you describe your action?" asked Nurse Theresa.

"Stop being naive, Nurse. I'm a journalist, and I earn a living from reporting what I see and what I hear," said Tina.

Tina hates being perceived as a lousy creep, because she considers her conversation with the nurse as nothing but idle talk. The conversation between the pair became a bit intense since courtesy has been thrown out through the window, yet the nurse was bent on asking Tina if she must report whatever she sees and hear irrespective of how the news impacts on the persons concerned.

Tina seems to have come to the realisation that the nurse isn't just out to pick a bone with her but to lay bare the enormity of her action, and couldn't help herself but apologise to the nurse for her action if she feels offended, yet made it known to the nurse that she's just doing her job and will continue to do so.

"I've a question for you?" asked Nurse Theresa.

"You can go ahead with your question." said Tina.

Nurse Theresa went ahead to pull Tina's leg as she asked what if the news she just reported isn't correct since she picks her news from conversation between people whether they're correct or not. Sad for the nurse, Tina's knowledge of her craft isn't limited because she knows her onions as she told the nurse she isn't stupid. She didn't hesitate to remind the nurse that the moment she mentioned the professor's name, she went into the ward to make sure he's the one and verify what she has heard.

"Ok, thank you, just know that we'll not give you another opportunity to sneak around again in our clinic," said Nurse Theresa.

By the evening of the same day, Doctor Shekuh finished with a surgery that has taken quite a long day, he then walked to the professor's bedside accompanied by Nurse Theresa, and inquired from the Professor to know how he's doing.

"I'm fine, but I am put off by what happened here yesterday," said Prof. Church.

"I was told you wanted to see a doctor, and I instructed the doctor on duty to leave this matter for me to address," said Dr. Shekuh.

Sadly, the doctor is already on a back foot, as he's now outmanoeuvred by Tina Mbolelu, and the Professor thinks there's nothing to address, and after all, his medical details are all over the news making the headlines. Doctor Shekuh made it clear that his involvement at this point isn't some form of Trojan horse, as he said that it's glaringly obvious that the deed has been done and he's willing to accept responsibility for his hospital's failures.

Doctor's Shekuh's words didn't seem to soothe the professors' emotional trauma precipitated by the awful leak by Tina. The Professor had to take the doctor on a guilt trip as he continued to emphasise the hospital's negligence, reminding them that since they knew the woman is a journalist and reports anything that crosses her eyes, then due care should've been taken whenever she's in their premises.

"We've called to let her understand the gravity of her action," said Dr. Shekuh

The news of his health making global headlines isn't the only worries of the professor, sadly, journalist are now camped in the front of the hospital where the professor is being treated, and he didn't hesitate to express his concerns with Doctor Shekuh. "What's it about journalists hanging around the hospital, and wanting to get more to report about me?" asked Prof. Church.

"They've been around for some time, since this news broke out, and even when I came in about an hour ago" said Bolo. "I've seen them as well, and I intend to address them shortly," said Dr. Shekuh. The professor turned to Bolo and said he believes the news headlines have attracted the local media to him and asked Doctor Shekuh what he intends to say to them.

"I know what to say to the press, Professor. When I'm finished with them you won't find any of them around," said Dr. Shekuh. Bolo then pleaded with the doctor to do something fast to help take away the emotional stress from this critically ill professor.

Later that night, Eileen walked into her mum's bedroom as her mum packs her bags, and getting ready for the Zimbabwe trip before going to bed. "Mum, I supposed you've finished packing?" asked Eileen.

"I'm getting my things ready for the trip to Zimbabwe," said Nora.

Eileen sat on her mum's bed fiddling with her mum's bracelet while her mum continued packing her stuff. She then reminded her mum that she and Joe have finished packing their things and are ready for the trip, and they're only waiting for her so they can book flights together. Funnily, Nora has something else in mind.

"That won't be possible, and I'm going with Stone Walker as I mentioned to you in the morning," said Nora.

"Why're you going with dad's friend, and not us? He's our dad, and we have every right to see him and know how he's doing," said Eileen.

"Eileen, I'm not prepared for this court session with you, your dad has caused me enough trouble," said Nora.

Eileen was irked by her mum's bully-boy strike bursting tactics as she made it plain and simple to her mum that it isn't up to her to decide who visits her dad. Sadly, Eileen is never known to mince words as she protested the manner in which her mum pontificates on this matter, she then reminded her mum that it's her right to see her dad. Joe was attracted by Eileen's raised voice and walked in on the conversation between the pair and asked his sister what the problem is and why is it that she's so upset. "I don't know what mum is talking about and I'm not taking any more of this," said Eileen.

"What's she saying that you haven't said?" asked Joe.

"She said she's going to see dad alone," said Eileen.

"I know mum won't do a thing like that, mum and dad can't continue to make us victims in this house," said Joe.

Nora's disposition changed as her children went on the rant over her decision to travel without them, and funnily, she seemed to have heard enough and immediately decided to exert her authority to shut down every dissent. She then turned to Joe whose utterances she finds spooky and asked him to quietly leave her room if he doesn't have something nice to say.

"I never caused any of this; dad was obstinate and decided to go into the wild, running around with animals despite pleas to make him change his mind," said Joe.

"I don't want you making this already difficult situation more difficult for me," said Nora.

Unsurprisingly, Joe revisited his earlier assertion that life isn't all about serendipity, insisting that his mum should equally share in the blame. He quickly expressed his exception, stressing that instead of dreaming of where the President of the United States is giving his dad an award, all his mum could dream of was about leopards attacking his dad. He emphatically stressed that if his mum had dreamt something else, this wouldn't have happened and the outcome would've been different.

"Instead of talking about joining mum in Zimbabwe, you're busy talking trash," said Eileen.

Nora interjected by reaffirming her earlier position on the matter that she and Professor Walker are bringing their dad home, and her children can't go with her because of travel visas restriction.

"I know we can't travel without a visa, but since the foreign office is assisting you, they can as well assist us," said Eileen.

"This is not as easy as you think," said Nora.

Eileen is now becoming agitated by her uncooperative stance, as she inquired from her mum to know why it is difficult for the home office to give a little help. The drama between Nora and her children persisted and seem to have shifted away from the calamity that befell their dad and how to deal with the adventurous Professor Church. They're rather beginning to burn their energy over who travels to Zimbabwe and who stays back. Nora tried managing this ensuing kerfuffle as she tried calming the situation by sweet-talking her children into staying back while she get their dad straight to the hospital, and then they can spend as much time with him as they want.

"Ok, I'll spare you this time, just understand we have just as much right to see dad as you do," said Eileen.

Nora looked around and didn't see Joe and she didn't see him leave her room either. She then asked Eileen of Joe's whereabouts. "He left, maybe he's in his room or somewhere," said Eileen.

Nora immediately left what she's doing in search for Joe but met Joe playing a computer game in his room, and she didn't hesitate to ask him why he left, but Joe's response was startling to his mum. "Do you care?" asked Joe.

"Of course, I do care about how you feel, and how this whole saga is affecting our lives," said Nora.

"I'm tired of you, mum. Soon, I'll sever ties with you, just as I did with dad," said Joe.

Nora became quite emotional as she finds Joe's subtle threat to be cruel and forbids him from saying a thing like that. She then sat down in the sofa in Joe's room as she urged him to let her know what the problem was. Now that Nora is seated and ready to listen, Joe quickly reminded her that his parents have been taking decisions, and it hasn't augured well for the entire family, and sadly, this is where that has led them. Joe urged his mum to do them the privilege of being a part of the decisions that happens in the house.

"Ok, I'm all ears. What contribution do you want to make?" asked Nora.

Now that Nora passed the ball to Joe, as she asked him to make his contribution, Joe decides that the situation is already inflamed as it is, then suggested he will go by his mum's decision and he doesn't have anything to say for now.

Nora tried creating a friendly ambience after the cantankerous atmosphere precipitated by the debate over who gets to travel to Zimbabwe, as she told Joe that she wouldn't want to leave for Zimbabwe knowing that her kids have some animosity towards her.

"We're all square, mum. You should go and continue packing your bags. Do you want me to give a hand?" asked Joe.

"Your sister is already doing that," said Nora.

The next morning Nora and Professor Stone Walker joined the morning flight and arrived in Zimbabwe later in the evening of that day after a long-haul flight.

Sadly, the embassy staff meant to pick Nora and Professor Walker on their arrival at the airport wasn't there as at the time of their arrival and this sort of put Nora off because her patience was already thin. Professor Walker suggested they wait at the airport for the embassy staff that will be joining them at the airport. Nora stood there at the entrance of the arrival lounge leafing through a guidebook she finds handy and thought it might be helpful in navigating her way through the city to the hospital where her husband was admitted.

"I want this whole thing managed properly, I don't want it to be shambolic," said Nora.

"This won't end in shambles, let's just keep calm," said Prof. Walker.

"It's already getting late, and why aren't they here waiting for us before our arrival?" asked Nora.

While Nora was itching to go it alone without the embassy staff that was meant to provide consular assistance, Professor Walker kept her on a tight leash as he held her back and reminding her that the embassy has already established contact with her husband. The professor stressed that it will make the job of locating him easier. Interestingly, Nora pestered him further that she's eager to see her husband, and that she thinks they should be able to locate the clinic without the embassy's assistance, yet Professor Stone Walker pressed her to be patient.

While they had their conversation, a car pulled over in front of them as they talked, and Bill Alfred stepped out of the car. "Professor Walker and Nora Church?" asked Billy Alfred.

"Yes, of course" said Prof. Walker.

"I'm Bill Alfred an embassy attaché, please get in and let's go," he said. They shook hands as they exchanged pleasantries, and Billy collected their bags and loaded them into the boot of the car. "What's the nature of the hospital where he's receiving treatment?" asked Nora.

Billy who is resident in Zimbabwe was on hand to provide Nora with a response as she told her the hospital where her husband was admitted to isn't the best of hospitals by all standards but the hospital is still ok.

"I suppose you're aware we'll need your assistance in returning my husband to the United States immediately," said Nora.

This warm ambience was short-lived as the conversation quickly went sour because Billy stopped short of giving Nora the kind of response she seeks, as he said its best to consider medical advice before deciding on the next step to take. Sadly, Billy's response got Nora incensed and she quickly turned the heat on Billy over his tacky response, asking him what the hell he's talking about. She reminded Billy that her husband will need specialist treatment, and she can't let him undergo any brain surgery procedure here in Africa.

"What if the doctors advise that it'll not be safe for him to fly because of his condition?" asked Billy.

"The United States government should be able to fly my husband home with an air ambulance. After all, this man has contributed a lot to his nation," said Nora. Billy considered Nora's assertion to be a big jump, and took exception to Nora's appraisal of her husband as he quickly reminded Nora that her husband's decision to travel all the way to Africa and live in the midst of wildlife cannot be regarded as a contribution to his nation. It didn't take long before the temperature in the car became fever-pitched as Nora flared up and asked Billy to stop being hypocritical. Nora insisted that Billy Alfred didn't have to say a thing like that to her face because she considers it cruel and belittling.

"I'm sorry, Nora; it's just that your comments are fallacious," said Billy.

Professor Walker tapped Nora on the shoulder, trying t make her stop picking quarrels with Billy, and reminded her everything will be fine. An hour later, they arrived the Wonder World Clinics, and walked straight to the receptionist. "Hello, good evening," said Nora.

"Good evening, what can we do for you?" asked the receptionist.

"We're here to see the Professor," said Prof. Walker.

Unfortunately for Nora, the receptionist mistook them for journalist fishing for more info about the professor and she quickly dismissed them as she turned to Nora and told her she's sorry she can't see him. The receptionist reminded them she was instructed not to allow anyone in.

"Why can't I see him?" asked Nora.

The receptionist continued with her line of conversation saying, "you journalists have done enough damage already and this hospital doesn't want any more trouble." Nora on the other hand, was already incensed by her heated exchange with Billy moments earlier, and wasn't in any mood for further delays. She then tried clarifying any misconception of the receptionist by letting her know they are from the United States, and she's his wife, and needs to see him urgently.

"Sorry, I don't intend to be rude, and I need to see your identification to be sure, because I don't want journalists passing off as family," said the receptionist. Nora then brought out her passport. "Enough of this drama! I didn't travel all the way to Zimbabwe to be interviewed like this," said Nora.

"I'm Professor Walker, Professor Pratt Church is my colleague, and this man here is an attaché to the United States embassy," said Prof Walker, as he also displayed his passport.

"Ok, you can go in," said the receptionist.

"Where is he and how do we locate him?" asked Nora.

"Go upstairs, first floor, and turn right, he's in bed ten," said receptionist.

Minutes later they are all by the professor's bed side, and Nora began to sob "Oh, honey is this you?" asked Nora.

"Err.., Nora, you came, but I told you not to bother so much about me," said Prof. Church.

"Stop being silly, why do you choose to cause us so much trouble? This isn't what we agreed when we were getting married," said Nora.

Professor Church tried making light of the situation as he asked his wife Nora to calm down. Nora seems not to be having it, as she reminded her husband this whole debacle is precipitated by his sheer arrogance and vanity.

Professor Walker allowed Nora to finish getting off whatever emotion she has in her chest before exchanging pleasantries with his professor friend and asked how he's feeling.

"I'm fine, Walker. How're Gloria and the kids," asked Prof. Church.

"Gloria is fine, let's focus on you for now, how did this happen?" asked Prof. Walker.

Professor Church felt it appropriate to introduce the friends he made in Zimbabwe and he first introduced Bolo Baum and then his son Jonas Baum. He then asked his wife to help him thank this father and son for all they did for him.

"The mention's of Jonas's name clicked in Nora's memory, and she turned around facing Jonas, then asked her husband if this is the Jonas he mentioned to her on the phone as his guide.

"Hmm, I've mentioned him to you already, yes, he's, and that's his dad, and they're the reason I'm alive," said Prof. Church.

Nora's disposition changed immediately, and she looked to Jonas with some ferocity, and she told him off by reminding Jonas that as her husband's guide, he's meant to keep him safe. She didn't stop talking tough as she blamed Jonas for taking her husband to big cats' infested forest where he could be killed.

"Madam, that isn't how the whole thing was, it isn't my fault," said Jonas.

"Then whose fault is it! My husband could have been killed, and you're telling me it's not your fault?" asked Nora.

Bolo looked on as Nora tongue-lashed and gave his son the dressing down, he couldn't help but step in, and tried toning down the temperature by accepting the blame for everything, especially now that he just realised Nora's blood is too hot to handle. "Madam your reaction isn't misplaced, any sane person would react the way you just did," said Bolo.

Sadly, the gloves are off, and platitudes won't do the trick because Nora isn't ready for any rhetoric or sweet talk, as she quickly dismissed Bolo' submission in the matter and told him not to patronise her because she isn't happy with him and his son.

"It's ok, Nora," said Prof. Church.

Professor Church had no choice but to set the record straight to take the heat off this family that has graciously hosted him and shown him nothing but kindness, as he told his wife that none of this is Jonas's fault. He unblinkingly told his wife that the fault is all his and he should be the one apologising to Jonas and also thanking his father for his generosity.

"Why? Jonas is your forest guide, and he's meant to guide you through the forest safely," said Nora.

Professor Church painstakingly gave his wife the granular details and the chronology of event leading to the leopard attack as he quickly narrated to Nora that he's is actually the one who put Jonas in danger. He made them understand that Jonas warned him of the possibility of a big cat by the stream and insisted they stay away, but he refused and told him he loves to enjoy the company of the animals.

Nora held her hand over her mouth and cried the more as she asked her husband why he would want to put himself in such danger.

"It was even the same Jonas that saved me from the leopards and took me to his dad, who stayed away from his farm and stayed with me, he even made the deposit payment for my treatment," said Prof. Church.

Nora was taken aback by the generosity of this family towards her husband and felt bad over her earlier rant at Bolo and Jonas and asked in surprise. "You did all that for us?" asked Nora.

"Let's be happy he's stable; when he was brought to me; all he said was 'please save me'," said Bolo. Like always, Bolo espouses pragmatism, but this time he empathised with this family and bears no grudge over a premature rant.

"I'm so, so sorry, over my reaction, I'm just mortified and sick over all this," said Nora. Bolo Baum wants the focus to be on the professor's health as he steered the conversation away from who did what, and felt it's good to state the fact, as he told Nora that he equally blamed his son over the attack before he knew the truth.

"Jonas, I'm so, so sorry, and thank you for everything," said Nora.

"You shouldn't have come, I would've managed," said Prof. Church.

"See where your stubbornness has led us. How can a man run away from a career, a family and a normal life just to live among wildlife?" asked Nora.

"That's my fantasy, and I still intend to continue doing so," said Prof. Church.

Nora dismissed as utter nonsense her husband's blab about his fantasy of living in the wild. She made it clear that she isn't inclined to listen to any of his drama. She moralised the situation by reminding him he'd a career, a normal life and a family, and these things are in short supply. Though, he had all of it, but he underestimated them by choosing to live in the wilds of Africa.

"We need to see the doctor because you're leaving with us immediately," said Prof Walker.

"Professor, should I wait or leave, and return to you tomorrow?" asked Billy.

Professor Walker urged Billy to hang around to help facilitate Professor Church's travel to the United States, as he said they might start planning their return immediately after meeting with the doctor.

"Jonas, please take them to the doctor's office," said Prof. Church.

Jonas stood up, and then turned to Nora and Professor Walker and asked them to please come with him, and they all walked to the Medical Director's office.

"Jonas, is the professor ok and who are these people?" asked Dr. Shekuh.

"My name is Professor Stone Walker, Professor Pratt Church is my colleague and this is his wife, Nora. This man here is Billy Alfred, he's an attaché at the United States embassy," said Prof Walker.

"You're welcome, Professor, and madam you're welcome," said Dr. Shekuh.

Nora didn't hesitate to ask the doctor to brief her on her husband's medical condition, because she has come to take him with her to the United States.

"I understand your concerns, but I can't do that without his consent," said Dr. Shekuh.

Unsurprisingly, Nora isn't one to be lectured about consent as she quickly reminded the doctor that he gave her husband details to a journalist without his consent from what she understands, and questioned why he's now stalling, and talking about consent.

Doctor Shekuh remained calm even as the professor's wife was kicking off, he'd to calmly inform her that the circumstance of his medical record getting to the press is quite different, and he thinks that obtaining her husband's consent is the right thing to do.

Professor Walker understands that the doctor is doing exactly what he ought to do, considering the circumstance, he then tapped Nora by the shoulder as he tried to make her stop the back and forth conversation with doctor. "It's ok, doctor, let's meet him and discuss it with him, I know he won't object to that," said Prof. Walker.

"Wait for me by his bedside, and I'll be with you in a few minutes," said Dr. Shekuh.

"Ok, Nora, let's wait for him in the ward," said Prof Walker. They all went back to the ward and waited by the professor's bed side, and it didn't take long Doctor Shekuh was on hand with the details of the professor's medical record. "Professor, your wife and friend want me to brief them on your condition," said Dr. Shekuh.

"Do I've a choice?" asked Prof. Church.

"Of course yes, you do have a choice," said Dr. Shekuh.

Professor Church smiled and told the doctor he doesn't seem to have a choice, particularly now that his wife is standing right by his side. He then urged the doctor to tell them everything without any reservation. Doctor Shekuh then asked Nora and Professor Walker to join him in his office, so they can go through the professor's file together. Minutes later, they're in the doctor's office and Nora asked the doctor to be fast about it. "As you can see, for now, he's stable, but his condition is still critical because of the bleeding in his brain," said Dr. Shekuh.

"Oh my God!" exclaimed Nora.

"He has been in and out of consciousness and also dizzy most of the time," said Dr. Shekuh.

"What do we do about that?" asked Prof. Walker.

"The bleeding will surely stop once he undergoes brain surgery," said Dr. Shekuh.

Nora sensed this doctor is a quack and her perception of the hospital where her husband was admitted seems to have blindsided her judgement. She didn't hesitate to tell the doctor to his face that she's in doubt of his medical experience and can't trust his diagnosis of her husband condition. Typically, she'd to take every word coming from the mouth of this doctor with a pinch of salt.

Doctor Shekuh immediately interjected and reminded Nora that he's aware that she has been very rude since she walked into his hospital, and even to the very family that saved her husband's life, it's a pity she's as stubborn as her husband.

"What the hell are you talking about? How am I to be sure you aren't a quack?" asked Nora.

The doctor became furious, and pointed at a framed certificate. "Look at that. That's an award given to me by the British Medical Association, I worked as a consultant in the biggest hospital in England, why would you just walk in here and insult me because I'm an African," said Dr. Shekuh.

"Sorry about that doctor, she's just curious," said Prof. Walker.

The doctor was disconcerted because he felt Nora's comment was everything but benignity, and the insult got to him. He made it clear to them that there are ways people satisfy their curiosity and it isn't out of place to ask questions about his medical expertise, but that should be done politely. Nora toned down the rhetoric's but there was no remorse inside her, and even when she chose to drop the criticism, she still thinks the hospital is dirt-cheap, and the doctor is nothing but quackery. She's just having a laugh at how Doctor Shekuh prides himself. Professor Walker interjected as he tried calming the highly inflame situation, as he told the doctor his experience isn't in doubt, it's just that Nora has been through a lot.

"We stitched twelve places where his flesh was ripped apart by the leopards, but the attack on the skull has resulted in a bleeding in his brain," said Dr. Shekuh.

"Is he safe enough to fly? We will be taking him back with us today," said Prof. Walker.

"His condition is still critical, and travelling isn't a good idea, though he can, provided a medical person accompanies him," said Dr. Shekuh.

"You're his doctor, and you're already handling his case, why not accompany him?" said Prof. Walker.

Considering the flurry of attacks he received from Nora, the doctor wouldn't want to touch anything concerning Nora with a ten-foot barge pole. He obviously isn't in any mood to be involved with this professor any further as he's keen to wriggle himself out of this drama. He didn't hesitate to tell Professor Walker that he has other patients, and he doesn't think it'll be proper to put the lives of other patients at risk. Professor Walker decides to up his persuasive skill as he tried patronising the doctor with encouraging promises that he'll book a flight that enables him to return to Zimbabwe immediately they arrive the United States. He also promised to arrange for a medical team to wait for them at the airport, to take over from where the doctor stops.

"We will get you a first-class flight to help you relax," said Prof. Walker.

Faced with the stark reality before her, Nora's moral view as an ardent purist began to dissipate as she realised her husband's travel might not happen unless she tried being a little nicer to this potential angel. "Doctor, please, I know we started on the wrong note but do this for me, I beg you," said Nora.

Doctor Shekuh became silent for a while and decided he'll help to finish what he has started, even though this is a difficult one. Nora was relieved as she thanked the doctor with a smiled. "Thank you, and I'm so sorry for everything," said Nora.

They returned to the ward after they finished with the doctor, and Nora didn't hesitate to break the news to her husband that they're leaving the next day, and the doctor has agreed to go with them. "Did you bother to find out, if that's what I want?" asked Prof. Church.

"What you want doesn't matter anymore. Look at where what you wanted landed you," said Nora.

Professor Church is now the underdog, who finds himself on a back foot because what he thinks doesn't matter any longer. It's now up Billy to arrange an emergency travel, now that it's glaringly obvious that the professor will be travelling the next day. He then told them he will need the professor's travel documents to help book his flight and prepare for the next day.

"I don't think my travel documents are here with me," said Prof. Church.

"Then where did you leave them? Honey, we need to start getting ready, and there isn't any time to waste," said Nora.

"It's all in my bag, and my bag isn't here," said Prof. Church.

"Where are your bags then," Nora then turned to Jonas "do you know where his bags are?" asked Nora.

Jonas replied Nora that the professor's bags are in the forest, and because he rushed him straight to the hospital after the attack, the things are still in the forest. Nora became worried about the safety of the items in the wildlife infested forest, and asked Jonas how sure is he that her husband's things are still intact and safe. Nora didn't stop short of reminding Jonas that he should've gone to get them.

"I told him to wait; when I'm fine we can go and get them together," said Prof. Church.

"You aren't going back to that Leopard infested forest," said Nora.

Billy Alfred then suggested an alternative to dealing with the situation at hand, as he hinted that if they can't find the professor's passport, he'll arrange something that'll enable him to travel the next day.

"Why can't you sort the paperwork tonight?" asked Nora.

"It's late already; can't you see what time it is?" asked Billy.

Nora seems to have lost track of time, but Billy's reminder brought her back to come to her sense of time. "Oh, you're right, Billy," said Nora.

"Getting this done tomorrow will cause us a little delay," said Nora.

Billy Alfred promised to get all paperwork ready by 10.am the next morning, stating he didn't expect that the professor's travel documents will be in the forest and the setback wasn't expected. He's now to improvise, to enable this trip for the next day without further delay. "Then we've got no choice than to take things as they come," said Nora.

Bolo interjected and told Nora not to worry that they'll send the professor's bags across to him the moment they recover them from the forest.

"When do you intend to do that?" asked Nora.

Bolo didn't hesitate to let Nora know it isn't all about her as he reminded her that they have all abandoned their routine to watch over her husband since the attack, but now that he's returning to the United States. He promised Nora his son should be able to retrieve the bags from the forest latest by the day after tomorrow. Funnily, Professor Church's vanity means he's still held bound by his obsession for the wild, and he has something else in mind. He quickly interjected and asked Jonas to keep his bags with him and not send them over to the United States, because he'll need them when he returns to the wild.

"Stop being ridiculous, Professor. The ensuing melee from your first week in the forest should be enough lessons to help you reverse your course of action from the wild to the city," said Prof. Walker.

"That won't happen, you're leaving with us, and you aren't coming back. Jonas, I'll give you some money to help transport his things to the embassy," said Nora.

Billy Alfred brought out his card and hands it to Jonas. "Here, this is my card, just bring the bags to me, and when you get to the embassy ask of Billy Alfred," he said.

Jonas agreed to do as discussed, but Professor Church isn't having it, as he insisted on getting his bags himself. It was as if the attack wasn't enough message to the professor, this attack is just a minor setback that won't stand in the way of his dream to keep animals safe in the wild.

"I don't want any lame excuses, Jonas please just do as we just agreed," said Nora.

Jonas is now boxed to the corner, as he faced with two competing instructions, and worried about whose instruction to adhere to, but while he was busy racking his brains on how to deal with the conflict, Nora received a call from Eileen.

"Hello mum, where are you?" asked Eileen.

"I'm in Zimbabwe, and I'm already at the hospital where your dad has been admitted," she said.

"Did you see him?" asked Eileen.

"Yes, I've seen him, and I'm even with him as we speak," said Nora.

"How's dad, is he ok?" asked Eileen.

Nora told Eileen that the media report about her dad is correct, but they're bringing him over, for surgery. Eileen began to sob as she just can't believe this is happening to her family. Nora did all she could to make Eileen stop sobbing as she assured her that though her dad's condition is critical but he's stable and he'll need surgery immediately. "Can I speak with dad?" asked Eileen.

Nora made Eileen promise she will stop sobbing before handing the phone to her dad and she promised to do just that. Nora then handed the phone to Professor Church, and told him Eileen is on the phone and wants to speak to him. The professor isn't out of the woods yet as his voice was still faint even as he spoke to his daughter.

"Dad, is that you?" asked Eileen.

"Yes, it's me, Eileen. Why're you crying? Don't worry I'll be fine," said Prof. Church. Sadly, Eileen couldn't keep her promise as she continued to weep and couldn't speak until Joe came to take over the conversation.

"Hello dad, it's me, Joe," he said.

"I thought you wouldn't call, it's good to hear your voice," said Prof. Church.

Interestingly, Joe was quite courteous and benign with his choice of words this time as he told his dad there's no way he wouldn't call him, particularly at a critical time as this. Professor Church chuckled as he told Joe he thought he wouldn't call him yet told Joe he understands that they don't see eye to eye on a lot of things, but the truth remains that he has always loved him.

"Maybe you and I've a lot in common, it's like we both hide our love for each other," said Joe.

Professor Church smiled as he reminded his son that it must be serendipity, or probably a strange coincidence that's quite difficult to explain. But Joe decides to make a joke about the whole conversation with his dad, saying maybe that's the best way to describe it. Joe didn't want to hold his dad in a long conversation as he told him he already knows he isn't feeling great, and so wouldn't ask how he's feeling.

"Your guess is as good as right, and I'll be coming home with your mum tomorrow," said Prof. Church.

"Ok, stay safe, and we'll be expecting you. Please give the phone to mum," said Joe.

Professor Church then handed the phone back to Nora who's was seated by the professor's bedside, and funnily, Nora thought it was still Eileen on the phone. "Hello Eileen," said Nora.

"It's me Joe, mum how's it going?" asked Joe.

"We're doing everything we can to bring your dad home," said Nora.

"Is everything in place, or there are still grey areas that still needed to be worked on?" he asked.

Nora assured Joe that everything is in place except for the fact that his dad's travel documents are still in the forest, Joe became worried that this little itch could mean the trip won't go ahead and suggested to his mum to ask someone to go and get the documents immediately. Unsurprisingly, Nora had to lecture Joe about the reality on ground, as she told him people don't just walk into a leopard infested forest at their whims and caprices and come out unscathed. She then proceeded to say this requires a hunter to get his things out of the forest.

Joe was confused as to the possibility of his dad making this trip without his travel documents, Nora had to allay his concerns as she told him the embassy is working out something that'll enable him to travel tomorrow.

"That won't be a bad idea, but is there any arrangement to retrieve the bags from the forest?" Joe asked further.

"Yeah, arrangements are in place, to get that done. The bags will be sent to the embassy, and they'll eventually get to us," said Nora.

"Then that's perfect, and we'll be waiting for you at the airport tomorrow," said Joe.

By the night of the next day, Nora and her husband, accompanied by Professor Stone Walker and Doctor Shekuh arrived in the United States, where an ambulance and a medical team were waiting. Minutes after their arrival, Professor Stone Walker called his wife, Gloria, to inform her of their return to the United States.

"Hello Gloria, we're back," said Prof. Walker.

Oh, glad you're back but that's quick, and how's he?" asked Gloria.

"We just arrived the hospital, and we'll have to await the doctor's report," said Prof. Church.

Gloria wasn't impressed with Professor Church's decision to abandon his family for a romp in the wild, as she jocularly told her husband they should've taken Professor Church to the psychiatrist, and asking, what makes Nora think the hospital is what her husband needs.

Professor Walker scoffed saying that wouldn't have been a bad suggestion, but for now Pratt would need medical attention. Gloria couldn't help herself as she told her husband she's mad at his friend, particularly for the troubles he has caused his family.

"You're right; Nora is already an emotional wreck," said Prof. Walker.

"Does it mean the media reports about him are true?" asked Gloria.

"Of course, yes! All of it, except the doctors in the United States will say otherwise," said Prof Walker.

"I'm taken aback by your friend's carelessness and negligence for his family," said Gloria.

The medical team awaiting the arrival of Professor Church took over, and while Professor Walker was still on phone on to his wife, he spotted Doctor Shekuh and felt the need to have a word with him, so he can properly appreciate him for his willingness to accompany the sick professor to the United States. He then decided to end the conversation with his wife, and immediately walked up to Doctor Shekuh and thanked him for his help.

"I'm happy doing this for your colleague. Though, his wife seems not to appreciate the work I've done on her husband," said Dr. Shekuh.

Professor Walker apologised for Nora's insensitivity, yet tried to speak up for Nora, as he told the doctor that Nora's is a very polite woman who's under enormous stress. Doctor Shekuh made a joke about Nora's ingratitude and why he considers every act of kindness a fulfilment of his humanity. "Little acts of kindness like this one helps to keep evil out of a man's path, and that's why I did this," said Dr. Shekuh.

"Oh, I call them the little good deeds no one talks about," said Prof. Walker.

The doctor became philosophical as he said that these little good deeds keep evil far from people and their family, and he doesn't take them for granted. Funnily, Professor Walker laughed, and told the doctor he's right but bad things still happen to good people.

"Yes, you're right, but when bad things happen, these little good deeds as you call them will help you through those bad and difficult moments," said Dr. Shekuh.

"Doctor, you've an interesting way of presenting your arguments," said Prof. Walker. After his conversation with Professor Walker, Doctor Shekuh returned immediately to the airport, and boarded his flight back to Zimbabwe.

While Nora was waiting to hear from the doctor concerning her husband's condition, and an hour after they arrive the hospital, Lindsay Black walked up to Nora and introduced herself. "I'm Doctor Lindsay Black, and you're Professor Church's wife I suppose," said Dr. Black.

"Yes, I'm Nora Church, and I'm his wife. Maybe it's you I should talk to, and why're the press chasing us around?" asked Nora.

Lindsay Black smiled at Nora's naivety because she seems to forget that her husband's reputation precedes him, and his notoriety will attract heavy press presence. The doctor quickly reminded Nora that she should know that when the foreign office gets involved, the press also gets involved. Unsurprisingly, she went on to narrate her concerns with the press as she told the doctor that the press waited for them to arrive at the airport and now, they've followed them to the hospital.

"That should be expected because your husband has made the headlines," said Dr. Black.

"But the way they're hovering around us makes me uncomfortable," said Nora. The doctor had no choice in the matter than to advise Nora to ignore the presence of the media and focus on her husband's recovery. Immediately, after assuaging her worries of the press, Nora steered the conversation away from the press as she asked about her husband's condition. "We've just conducted another scan on your husband, and the result will be ready soon. We're waiting for our consultant who'll be here a few minutes from now," said Dr. Black.

"The consultant you're expecting, what about him?" asked Nora.

"When he comes, he'll discuss the result of the scan with you and discuss the options with you," said Dr. Black.

Nora was quite hopeful that the scan result will be different from the one conducted in Zimbabwe as she urged the doctor to discard the scan results from Doctor Shekuh because she thinks he's a quack and doesn't seem to know what he's doing.

"You mean Doctor Shekuh?" asked Dr. Black.

"Yes, he doesn't seem to know what he's doing, even the name of the clinic is just weirder than the services they render," said Nora.

The moment Lindsay Black saw Doctor Shekuh, there was a flicker of recognition. "I know Doctor Shekuh, I met him in London years back during an award ceremony, and he's among a handful of doctors awarded for their exemplary services," said Dr. Black.

Lindsay Black's appraisal of Dr. Shekuh came to Nora as a surprise, and she put her hand over her mouth. She felt bad because she didn't only underestimate Doctor Shekuh from the moment she set her eyes on him but explicitly called him a quack. Though, Nora opened up to Lindsay Black that Doctor Shekuh told her about himself, but she thought he was just bluffing. "Doctor Shekuh is a very experienced doctor, but I don't know why he chose to return to Africa," said Dr. Black.

"Can I quickly go for a cup of coffee before the consultant gets here?" asked Nora.

"You can but do that quickly. I know you must be tired and it's quite an exhaustive trip travelling from Zimbabwe down here," said Dr. Black.

"Oh, tell me about that, my legs are killing me," said Nora.

"I know, it must have been hard for you. Go, go get yourself a cup of coffee," said Dr. Black.

Nora asked the doctor for direction on how to get to the kitchen as she itches to get her cup of coffee. Lindsay Black took some steps forward using her hand gesture to give Nora direction, as she asked Nora to take a right and the coffee machine is there by the kitchen.

Minutes after getting her cup of coffee, Eileen called her mum to know if her parents have arrived. Nora calmly told her daughter her dad is fine, and he's being attended to, but Eileen is eager to see her dad and wants to come over to the hospital to join her mum. She inquired of the hospital from her mum because she wants to know the hospital her dad was admitted to.

"Come to Mary Bullion Hospital, and when are you coming?" asked Nora.

"Is that where dad is?" asked Eileen.

"Yes," said Nora.

"Can we come over to the hospital tonight?" asked Eileen.

Nora objected to having Eileen and Joe travel late into the night to the hospital, as she said she doesn't think it's advisable they hit the road, and moreover, it's already very late. Eileen concurred as she hopes she will be able to manage her anxiety about seeing her dad immediately, and said she thought as much. Though, she would've loved to come irrespective of what time of the night it is.

Just as Nora and Eileen continued their conversation, someone walked into her husband's hospital space, and she sensed it must be the consultant she has been waiting for. "No, leave it for tomorrow, you and Joe can come over, but I've to go now," said Nora. "Nora Church, this is the consultant that will attend to your husband," said Dr. Black.

"Hello doctor, good to see you," said Nora.

"Thank you, Nora Church, I suppose?" said the consultant, who then introduced himself as Doctor Norman Ramsey, but asked Nora to just call him Norman. After their formal introduction the consultant told Nora he will be back to discuss the Scan results with her, as he told her to wait by her husband's bedside.

"But we have been waiting for you, is it traffic that caused the delay or what?" asked Nora.

"I've been busy in theatre, and I just left the theatre twenty minutes ago," said Norman.

"Oh my God, when Doctor Lindsay Black said you're coming I thought you were outside the hospital premises," said Nora.

"It's ok Nora, I'm coming right away, let me get your husband's file," said Norman.

Minutes later Norman Ramsey walked into the ward with Professor Church's file in his hand. "Hello Nora, it's like your husband is asleep," asked Norman.

"No, he isn't, honey the doctor is here to see you," said Nora.

Professor Church turned around. "Err.., good morning, doctor," he said.

Norman Ramsey began by formally introducing himself to the professor, because he only introduced himself to Nora earlier. "I'm Doctor Norman Ramsey and I'm a consultant, just call me Norman. How're you doing, Professor?" asked Norman.

"As you can see doctor, I'm not doing great," Prof. Church said and chuckles.

"I know my question is rhetorical, but I'll need to know how you're feeling because it'll help us get you back on your feet," said Norman.

The professor seems to want to create a warm and friendly ambience as he took the responsibility of whose comment is rhetorical, and he accepted the blame for giving a rhetorical response. Norman Ramsey decides to go straight into the business at hand as he told the professor his scan result is out and he's there to discuss the implications of the result.

Unsurprisingly, Nora has been trying to prove her suspicion right about the zealousness of Doctor Shekuh and his work, despite her conversations about the Zimbabwean doctor with Lindsay Black. "Is the result different from the one conducted by the Zimbabwean hospital?" she asked.

"The result is the same, and the doctor did a good job to stop him from going in and out of consciousness," said Norman.

"Which means the bleeding in the brain is real?" asked Prof. Church.

"When do you intend to perform surgery?" asked Nora.

Norman Ramsey had to relate the obvious risk of undergoing this delicate procedure, as he told the professor that the hospital intends to perform surgery immediately but brain surgery is a delicate process, and usually has some side effects.

Nora has been quite afraid of what the possible outcome of a brain surgery might be. She was quite upfront this time as she asked to know what the possible side effects might be, and said the list of possible side effect read to her by the other doctor in Zimbabwe sounds vague.

"Let's hear the doctor out," said Prof. Church.

"The possible side effects could include, stroke, disoriented mentality and loss of memory," said Norman.

Nora turned immediately and looked at her husband and cried as the scare of the side effects of the surgery means that her family might laugh a little less. She kept saying she just can't get her head around what her husband wanted in the wild, if not to cause her heartache. Professor Church held and gave Nora's hand a small squeeze. "Calm down, Nora. Honey, you've to stop crying," he said.

Nora told her husband not to patronize her as she turned to Norman and asked what their chances of success would be if the surgery is handled by an expert.

"Your list of possible side effects has broken my wife, and I hope these outcomes aren't being exaggerated," said Prof. Church.

Norman Ramsey obviously made it clear that he doesn't intend to exaggerate or assuage their fears, and he's only out to tell them the obvious truth and that's his responsibility as a doctor. Professor Walker cuts into the conversation and asked Doctor Ramsey, what his friend's chances are in relation to these side effects.

"The whole thing is a fifty-fifty chance even if the surgery is carried out by the best specialist, but you should be positive," said Norman. "But there are people who undergo this procedure and come out ok, without any of these side effects?" asked Nora.

Norman Ramsey did a good job encouraging the professor and his wife to face up to the obvious with courage and a positive spirit, even as he told them a lot of people undergo brain surgery and come out without any side effect.

After being presented with the difficult option before them, Nora asked the doctor what he needs to commence the surgery immediately, and when does he intend to carry out the procedure. The doctor passed buck to the professor whose consent will be needed for the surgery to go ahead, yet said he's ready to perform the procedure tomorrow. Though, they'll need to perform a series of tests before then.

"Ok, please, we don't want any of the side effects," said Nora. After spending some time discussing the professor's health, Norman Ramsey left the ward, and Professor Pratt Church quickly turned to his wife and muttered saying this whole adventure has become uninteresting. Nora didn't hesitate to banter her husband as she reminded him that his glory days of being regarded as a responsible wildlife conservative advocate have elapsed. "Why the fuss about what I did or didn't do?" asked Prof. Church.

Nora became furious because she felt her husband seem not to understand the enormity of the troubles ahead and didn't hesitate to remind her husband that his posturing has moved from obsession for wildlife to insanity. Particularly depressing for Professor Church is the fact that his wife continues to give him the treatment of the bogyman in the basement.

"Why don't you avail me of all the support and encouragement I need in my quest to save wildlife?" asked Prof. Church.

"Have you thought about the analogy of a professor, who ended up half naked and running around in the forest with wildlife, in the headlines?" asked Nora.

Professor Church understands that getting at it with his wife isn't getting him anywhere, as long as they continue bantering each other. His wife is a purist, whose benignity shouldn't be put to test particularly in the face of a vain husband, whose interest is misplaced. "I hate it when you respond to issues in a dogmatic and biased tone," said Prof. Church. Nora suddenly walked away from her husband's bedside and to the hospital reception area to relive herself of the heat of the moment.

Eileen and Joe arrive at the hospital the next day. "Hello mum," said Eileen.

"Err.., Eileen, you're welcome, and did you get the things I asked you to bring for me?" asked Nora.

"Mum, how's dad?" she asked.

"Err.., your dad went in for the surgery about five minutes ago," said Nora.

"We missed him! We thought we could get here before he went in for surgery," said Joe.

"But that's quick, how come it's all so fast?" asked Eileen.

Sadly, Eileen missed her dad who has just been moved to theatre, and she's in panic over her dad's fate, as she expected to see her dad before he goes under knife on the surgical table. And she asked why the surgery happened sooner than planned.

Nora didn't hesitate as she opened up to her children that their dad didn't just go into the theatre for the surgery, he was actually rushed to the theatre. Their dad's surgery was moved forward due to some complications. Eileen became more worried as she couldn't just get her head around the nature of complication that got her dad rushed into surgery.

"He became unconscious, and I don't know what to say, I actually panicked before calling the doctors in," said Nora.

"I hope dad will be fine? It's just that dad doesn't listen, if he had listened, we wouldn't be here now," said Joe.

"Stop saying dad doesn't listen, just say men don't listen," said Eileen.

"Why're you trying to recreate my statement?" asked Joe.

Eileen unblinkingly told Joe that all men are the same and reminded Joe he's is a mirror of their dad, as they both are the same. While the pair is at each other's neck, Joe noticed that his mum was unusually quiet and asked her if anything is the matter.

"We all need to be positive, so your dad doesn't suffer complications from the surgery," said Nora.

"Did they talk about any possibility of such happening?" asked Eileen.

"This is brain surgery, it's bad when it goes wrong," said Nora.

Nora stood up quietly and took some steps away from where her children were seated, but she somehow began walking farther away, Eileen saw as her mum was walking away, and then rushed to catch up with her. "Mum, where are you going?" asked Eileen.

"You're just walking away without saying a word," said Joe.

Nora points to some distance away "I think there is a chapel over there, and I need somewhere to pray, if at all there's a God." Interestingly, Joe tried to make his mum rethink her move and he didn't hesitate to ask her what makes her think a God she doesn't pray to will suddenly answer her now.

"If you go in there, what will you say and how'll you start since you've never prayed before," asked Eileen.

Nora reminded her children she prayed when she was a kid, and still thinks she should be able to say something when she gets into the church. Sadly, Joe has a way of making his mum reverse her decisions.

"Mum, would you give things to someone who doesn't believe in you? You don't believe in God, and he won't answer," said Eileen.

"I want the two of you to go back to the hospital, in case your dad leaves the theatre," said Nora.

Eileen held her mum by the hand. "Mum, let's go back," she said. Funnily, Nora took the bait and they all returned to the hospital. Three hours later, Norman Ramsey was out of surgery and told Nora her husband has been transferred to the intensive care unit.

"How's he, and how did it go?" asked Nora.

"The whole process went well, but we will need to monitor his progress," said Norman.

Eileen interjected and asked if they can see their dad now, but Norman seems to think differently, as he said only their mum can go into the intensive care unit to see him for now.

Joe protested saying his sister and himself shouldn't be left in the dark when it concerns their dad. He then urged Norman to allow him and his sister see their dad. Sadly, Norman insists that intensive care unit isn't a place for crowd. "Eileen, you and Joe should wait let me go and see your dad," said Nora.

"Does it mean you don't want us to see our dad?" asked Eileen.

Unsurprisingly, Norman Ramsey has a soft side and gave Joe and Eileen the all clear to see their dad in the ward provided they act softly, softly. Interestingly, the surgery went well without the possible negative side effects, and the professor recuperated well after all.

A month after the brain surgery, Professor Church was due to be discharged and the first to-do list of Professor Pratt Church is making arrangements to return to the wild. His thought about having a breath of fresh air is living in the wild, and now that he realised he's out of the woods, the professor urged Nora to please send a message across to Jonas, and ask him not to send his bags over.

"Why? You know you're being discharged today, and you'll need your clothes," said Nora.

"I've some clothes here, and the ones with Jonas should remain with him," said Prof. Church.

"Why? We never agreed to pass your clothes and travel documents to Jonas," said Nora.

Professor Church looked at Nora without batting an eye and unblinkingly told her he's going back to wild immediately he leaves the hospital and he doesn't think sending his bags over to the United States is a good idea.

Nora is now beginning to find her husband insufferable, as she got fiery and quickly told him she isn't debating this with him. She reminded him he has caused them so much trouble, and he needs to get that into his thick skull.

Lindsay Black walked in while the pair was at each other's neck. "Hello Nora, how're you doing?" she asked.

"We're fine, and can't wait to go home," she said.

"Err.., tell me about it, and don't worry you're going home today," said Dr. Black.

The professor is now feeling better enough to go home but not without the very visible scars left by those leopards. Interestingly, if Professor Church's experience in the hands of those leopards didn't leave emotional scars inside the professor, it sure did leave physical scars that he has to carry with him wherever he goes. "Oh, I'm glad about that, please what about the scars on his body?" asked Nora.

"We've discussed that with him already, he'll need skin grafts, on his head, his face, his hand and leg," said Dr. Black.

"The scars are too much, and when do you think that can be worked on?" asked Nora.

"Let's say two months from now, but we'll monitor his progress to determine what happens," said Dr. Black.

The professor interjected and apologised to the doctor saying he doesn't think he'll be available then for the skin graft. The doctor was taken aback by the professor's hesitation, then asked why is it that he won't be available for the skin graft, and asked if he has any other appointment at that time.

"No, but I must return to the wild," he said.

Nora was wrought with fury over her husband's insensitive remarks, as she quickly asked what nonsense it is that he's going on, and on talking about the wild. She urged him to stop the gibberish because she isn't inclined to hear any more of this. Sadly, Lindsay Black couldn't help but get involved in this unfolding drama, as she quickly urged the professor not to return to the wild because he hasn't fully recovered. Even though the job of a doctor is treat patients and not to judge or delve into a family squabble that has nothing to do with her, Lindsay Black tried in her own little way to remind the professor to consider the trouble he has put his family through.

"I can't remain here while the poachers take over the forest," said Prof. Church. As far as the professor is concerned, the forest is there for the taking, and if he stays back poachers will have all of it to themselves, and he'll have none. "Professor, I suggest you see a counsellor," said Lindsay Black.

"What for! And what are you implying?" he asked.

"You don't sound rational, that's why she's recommending a counsellor," said Nora.

The fine art of satirical theatre isn't meant to be barged into, and so also is this delicate subject matter, and the frown in the professors' face is a subtle way of asking the doctor to back off. Things are beginning to get heated, and the professor seems to hold back his anger from turning on the doctor for her unprofessional advice, Lindsay Black had to wriggle herself out of this dramatic scene. "Nora, the nurse is processing his discharge, and she'll tell you all you need to know," said Dr. Black.

"Ok, Lindsay, thank you, but I'll follow up on the skin graft because he can't go about with these scars, they're scary," said Nora.

Two months after his discharge, the professor have been home recuperating and interestingly, his healing went quite well, without any obvious side effects. Sadly, all he does all day is imagining himself in the wild and relieving his wildlife fantasy. He then thought to himself that it's now time to act, but his first point of call will be to get Jonas on board. Despite intense opposition from his family, he decided to brave it this time as he picked his phone, and scroll through the contacts and then dialled Jonas's phone.

"Oh, Professor is that you?" asked Jonas.

"Yes Jonas, it's me and I'm fine," said Prof. Church.

Jonas sounded relieved to hear that the professor had pulled through the traumatic experience, as he quickly told the professor how glad he was to hear from the professor, but didn't hesitate to ask about his wife.

"My wife, Nora! She's fine and what about your dad? You know I haven't been able to say a proper thank you to him," said Prof. Church.

"My dad is fine and he'll be very happy to hear you're fine, at least our fears are over," said Jonas.

"You just said your fears are over, what fears are you talking about?" asked Prof. Church.

Jonas quickly reminded the professor that they were with him when the doctors mentioned the possible side effects of the surgery, and knowing he pulled through without any of these negative side effects is something worth celebrating.

"Now I understand your fears, but I'm glad none of that happened," said Prof. Church. Jonas told the professor he has sent his bags to his wife as agreed. Unsurprisingly, the professor has other things in mind, but that ship has now sailed. "Yes, I've seen the bags. Though, I never wanted you to send my bags over," said Prof. Church.

"Sorry, I'm not following, but your bags can't be here while you're over there," said Jonas.

"That's exactly what I was saying, because I intend coming back to the wild," said Prof. Church. Now that the professor has successfully steered the conversation away into a grey area for Jonas as he mumbled. It became glaringly obvious for the professor that Jonas was struggling to keep up with the conversation and the flow seems to have stall because Jonas told him outrightly, he doesn't think that's a good idea. Sadly, the professor remains dogged and ever resilient on getting what he wanted.

"Why do you think differently! Do you mean living out my fantasy isn't a good idea?" asked Prof. Church.

"I saw how your wife reacted when she came for you, and that tells me they aren't in support of your expedition," said Jonas.

Jonas's view on this matter seems to have a little or no impact on the Professor, it's seems like pouring water on a duck because he remained as stubborn as a mull. The professor isn't having any contrary opinion as he subtly told Jonas to have it in mind that he will be coming and has just informed him out of courtesy.

"And you still want me to be your forest guide?" asked Jonas.

"Of course yes, who best understands the forest more than you?" asked Prof. Church.

"Ok, I'll discuss this with my dad and get back to you, on the outcome," said Jonas.

Now that Jonas's comments seems to be shrouded in uncertainty, the professor asked if their working together requires deliberations, yet suggested he'll leave Jonas to handle this the way he understand best.

Jonas reminded the professor that deliberation with his family is very important, considering the flurry of attacks from his wife. He referenced the insults his dad received from Nora, yet appreciated the professor's prompt intervention to take the blame while his wife was at their neck. "Not when your dad was blamed for what he knew nothing about, I take responsibility for that," said Prof. Church.

"You have to bear with me, I'll get back to you," said Jonas.

"Ok, thank you, Jonas, please pass my warm regards to your dad," said Prof. Church.

Tina Mbolelu, the journalist that previously exposed the professor's medical condition to the world just rushed her mum back to the hospital after some health complications following her discharge, and this time she might stay a bit longer in the hospital than she previously did. This journalist has serendipitously become fond of this hospital that finds her insufferable.

Sadly, Eileen was lurking in the shadows as her dad discussed his return to the wild with Jonas, she was extremely patient and calm as she waited to get her facts right, and once the conversation was over she came out of the shadows and joined her dad in the living room. "Dad, I heard your conversation with that Jonas, and I think that was the guy that went into the forest with you," said Eileen.

"Yeah, he was my guide in my failed adventure," said Prof. Church.

Even as her dad was trying to make a joke out of the not-too-funny situation, Eileen didn't bat an eye as she sternly told her dad not to call it a failed adventure, because if he does, it means they're glorifying an ugly stunt he pulled that affected his family and friends.

"Why would you call living out in the wild an ugly stunt?" asked Prof. Church.

"Dad, what then would you call that?" asked Eileen.

"I call that living out my fantasy, and nothing else," said Prof. Church.

Eileen got all riled up, and her patience ran out fast even though she's doing a bad job in her attempt to make her dad get a grip. Yet, she did make sure she reminds her dad that his fantasy is weird and it's about to become weirder from the conversation she just heard.

"Are you eavesdropping on my conversations?" asked Prof. Church.

"No, I walked into your conversation, and this is my house isn't it? So, I don't eavesdrop," said Eileen.

Professor perceives that his daughter was quite hurt by these stunts, and the more he engages her further on the subject, the more she gets worked up, so to keep things civil, he told Eileen she won. But still felt the need to remind her, this is his house, and sadly she has now hijacked it to be hers.

"Dad, seriously, you aren't going to Zimbabwe, I suggest you advise your Jonas to look for a different person to work for," said Eileen.

"I'm concluding arrangements for my next expedition," he said.

"Dad, why're you doing this to us! Do you just want to waste your life and turn us into children without a dad?" asked Eileen.

"Stop making this whole thing more difficult, you keep talking as if your dad is about to die," said Prof. Church.

"Weren't you close to death before mum brought you here!

Just look at your body, what do you think about those huge scars?" asked Eileen.

Professor Church made a joke out of himself over the scars, as he jocularly said these are mere scars, and they'll go away, and they don't impact on his choices. But Eileen thinks they aren't mere scars, just that he has been beclouded by a strange obsession that has kept him bound and left people talking. Joe came in from visiting his friends and walked into the living room while still fiddling with his phone. Sadly, Joe was greeted by this unfriendly ambience created by his sister and his dad, but he didn't first get involved as he walked straight to the refrigerator.

"Where did this cake come from?" asked Joe. It's now glaringly obvious that the ambience in this household now signifies acrimony.

"Don't touch it, it's mine, you can eat every other thing in the refrigerator but not the cake," said Eileen.

"Knock it off Eileen! Why're you looking so tense? And I don't think your reaction is just about a little piece of cake," said Joe. "Just leave my cake, if you want to know why I'm tensed just ask your dad," she said.

"Dad is sick, so what did he do this time?" asked Joe.

Eileen laid it bare and told Joe that their dad is planning to return to Zimbabwe, and all his expression of love for his family is just a mere charade. Joe felt Eileen was just pulling one of the tricks up her sleeve because he didn't hesitate to tell his sister that can't be true, and she must be joking, yet turned to his dad to ask if what Eileen said is true.

"What's it about my expedition that I must answer for all the time?" asked Prof. Church.

Since the professor didn't give a straight answer to Joe, it now dawned on him that their dad will be returning to the wild any moment from now, and he's justifying this whole shamble as his fantasy. It's now glaringly obvious that Eileen was telling the truth, Joe interjected as he told his dad that if he's thinking of doing such evil then it'll be to his own peril. He further advised his dad to drop the idea because everyone in America thinks mum should've taken him to a psychiatrist.

"You mean, people think I'm crazy?" asked Prof. Church.

Joe got off rail as he became a bit rude to his dad, telling him to read the headlines himself, and that people don't think he's just crazy, they've actually concluded that he's crazy, crazy. But the professor didn't bother, as he quickly dismissed Joe's assertion by saying people have a right to their opinion and they can't live out his fantasy for him.

Joe laughed as he asked his dad if he intends to prove those saying he's crazy and should've been taken to the psychiatrist instead of the hospital right. Joe's irritation is precipitated by the feeling that his dad's smoke and mirror approach to manoeuvring his way back into the wild was quite unsavoury and has possibly put them on the back foot.

The professor's attempt to quell this opposition meant he had to end the conversation that's fast becoming a noise in his ears, he then spoke in an authoritative tone, and said this session is over, insisting he doesn't live by what people say or think about him.

"But you were among those that propagate the law of public policy, why're you now turning it on its head," asked Joe.

Eileen was forced to spit out the hurt she has been harbouring in her heart as she relates how her university lecturer described her dad in a very condescending manner. Funnily, the Professor chuckled as Eileen told him he was being talked about, yet he loved the idea as he felt he was stimulating conversation around animal rights.

"For your information, you're now a case study, and we, that's your wife and children are now the sample of the study," said Joe.

The Professor turned to Eileen and asked her to finish the conversation she started about how her lecturer described him. Interestingly, Eileen scoffed as she told her dad her lecturer described her dad as a man heading down the path of a sterile garden.

"What a description!" exclaimed Prof. Church.

"Now you know better," said Eileen.

Joe turned around and said he's retiring to his room and advised Eileen to stop flogging a dead horse. Joe's comment irked his dad as he angrily told Joe to check his use of words and asked if he just metaphorically called him a dead horse.

"This session is over, and I don't want to hear a single word from any of you," said Prof. Church. "I'm also going to my room," said Eileen.

"Good," said Prof. Church.

They both left their dad to himself and retired to their rooms. Later that evening, Nora walked into the house from work and asked her husband how he's feeling as she usually does.

"Oh great, but a little pain here and there still persist," said Prof. Church.

"Where's everybody, why're you all by yourself in the living room?" asked Nora.

"Oh, they're in their rooms," said Prof. Church.

Nora was relieved that Joe isn't up and about town gallivanting, not knowing he has just returned from walking out and about town. The moment Eileen sensed her mum is back home from work, she walked to the living room as she's eager to let loose, like a loose cannon. Nora sensed something isn't right from Eileen's disposition and didn't hesitate to ask why she's all worked up. Now that the opportunity to speak up is afforded her, all she could say was that their dad deserves to be by himself, and she thinks he loves it. Nora who'd no idea of the trouble brewing within her home, quickly cautioned Eileen, saying she has had a long day and she's not ready for unguarded utterances that'll put her off.

She brought out her car keys and handed them to Eileen and asked her to go to the car and get a bag containing groceries. "Oh, you went shopping?" asked Eileen.

"Of course yes, I'd to go to the grocery store to pick some things, make sure you season the salmon properly, Joe will give you a hand. You didn't season the last one properly and your dad didn't really enjoy it," said Nora.

"Mum, are you still worried about what dad enjoys or not?" asked Eileen.

"Why've you been going on and on about your dad today?" asked Nora.

Eileen quickly told her mum that her dad doesn't want to be with them, and sadly, he's going back to the wild. Nora thinks otherwise because she didn't bat an eyelid as she reminded Eileen that her dad has always talked about the wild, and that doesn't necessarily mean he's running off again to the wild.

"I'm sorry to disappoint you, mum, dad called that man, and I can't even remember his name, the one that was his guide in the forest," said Eileen.

"You mean Jonas?" asked Nora.

"Oh, yes that's him, dad told him to expect him in the next week or so," said Eileen.

Nora realised her husband have moved away from mere talking about returning to the wild, he's already acting out what she erroneously considers to be a mere blab as he puts his plans into motion. Sadly, she has come to realise that her husband's fantasy isn't anything like the cloak- and-dagger, and rather she immediately concluded that her husband is just an insane man who needed his brain checked out. Nora then turned to Eileen and asked if she's sure about what she just said about her dad's conversation with Jonas.

"Dad is here you can ask him, and you can also confirm from Joe, he'll tell you all about it," said Eileen.

"Honey, is it true? Please tell me it's a lie," said Nora.

"Actually, she's telling the truth, and I can't just sit around and watch poachers take over the wild," said Prof. Church.

Nora immediately gave him the dressing down, and reminded him this was what he said before he ended up in the jaws of those leopards. The professor jocularly told Nora that his encounter with the leopards is part of his wild experience and doesn't stop him from deriving the fun he wants from the wild.

The fear of the possibility of rushing to Africa to rescue her husband again gripped Nora, she quickly made herself clear as she reminded her husband that she isn't prepared to go through the kind of torment he put her through the other time. She then fixed her gaze on her husband and wondering, because she finds it particularly depressing that the husband she use to be quite proud of has now descended to a manner of madness that has gone suffuse, and quite unfitting for a professor.

Professor Pratt didn't hesitate to absolve himself of every blame as he laid it all at Nora's feet, accusing her that the torment she was referring to was because she allowed herself to be all worked up over his interest in the wild.

"Do you know how America describes you? They call you the crazy professor," said Nora.

"I'm unperturbed by what the press said and didn't say about me," said Prof. Church.

"What about us, your children and I, don't we deserve some peace and happiness, or do you want this family to return to the headlines again for all the wrong reasons?" asked Nora.

The professor seemed off, even as he's blind of the reality before him because he continued to insist that it'll be farcical for people to expect him to remain with his family while poachers are growing in their numbers. Nora finds her husband's excuses to be quite depressing and reminded him that it's his opinion, and at least he has heard and read the vile comments people have made about his family in the media.

"News about my going back to the wild to engage in a rat race shouldn't be considered as vile," said Prof. Church.

Unsurprisingly, the professor seems to be enjoying all the conversation precipitated by his adventurous moves irrespective of whether the comments are positive or not. Joe walked into the conversation trying to save his mum the heart ache of duelling with his adventurous dad, and advised her that his dad has made up his mind and sadly, he doesn't think there is anything anyone can do about this.

"Don't tell me what can or can't be done about this, and all I want is for your dad to reverse his decision," said Nora.

"Dad, your action is nothing but grotesque," said Joe.

"No, this is a bad joke becoming a reality," said Eileen.

Professor Church, at first dismissed the criticism from within his household, saying he doesn't respond to fables as he tried to surmount the army of opposition coming his way but failed, he then changed tact and decided to plead with Nora telling her he needed to do this, because it makes him happy. "We won't take this, and we won't allow you to turn our lives inside out," Nora said and walked away in anger. Even as Nora walks away the professor made a passing remark to her as he registers his displeasure about the opposition from his household. "Despite your disapproval of my trip, I expect my kids to be cool headed, suave and urbane when they engage me in a conversation," said Prof. Church.

"Why should that be, when you'v e made your kids loathe you?" asked Nora.

The professor was quite disappointed by the lack of support from Nora as he accused her of sitting on the critic's seat and fanning the wind of opposition against his every move and told her his children would've supported his moves if not for Nora's constant bickering.

Nora isn't having her husband's excuses because she's also claiming to be the victim in all of this. She reminded her husband that her bickering didn't in anyway make his children to loath him, and perhaps he should rethink his actions because he has done his children great harm in the most casual and cruel of ways. She reminded him it isn't too late to make amends, but effort to declutter the professor's mind of his obsession with the wild fell flat.

Nora angrily walked into her room because she couldn't get the thought that her husband is returning to the wild out of her mind. Though, embarrassingly obvious, the thought to seek help from Professor Stone Walker to help talk some sense into her husband came to her mind. She quickly reached for her phone and dialled Professor Stone Walker. Sadly, Walker wasn't available to pick up the phone, it's Gloria who did.

"Hello Nora, my husband is in the bathroom," said Gloria.

"I need to speak with him because my husband is at it again," said Nora.

"What's going on, is he ok?" asked Gloria.

"Yes, he's ok, but he's preparing to run off to the wild," said Nora.

"What do you mean run off to the wild?" asked Gloria.

Nora told Gloria her husband is going back to the wild, and he seems to have made arrangements, and sadly, she began to sob as she asked why her husband will choose to do a thing that hurts this much to her. Gloria wasn't particularly a fan of Professor Church not just because of his rustic ways, but merely over his choice to live in the wild and also the hurt on his family. She angrily exclaimed over the phone saying this is becoming too much, and something needs to be done to stop this.

"What can we do? Please tell me what to do, just say something because I can't do this anymore," said Nora.

Sadly, while the women were planning their coup on how to keep Professor Pratt Church in a tight leash, Professor Walker walked out of the bathroom into the bedroom and asked who it was on the phone.

"It's Nora, and you need to hear this," said Gloria.

Gloria then informed Nora that her husband is here, and that she can now speak with him. Nora basically broke down as she told Professor Walker that she's tired and doesn't think she can do this anymore. Professor Walker was lost as to what Nora's troubles was, as he interjected and told her he has no idea of what it was she was talking about.

"Your friend is running off to the wild and he has made arrangements," said Nora.

Professor Walker hinted Nora that he can recall Professor Church's mention of returning to the wild the moment he's back on his feet but he took all of it as a joke, and asked Nora if her husband is actually serious about this.

"Yes, I was surprised when my children told me they heard him making arrangements, and he confirmed it," said Nora.

Professor Walker didn't mince words as he puts this new unfolding drama into perspective and he told Nora that if his friend's last experience in the wild couldn't stop him from going back to the wild, then nothing can. "What are you saying, Walker! Should I just sit on my hands and watch my husband continue in this blind obsession?" asked Nora.

Professor Walker tried making himself clearer as he quickly told Nora that he isn't implying they sit on their hands and watch the professor continue in this obsession that's leading him down the garden path. He rephrased his earlier comment, saying he's just stating the obvious by saying the jaws and claws of those leopards should be enough lessons for a sensible man.

Since the lessons from the jaws of those leopards didn't do enough to make the professor change course, Nora is now confused as to what to do about this. Then the thought of asking for a divorce so her husband can be free to roam the wild as much as he wants came to her mind.

Professor Walker couldn't afford to see this family whom he's closely knitted beak-up, and he quickly interjected and reminded Nora that divorce isn't an option. He made it clear to her that if she divorces her husband, what about her children, and asked if they can as well divorce their dad.

"But something must be done, and this mustn't get crazier than it already is," said Nora.

Professor Walker asked Nora to calm down, promising to have a word with Professor Pratt Church, but equally advised Nora to let her husband go if he insists. Immediately after his phone conversation with Nora, Professor Stone Walker then puts a call through to Professor Pratt Church. "Hello Professor, how're you?" asked Prof Walker.

"I'm fine, Walker, how's Gloria?" asked Prof. Church.

Professor Walker didn't mince words as he told Professor Church that Gloria is fine but he doesn't think she's happy with him.

Professor Church felt lost because he doesn't have any personal squabbles with Gloria and wondered why Gloria is mad at him. He told Professor Walker he knew he hasn't visited for some time now and asked him to tell Gloria to bear with him.

Professor Walker side-stepped the platitudes and burst his friend's bubble as he claimed ignorance of the reason for Gloria's anger. He quickly reminded him that his not visiting them isn't the problem, it's just that Gloria isn't a fan of his uncanny moves, and she's mad over his plan to return to the wild.

"Err.., Nora has told you about it already, and when did she do that?" asked Prof. Church.

"When she did that shouldn't be the bone of contention, rather your obsession with the wild should be," said Prof Walker.

Professor Church took exception to Professor Walker's comment about his adventure saying it's curiously lacking in perception and had to call Walker's attention to the fact that it's him alone that understands his protection of the wild to be an obsession or some curiosity of a sort that needed to be satisfied.

"Then what do you call your actions?" asked Prof. Walker.

"I know you call it obsession, but I call it a dream," said Prof. Church.

Professor Walker scoffed at his friend and asked him why he's quite condescending of wisdom and apathetic to the reality before him. This whole thing has gone suffuse, and his friends are now spiting fire. Professor Church went silent for while even as Professor Walker waited a while for response and sadly, the response was more of an accusation than a mere response, as he described Professor Walker's comments as one expected from a rabble-rousing and inflammatory character.

Professor Walker smiled and urged his friend to stop making a mountain out of a mole-hill, because his comments are of sincerity of heart, and as he can see the relationship between him and those around him is already tenuous.

"Stop pulling the wool over my eyes, Walker," said Prof. Church.

"Do you know the whole world watches you with bated breath as you act out in the wild?" said Prof Walker.

Professor Pratt Church isn't ready to be lectured by his friend, and particularly hates being metaphorically described as one humpty dumpty who has lost track of time. Though, Professor Walker did a good job of disabusing his friend's mind that he isn't an anarchist, yet dug in further as he asked Professor Church if he realises how this fantasy of his impacts on his wife and children.

Professor Church was already beginning to find this conversation to be boring, he thought of ending the phone call abruptly, but realised it might be considered bored rude. He then subtly told his friend that he just doesn't understand what the fuss was about, and he reminded him that his children, Eileen and Joe knew too well that he's an animal rights advocate and that his love for the wild is what he expresses through advocacy. It suddenly dawned on Professor Walker that this is a lost fight, and nothing will stop this 'two birds' one stone kind of man' who uses advocacy for animal rights as a ploy to live among wildlife.

"So, you don't care what a negative press would do to your family?" asked Prof. Walker.

"Who is perturbed about what the press say or don't say? I equally expect them to ignore the press as well," said Prof. Church.

Professor Walker became furious as he thinks Professor Church is somehow elusive and remains as stubborn as a mule. He then lashed out at his friend as he frankly told him he's tired of going over this matter with him, and he thinks he's done trying to stop him from doing whatever he wants.

CHAPTER

SEVEN

The Return to the wild

Two weeks later, it's time for Professor Church to attend to his appointment with Jonas in Zimbabwe, and after packing his bags, he turned to his wife and said he's about to leave for the airport. Sadly, Nora remained statue-still without any emotion, as she told her husband that his trip to Africa isn't news that interests her, and she went further to ask what's it he wants her to say.

"I want you to say something, goodbye, stay safe or whatever, but just say something," said Prof. Church.

"I can't say any of that, because I'm filled with so much bitterness right now," said Nora.

"But you don't have to be, all I want is your understanding," said Prof. Church.

"Why do you always want to be understood, without putting yourself in our shoes, do you even realise you need a skin graft?" asked Nora.

Professor Pratt didn't hold back as he told his wife he no longer belongs to the city because he knew a lot of people now call him the scar face, and the scar face thing isn't his worry. He turned and told his wife he's just going to inform Eileen and Joe he's leaving.

"Is that all you've to say about this! Does it mean you don't need the skin graft?" asked Nora.

"I don't know what to say, Nora, I'm returning to the wild and I don't see how a skin graft will improve my efficiency in the wild," said Nora.

Professor Pratt walked to Eileen's room and stood by the door but Eileen felt her dad is having a laugh for having the guts to come to her door, her dad stood and she kept him standing, but after a while he asked if she knew why he's in her room.

Eileen made it clear that she's quite aware of the reason he has come to see her, but asked why she should let him into her room as if he's a man who cares. Her dad took all the insults on the chin, he then smiled and told his daughter that the fact that he's returning to the wild never meant he has stopped loving her.

"I thought it was a joke when Joe was saying it, but I now realise you don't need us and I don't think we'll need you either," said Eileen.

"So, what are you implying?" asked Prof. Church.

"Goodbye, dad, I don't want to see you again, just go away," said Eileen.

Eileen banged the door to her room to keep him out and left her dad to indulge in a guilt trip. Professor Pratt Church then walked to the door of Joe's room and wanted to tell him he's leaving but suddenly developed cold feet because he realised he could get worse treatment compared to the manner Nora and Eileen treated him. He walked back to the living room, reached out for his bag and left for the airport.

Professor Church arrives in Zimbabwe and goes straight to Jonas's place. "Hello Professor, you're in Zimbabwe!" exclaimed Jonas.

"Yes, Jonas, how're you?" asked Prof. Church.

Jonas welcomed the professor as they exchanged pleasantries with the each other yet reminded the professor, he wasn't expecting him because he never told him he's on his way to Africa. Professor Church craftily avoided telling Jonas he's on his way to Africa because Jonas didn't quite give him the green light to come over when they spoke earlier. The professor wasn't economical with the truth either as he told Jonas he felt it was necessary to keep things under wraps because he has had enough opposition concerning this trip.

"Oh, does it mean you deliberately kept me in the dark?" asked Jonas.

"I didn't keep you in the dark, Jonas. I told you about my coming the other time," said Prof. Church.

Jonas asked the professor that now that he's here, is he planning on returning to the wild, because his visit seems to take him by surprise. The professor chuckled and then told Jonas he's of course returning to the wild, and if not, what else will make a scar-faced professor travel such a distance to see him. Sadly, Jonas's family got burnt by their last involvement in the professor's adventure, and he quickly told the professor he doesn't think this will work out because his dad doesn't think it's a good idea.

"Your dad might think differently, but it's my choice to make," said Prof. Church.

Jonas didn't hesitate to put the professor in his place as he turned the phrase around and gave it back to him and told him he's right, but just as the professor's decision is his to make, and so does he have the right to his own decision. "What are you saying Jonas?" asked Prof. Church.

"My dad wants you to get someone else to be your guide," said Jonas.

The professor quickly changed tack to keep Jonas on side, and said he never said his work wasn't good enough, and asked why he has chosen to take this harsh decision. Jonas told the professor his dad believes the professor is a moving accident waiting to happen, and he's careless and too obsessed with the wild that he forgets about his safety and the safety of those around you.

"I realise my actions actually endangered you, but I now know better," said Prof. Church. Sadly for the professor, too much water has passed under the bridge as Jonas said it's no longer about him but it's about his dad's decision and he doesn't want Nora coming to embarrass his family any further.

"But that confusion has been cleared and sorted," said Prof. Church.

Jonas sternly reminded the professor that what happened was beyond confusion and shouldn't be described as a mere glitch. He described what happened to be more of a theatre, and insists his family shouldn't be the victim of any vile words. Jonas described the precarious situation his family found themselves and how they narrowly wriggled out of the professor's wife's wrath.

"Jonas, I'll need to see your dad, and clear the air, so we can all move past this, will you take me to him?" asked Prof. Church.

"I don't mind," said Jonas.

Professor Church and Jonas continued their conversation and spent a short while having some light refreshment before setting off to see Jonas's dad. "How far is your dad's place?" asked Prof. Church.

"It's a short distance away from here, just a stone's throw," said Jonas.

Just as Jonas and the professor stood up to leave, Jonas received an unexpected phone call from Nora, and he then stepped a few meters away to take the call. "Hello, who am I speaking with?" asked Jonas. "Hello Jonas, this is Nora, don't you have my number?" she asked.

"No, I don't have it on my phone," said Jonas.

Nora reminded Jonas that she gave him her phone number in their previous meeting and he did call her with it. Jonas didn't actually want much to do with Nora, considering the flurry of attacks he received from her in their previous meeting, he told her that he only had her number on paper and didn't save it on his phone. Funnily, while Nora was trying to be more engaging on the phone, Jonas was quite cold towards her and eventually told her blankly that he really didn't bother to save her number on his phone.

"But you should've saved it on your phone, at least you knew I would be calling you again," said Nora.

"No, I didn't expect you to call me after the scorn you poured on my dad and I, despite all we did for your husband," said Jonas.

"But I've apologised to you and your dad, and I expect you to move past that," said Nora.

"Whatever! What do you want this time?" exclaimed Jonas.

Nora sensed that Jonas isn't particularly interested in speaking with her, so she decided to change tact by becoming exceptionally nicer on the phone because she's seeking to create an alliance with Jonas to help dissuade her husband. She told Jonas it's obvious that her husband will come to him as he's planning to return to the forest, but he shouldn't give him any assistance.

"He met with me and I told him I'm not interested in going into the wild with him," said Jonas.

"Oh, that's good, where's he now?" asked Nora.

Jonas told Nora he has played his part by refusing to work with her husband, but it now behoves on his dad because the professor has gone to convince his dad who actually instructed him to stay away from working as his tour guide. Unsurprisingly, Nora didn't hesitate to express her hopes as she made it clear that she hope that Jonas's dad would turn her husband down just as Jonas did, and maybe that'll make him return to them.

"Let's hope that happens, though I'm afraid for your husband," said Jonas.

"What do you mean you're afraid for him?" asked Nora.

Jonas thought it right to tell Nora the obvious truth as he told her that even if they turn him down, he might go into the wild alone and that could be fatal. This professor is now known for having a talent for attracting trouble, and sadly the African grassland is now the professor's baby and asking him to stay away is like asking him to stop breathing.

"You're making sense, if you're certain he'll go into the forest alone then I'll still need you to be there with him," said Nora.

Jonas took the pains to lecture Nora about her husband's obsession with the wild, saying he's very careless when it comes to staying alive in the wild, and he has equally put the lives of others at a risk.

"If after meeting with your dad, he insists on going into the wild alone, please let me know," said Nora. Jonas didn't just want to be some kind of errand boy for Nora, he made his position clear, and said letting her know about her husband's decision doesn't change anything. He then asked if she intends to join her husband to keep him safe.

"Maybe you and I will work together, and I'll give you some money for phone calls and for your troubles," said Nora.

"You mean I should be calling you? He wouldn't like the idea because I noticed he doesn't want you knowing much about his escapades," said Jonas.

Nora told Jonas that this isn't about what her husband wants, it's now about keeping her husband safe and alive, and she believes Jonas would want to stay safe as well. Jonas was rather more pessimistic than optimistic about this dual relationship with Nora, and then her husband. He was particularly lost as to what part he has to play in all this, he then asked Nora what it is she wants him to do.

It's now glaringly obvious that Professor Church isn't going to literally pivot and return to his family. Nora now pleaded with Jonas to give her a regular update about her husband yet advised Jonas to be discreet about it and shouldn't let her husband know about it.

"Ok, I'll do all I can to help," said Jonas.

"Thank you Jonas, but just don't let him stray into the forest alone," said Nora.

Just after the phone call with Nora, Jonas drew closer to Professor Church who didn't hesitate to hint Jonas that he knew it was his wife he was speaking with on phone. "What makes you so sure she's and how do you know?" asked Jonas.

"From the line of your conversation I knew it was Nora on the phone. Though, what did she say?" asked Prof. Church.

"Nothing serious, she just wants to be sure you had a safe trip" said Jonas.

"Oh, that's Nora for you," said Prof. Church.

Minutes later they arrived at Jonas's Dad's place but met his mum as they entered the house "Hello mum, is dad home?" asked Jonas.

Jonas's mum, Esther, spoke to him in their native language and asked if this isn't his friend that was attacked by leopards. The truth is that Esther only met the professor briefly, when he was all bandaged up, and she really didn't have a good grasp of what his face really looks like.

"Yes, he is," said Jonas.

"Oh, I'm glad he has recovered, he almost died from that attack, but what's he doing here?" asked Esther.

"He's here to see dad," said Jonas.

Sadly, Esther wasn't spared the raw details of Nora's rant on her husband and son, and she didn't hesitate to ask Jonas if he has forgotten the trouble the professor's wife almost caused him.

"Hello madam, how're you doing?" asked Prof. Church.

"I'm fine, and you're welcome," said Esther.

Even though the professor had no knowledge that Jonas's mum isn't particularly impressed with his visit. He began by thanking Esther for saving his life and reminded her that the manner with which he returned home the other time didn't really give him this opportunity to say a proper thank you.

"Oh, good to hear you understand we actually tried to save you, but why did your wife engage my husband in such an asinine rage?" asked Esther.

Professor Church is now beginning to face the obvious, because he now knew his wife's rant actually touched this family's nerves. The professor is now grasping at straws as he quickly tried calming frayed nerves by reminding Esther that he intervened immediately to absolve her husband and son from any responsibility as regards the attack.

Jonas saw that his mum's line of conversation could make their guest uncomfortable, he then quickly spoke in his native language to his mum and told her he just spoke with the professor's wife, and they've settled their differences.

"Ok, just that I don't want any trouble and my family shouldn't suffer over their acts of kindness," said Esther. Bolo Baum walked into the conversation from inside the house, and was quite ecstatic to see the professor, because the last time he set his eyes on the professor, he was sick and waiting for brain surgery. He now jokingly asked the professor if that's him.

"Yes, Bolo, it's me, our first meeting on my previous visit was quite a bizarre one," said Prof. Church.

"I'm glad you're fine, and how did the surgery go?" asked Bolo.

"My standing right before you, says it all," said Prof. Church.

"My son has sent your bags across to your wife, and I hope you got them?" asked Bolo. Professor Church understood Bolo's comments concerning his bags to mean, he doesn't have any reason to be in Zimbabwe particularly when the items he left behind has been returned to him. Without any further dawdling, the professor didn't hesitate to hit the nail on the head as he told Bolo that he didn't come for his bags, rather he has come to thank him for his selflessness and kindness towards him.

Bolo knew very well that the professor didn't travel all the way to Zimbabwe just to say thank you to them, he then advises that the professor should've stayed a little longer with his family and healed completely before coming over to express his gratitude to them.

The professor has no choice than to hit the nail right on the head as he interjected and told Bolo he's actually returning to the wild, and he felt he should settle old commitments before his new expedition kicks off.

"Thank you for your gratitude, but I don't think it's a good idea for my son to remain as your guide," said Bolo.

The professor couldn't help but address the elephant in the room, and said he knew that Bolo's decision is based on his wife's reaction towards him and his son. He then said his wife has apologised, and he expects that by now they've moved past that.

Bolo's last experience meant he had to tread cautiously in his dealings with the professor, and that implies that the professor's wife must give the green light for their involvement. Bolo was thrilled that the professor recognised the place of gratitude, and nonetheless he asked the professor if his wife sanctioned this trip.

He thinks this is important because he doesn't want his son being caught up in a web of confusion.

Jonas quickly intervened and spoke to his dad in their native language, telling him the professor's wife called him and asked him to watch over her husband. Bolo remained sceptical with Nora's assurances and gave a word of caution as he said he hopes the professor's wife won't turn on Jonas when things go south. "No, she was quite polite this time, and really wanted my help," said Jonas.

After learning of recent developments from Jonas, Bolo turned to the professor and told him his son said he just spoke to his wife.

"Ok, what does that imply?" asked Prof. Church.

"It means I've released my son to work with you, but I don't want you engaging in doltish acts," said Bolo.

"Oh, thank you, and no worries, I now understand the forest better," said Prof. Church.

Esther wasn't particularly impressed with her husband's decision to allow his son to return to the wild with the professor, because as far as she's concern this professor is trouble and nothing but a minefield. She quickly interjected and spoke to her husband in their native tongue. She pleaded with her husband to lay more emphasis on the fact that they don't want any puerile or fatuous act that'll endanger her son.

"I've told him about that, and there isn't any need nagging over that," said Bolo.

"Let me know when you're ready to leave, I'm going inside the house for a cup of water to quench my thirst," said Jonas.

The professor can't wait to feel the fresh air in the wild, and there isn't any need for hesitation. He told Jonas there's no time to waste and he's ready to get going and he just can't wait to see the wild and experience its freshness. Bolo sensed the professor is overtaken by his obsession for the wild, and in his heart, likened the professor to a child on a sugar rush, and then turned around, looked at his wife and smiled.

"Ok then, just give me a minute," said Jonas.

Later that day while Jonas and the professor stepped into the forest to start their lives afresh in the wild. It didn't take long after their arrival that Nora's phone call to her husband came in and she went on to ask her husband of his location.

"Ooh Nora, I thought you were still angry with me?" asked Prof. Church.

"I'm not just angry with you. I'm mad at you," said Nora.

"But you don't have to be angry, I'm only living out my fantasy and equally matching advocacy with work," said Prof. Church.

Nora's knack for timing matters a lot as she had to follow every of her husband's moves. She was hoping that Jonas's dad will refuse her husband the help he seeks but sensed his deal fell through since he's now headed for the wild. She furiously told her husband to stop reminding her of his witless and insane fantasy that has made his family an object of mockery. Funnily, the professor asked a question that got her hopping mad, as he asked if anyone is mocking her and the children, and if they do, then that'll be wrong.

"Stop being naive, didn't you see the headlines yourself, how'll you make meaning out of those headlines when your sense of judgement has been beclouded by your obsession?" said Nora.

"What about my children, how're they doing?" asked Prof. Church.

"Did you tell Joe you're leaving?" asked Nora.

"I'd wanted to, but changed my mind," he replied.

"You changed your mind about telling your son you are travelling? That's ludicrous," asked Nora. The professor tried explaining himself better and said his action can't be said to be absurd and that he took that decision after the cold treatment he got from her and Eileen.

"So, when did the children you care less about suddenly become so important to you?" asked Nora.

"It isn't out of place for a father to inquire of his kids' welfare," said Prof. Church.

"Sorry, your interest in your kids at this point is more of a misplaced priority," said Nora.

The professor tried making Nora understand he cares, and that he isn't an absentee dad who's just a waste of space. He went on insisting that all he wanted is for her to understand how much this means to him. Nora wasn't impressed as she asked her husband if he expected to be awarded a medal of honour for going above and beyond the call of duty that didn't stop even a single poacher from having their way in the forest. She then scoffed at the lameness of his excuse because her husband did a bad job of it as he tried selling his adventure to her, and it's now obvious in her husband's tone that he's just grasping the heel.

"You can call your children yourself, instead of asking about them from me," said Nora.

Professor Church is just trying to avoid any potential awkward moment that'll further add salt to injury, as he specifically told his wife he can't pretend not knowing things have gone south between him and his children. Despite the relentless onslaught of criticism on the professor, he never reeled, neither did he lost his cool but took it on the chin.

"Who is with you there?" asked Nora.

"Err.., Jonas is with me, and he'll remain my guide," said Prof. Church.

"You must be careful and stay safe," said Nora.

"Yeah, I will," said Prof. Church.

An hour later after they arrived in the jungle the professor pointed to a spot and reminded Jonas that he thinks this was the very spot they pitched their tent the other time. "Yes, you're right, you've a good memory," said Jonas. "Let's pitch our tent immediately, because I'm eager to walk around to catch a good view of the wild," said Prof. Church.

Jonas isn't ready to be out and about in the grassland immediately the tent is up, yet the professor's constant pestering meant he would want to have it his way. Moments after the tent is up and standing, Jonas didn't hesitate to remind the professor when they finished pitching the tent, they'll have to rest. After all, they aren't rushing anywhere.

Sadly, the professor has this endless craving for what's out there in the wild, and he isn't ready for any dawdling around and won't allow a single minute pass by without enjoying the fun of the wild grassland. He unblinkingly told Jonas he isn't sitting idly in the camp because he didn't come into the wild to sleep or rest. Jonas looked on, as the professor emphatically stated his position, and made it clear to Jonas in no uncertain terms that the primary essence of this adventure is to enjoy life in the wild and have a feel of the wild.

It has now dawned on Jonas that the professor's anxiety has morphed into a banal obsession with the wild, and this obsession has suddenly taken over the professor. He then asked to know why the professor is in a rush since he isn't going back to his country any time soon. "Allow me to satisfy my curiosity, Jonas," said Prof. Church.

"Do you know you surprised me, because I noticed a sudden change in your disposition the moment we entered the wild," said Jonas.

"Are you saying I lost my cool? But that should be expected. Why shouldn't I be filled with excitement knowing there's wildlife all around me?" asked Prof. Church. Jonas didn't hesitate asking the professor to check his appetite for freedom in the wild, and frantically reminded him of the implication of losing his cool because that could put both of them in danger.

"Don't worry, I'll avoid any action that could jeopardize our safety," said Prof. Church.

"Please do, because I promised my parents I'll stay safe, and I don't want your wife hurling insults at me or my family," said Jonas.

Minutes later the tent was set, up and standing, and they moved their things inside and made themselves comfortable. The Professor brought out a medium sized bottle of whiskey from his bag and handed it to Jonas, he then asked Jonas to open it.

"Err.., whiskey, do you want us to drink it right away?" asked Jonas.

"Of course yes, why else would I ask you to open it?" asked Prof. Church.

Jonas tried to talk the professor into drinking with caution as he quickly advised that they drink less because they're in the forest. "I know you want us to be alert, but a little whiskey won't hurt," said Prof. Church.

"I know, but I'm just letting you understand what it means to be here," said Jonas.

To avoid any hard feelings, Jonas sipped a little from the bottle of whiskey and held onto the near-full bottle of whiskey for a while without taking any further sip from it. The professor then asked Jonas to pass him the bottle of whisky so he can sip a little as well, and funnily, Jonas passed the bottle of whiskey to the professor, and he gobbled the whole thing in one. "Do you have to drink all of that? What if our tent is visited by a big cat, how can you be alert to keep safe?" asked Jonas.

"I need to lie down and rest, but this quantity of alcohol isn't enough to make me drunk," said Prof. Church. The professor is now gullible as he became a bit intoxicated within minutes, and now feeling the need for an urgent nap as he told Jonas he needs to rest his head for a while.

"Ok, you can relax while I keep watch over our tent," said Jonas.

"Where are you going, Jonas?" asked Prof. Church.

"I'm here keeping watch outside, the two of us aren't supposed to be inside the tent without a proper view of what goes on out there," said Jonas.

Professor Pratt suddenly told Jonas he's coming with him, and then stood up immediately and followed Jonas outside the tent, and sadly, instead of staying with Jonas just in front of the tent, the professor began to wander further away into the forest.

"Where are you going? I thought you wanted to join me to watch over our tent, you just don't walk into the wild like that," said Jonas.

"Let me just have a stroll around, you can join me if you like," said Prof. Church.

Jonas felt the sting of frustration precipitated by the professor's too many twists and turns, and he didn't hesitate to tell the professor he doesn't think this is working out. Jonas hit the nail on the head as he asked him why he chose to make working with him so difficult.

"I just can't remain in the tent, I felt I should see some of this wildlife on my first day in the forest," said Prof. Church.

"You aren't armed, so why should you walk into the wild naked?" asked Jonas.

"Why did you say I'm naked? I'm dressed," said Prof. Church.

"Entering into the wild unarmed means you are naked," said Jonas.

The professor continued straying further down into the wild as Jonas followed him from behind and tried talking him out of going ahead unarmed. While their conversation continued, the professor saw an African Skunk, a striped polecat and walked close to it. "That animal will make your life uncomfortable, I suggest you keep a safe distance from it," said Jonas.

The professor exclaimed, saying he has come across skunks in the past, but none as beautiful as this one. He was drawn by the strippy colours of this beautiful grassland creature. "I know it's beautiful as you said, but don't get any closer, just appreciate the animal from some distance," said Jonas.

The professor didn't heed to Jonas's instructions not to get any closer to this animal, he continued, as he came across as toned-deaf. He remained as stubborn as a mull as he continued with his rhetoric of reminding Jonas that this is the wild, and they're meant to co-exist with these animals peacefully. He went closer without adhering to Jonas's advice and unsurprisingly the Skunk sprayed him. "Ooh, ouch, ouch," the professor screamed.

"I told you not to get any closer to this animal," said Jonas.

The spray from this skunk kept the professor screaming as the irritation made him quite uncomfortable. "Please do something about this, quickly," said Prof. Church.

"I hate all this confusion," said Jonas. The professor didn't stop asking Jonas to do something to relieve him of the discomfort. Jonas continued to mutter in frustration, as he looked around then rushed to get some leaves, and he then squeezed them together before applying the juice on the professor.

"I've heard about how bad the spray of a skunk could be, but I never knew it'll be this uncomfortable," said Prof. Church.

Jonas told the professor that the juice of these herbs will help calm the irritation. Though, it will take a few minutes, yet the professor remained delusional as he asked why the animal should spray him even when he was only being friendly. "How did she know you were only being friendly! Aren't you a professor? You should know all this by now," said Jonas.

"Don't make me look daft, Jonas. I know that Skunks spray people in self-defence but I expected them to be nicer when you're friendly," said Prof. Church.

The professor tried to manage Jonas's rebuke of 'I told you so,' and insists there's nothing wrong with being a bit old-fashioned, Jonas then reminded the professor that the Skunk has proved him wrong, before asking to know how he's feeling. "I still feel the sensation, and is there something you can still do about this?" asked Prof. Church.

Jonas told the professor to give it a little while and he will be fine. The frustration got to Jonas and he suddenly turned around and told the professor he's returning to the tent because he has had enough for one day.

Just as Jonas turned around and took some steps in a bid to return to the tent, the professor beckoned and asked to know where he's going. He then urged Jonas to hang on so they will walk around a little bit more when this irritation subsides. Jonas didn't bat an eye as he told the professor he's sorry if he ruined his fun but he's returning to the tent, and he's no longer ready for any more drama. Sadly, Jonas didn't quite see the professor's obsession as a banality of evil but rather, he considers it as plain stupidity.

"But you know I'm not meant to walk around alone," said Prof. Church.

"Then join me in the tent," said Jonas. The professor's strove to impress Jonas meant he'd to corporate by being temporarily cool headed, he then muttered in frustration, and followed Jonas from behind as they head to the tent, and minutes later, they were in the tent. "Oh, I feel better now. You sure have a good idea of the wild," said Prof. Church.

"Why did you say that?" asked Jonas.

"Your understanding of herbs startles me, can't you see how better I'm feeling now?" said Prof. Church.

"Good to hear that, let's take some rest for today and continue tomorrow," said Jonas.

Nora continued keeping tab on her husband through Jonas, and later that day, she called Jonas for an update. The moment Jonas saw Nora's phone call, he walked outside the tent, because Nora urged Jonas to update her discreetly about her husband.

"Hello Jonas, how're you?" asked Nora.

"Hello Madam, I'm fine, but your husband is so stubborn and I don't think I'll continue working with him," said Jonas.

"Is anything the matter, is he okay?" asked Nora.

Jonas narrated to Nora how the professor lost his composure the moment he entered the wild, and insisted that her husband's disorderly conduct in the wild is putting him under intense pressure. Nora cried, saying she doesn't know why her husband is like this. Jonas tried calming Nora as he promised to help watch the professor's attitude within the next few days but stressed if he doesn't change then he will have no choice but withdraw from him.

"Please don't do that yet, he has a poor assessment of danger when it comes to the wild," said Nora.

"He's equally putting me in danger," said Jonas.

Nora did all she could to let Jonas know she understands his predicament yet pleaded with Jonas to please let her know whenever he intends to withdraw his services from her husband. Nora didn't stop short of reminding Jonas not let the professor know she called him.

"Ok, I've heard you," said Jonas, who then walks back into the tent after the phone call.

The professor didn't hesitate to ask Jonas who it was that's on the phone the moment he returned to the tent, and funnily, Jonas told the professor it was his girl friend that was on phone. "Why don't you invite her to join us in the wild?" asked Prof. Church.

Jonas smiled and said his girlfriend doesn't seem to share his interest in the wild, and wouldn't be interested in being a part of this party. They both made themselves comfortable as Jonas did a good job of keeping the professor on a tight leash, and decided against going into the wild for the rest of the day.

CHAPTER

EIGHT

The Second Tour

The next morning, the professor and Jonas made a fire to keep warm in the front of their tent as they enjoyed their cups of tea. Unsurprisingly, the professor passively asked Jonas what direction of the forest he suggests they go today. "Hmm, when we go down to the plain, we'll decide that," said Jonas.

"Why can't we decide that right now? That's what we call planning," said Prof. Church.

Jonas quickly reminded the professor they aren't hunters, and after all, they're just people without a defined purpose who dwell and walk around in the wild, and as a result the direction they'll go depends on the degree of danger on the ground. Jonas's mention of danger irked the professor, and he quickly accused Jonas of being muggy, and that puts him on a collision course with Jonas. He then furiously asked Jonas what he meant by the degree of danger on the ground, Jonas responded to the question, yet remained calm as he avoided being sucked in by the professor's grumpiness.

"If we're going down the valley and you see the prints from lions, you'll change course, won't you?" asked Jonas.

"Ok, you've made your point, but we should start going," said Prof. Church.

"When, right now? We should stay a little more," said Jonas.

The professor continued being jumpy, and Jonas continued to restrain his anger even as he plays the big brother in this partnership. An hour later, Jonas then suggested they make the trip down the valley and stressed they need not rush to experience what the morning looks like in the wild. It's embarrassingly obvious that the professor wants to be in the valley where the action is because he's keen to have a real wild experience. Jonas on the other hand is keen on safety. He reminded the professor that he could still catch a good view of the forest from this vantage point and that's the reason they pitched their tent on a hill, because it will enable them detect danger when it approaches.

"No, Jonas, I prefer to be part of what's going on in the forest, and I want that at close range," the professor insists.

Forty-five minutes later, the professor and Jonas got prepared and began their tour of the wild. Just as they touched down the valley, Jonas turned to the professor and asked if his gun is loaded and ready. "I've my gun, but I don't think loading it will be necessary," said Prof. Church.

"Why, Professor? Then let's go back if you won't load your gun," said Jonas.

"My bullets, and all I would need are all here," said Prof. Church.

Jonas reminded the professor that bullets and cartridges aren't meant to be in his pocket because danger doesn't give notice. He reminded the professor that when it comes to the wild, danger is already lurking. "Don't worry; I'll load my gun, if necessary," said Prof. Church.

"Oh, I'm tired of this, let's just continue," said Jonas.

Minutes later they spotted animal dung, walked closer and the professor asked Jonas which animal did that and he told him they are from Zebras. While they continued their tour the professor points to some hoof prints on the ground.

"These prints are different from the other ones," said Prof. Church.

"Yes, they're, they're made by giraffes and they're fresh, which means these giraffes should be close," said Jonas.

The professor looked around and saw some giraffes at a distance and told Jonas to look over there as he pointed to a herd of giraffes, and then told Jonas he's right. Sadly, the professor wanted more as he told Jonas he likes the sight of that and wants to get closer. Jonas agreed and they moved closer to where the herd of giraffes was, but Jonas advised the professor they keep some distance to avoiding spooking the animals, so they don't hurt him.

"Why can't we get closer? Giraffes aren't big cats, so they can't be aggressive," said Prof. Church.

Jonas took time to narrate the risk of getting too close to the heard of giraffes as he reminded him that a single kick could send him to an early grave or the hospital. After spending some time with the giraffes, they moved farther down the forest as they continued their tour of the forest, and then they saw it.

"What happened here, it's as if the world came to an end here?" asked Prof. Church.

"These are prints from a pride of lions, they hunted here last night and it was a dramatic hunt for buffalos," said Jonas. The sight made Jonas uncomfortable because it produced a still eerie feeling inside him that signals danger. This time, Jonas isn't muggy for nothing. The professor smiled with his face wreathed in smiles, his disposition is more likened a child who just found a lost treasure. He thought to himself, this is exactly what I wanted, and didn't hesitate to remind Jonas that he wished he'd been here to witness this chase and experience it first-hand.

Jonas was surprised to hear the professor's wishes which he considers gibberish from a man on a suicide mission. He then stopped and asked the professor if he's wishing himself death. "Do you know what it means to experience a pride of lions around you?" asked Jonas. Immediately after rebuking the professor, Jonas made a sudden turn and began walking back to the tent.

"Where are you going?" asked Prof. Church.

"I don't feel good about this, my instinct wants me to go back, so let's go back," said Jonas. The professor continued to dawdle around as he hesitated, but Jonas isn't having any of it, and sadly the professor told Jonas they're just beginning to have their fun, and this big cat territory is where the fun is.

"No, it isn't, I can sense death and immense danger, if you wish to die today and bring your expedition to an abrupt end, stay here an hour longer," said Jonas.

"Why're you moving so fast, let's go over to the giraffes or we can look for the zebras," said Prof. Church.

Jonas stopped to lecture the muttering professor whom he now finds insufferable that the pride of lions in question didn't succeed with the buffalos last night, so they returned hungry, and they might come out for these zebras or the giraffes as the case maybe any moment soon. Hence hanging around these zebras and giraffes could put them in the firing line.

"Err.., you're right, but your assessment of risk is too high, I hope you understand we need to take some level of risk?" said Prof. Church.

As they retreat from that area of the forest, the professor turned in a dramatic twist and headed in a different direction.

"Professor, where are you going?" asked Jonas.

Sadly, the professor turned and faced the direction of the stream where he was attacked by leopards previously and he blatantly told Jonas he's heading to the stream, and he just can't return to the tent without enjoying the sight of wildlife in their natural habitat.

While the professor continues playing the loser, as though he's being victimised and denied access to the fun in the wild. Jonas couldn't help but emphasise that the professor has just spent some quality time around a herd of giraffes, and reminded him has seen some gazelle today, before asking what else he needed for a fun-filled day.

"I want to see more of them, what about the Wildebeest, I want to see the elephants, I want to see the rhinos and even the big cats," said Prof. Church.

Jonas tried explaining to the professor that they now live in the wild and will definitely see all these animals and wondered why the professor was in a rush, he then cautioned that they don't have to see most of this wildlife at the expense of their lives.

"Let's go to the stream, we might find some of them by the stream," said Prof. Church.

Jonas, though, wasn't surprised at the professor's lack of candour because he saw this coming, but now that the professor seems to be attracted to danger, he felt like asking the professor if he has a short memory, but realised it might come across as rude. Yet, decided to remind him that it was beside the same stream that he was attacked by leopards.

"I'm certain those leopards will not be there this time," said Prof. Church.

After trying to subtly make the professor change course, Jonas then sternly told the professor he's sorry he can't go with him to the stream. Sadly, the professor didn't give in to Jonas's persuasion and warnings, and he didn't hesitate to let Jonas know he's going ahead without him. After all, he would have his fun alone and Jonas won't share in it.

The professor kept his word and was keen to continue to the stream alone and without Jonas, but Jonas didn't hesitate to give the professor a parting advice as he told him to make sure his gun is loaded in advance as he heads for the stream. "I don't think I'll need it, Jonas. Just wait for me in the tent," said Prof. Church.

Jonas continued in the opposite direction and minutes later Jonas had a change of heart and rushed back to the professor whose eyes are set for the drama around the stream. Jonas called out to the professor to wait for him as he rushed to catch up with the professor, but sadly, the professor has already gone some distance and he's just meters away from the stream and didn't hear Jonas. Unsurprisingly, Jonas ran as fast as his feet could carry him and joined the professor minutes later. "Why're you so stubborn, Professor?" asked Jonas. The professor continued pushing his luck as he continues pressing Jonas's button with his twists of stubbornness. Jonas remained worried sick that the professor's luck might not be anything compared to the three blind mice, and even the four-leaf-clover might not do the trick of bringing the professor the good luck he will need when rubber hits the road. The professor was polite anyway as he reminded Jonas that he isn't stubborn, but not without expressing his prejudice that he wasn't impressed with Jonas because he seems to be exaggerating the presence of danger. He'd to make it known to Jonas that he's making this whole idea of the wild uninteresting for him. Jonas tagged along as they continued their conversation, but as they drew closer to the stream Jonas saw some prints on the ground and quickly alerted the professor to them.

"Stop, just stop, can't you see these prints?" said Jonas.

"What prints are you talking about? There are many prints here," said Prof. Church.

"Yes, there are many prints here but these ones here belong to a Lion and they're fresh," said Jonas.

Professor Church looked around and saw nothing and the professor immediately told Jonas he can't see any Lion around and didn't stop short at accusing Jonas of making things up. "The Lion is very good at camouflage, and we're already its target" said Jonas.

"What do we do now?" asked Prof. Church.

Jonas's hunter's instinct kicked in immediately, and this time, Jonas isn't just the tour guide, he's assumed the posture of a hunter, as he began positioning himself and told the professor he will kill the animal, if he can. Sadly, the professor unblinkingly gave Jonas a stern warning as he promised him if he shoots the lion he will help see to it that Jonas ends behind bars because putting away those hurting innocent animals is the reason he's here.

"Then you just have to turn back and run," said Jonas.

The professor and Jonas turned around and ran as fast as they could and suddenly there's a lion chasing after them, but Jonas was quicker on his feet than the professor. This time the possibility of pulling a rabbit out of the hat is slim, particularly now that it's a lion that is unto them. Sadly, the lion was close to the professor when he unfortunately fell into a ditch, and the lion was looking for the best way to get the professor, but Jonas had to shoot at the lion to scare it away.

After successfully scaring lion away, Jonas made sure the coast was quite clear before he rushed to the ditch where the professor was and as he looked at the professor inside the ditch, he asked the professor if he's ok.

"That was a close call, Jonas," said Prof. Church. Sadly, the professor lay motionless on the floor of the bushy ditch.

"I'm done working with you, professor. It's like you brought me here to watch you die, and to kill me as well, why aren't you getting up?" asked Jonas.

Professor replied Jonas saying he can't move and he seems to have broken his shoulder. Jonas became very concerned and exclaimed.

"Oh my God! I'm coming in to lift you out of the ditch, and we've to be fast about this before this lion take us unawares," said Jonas. Professor Church is known to be quite an assuming man, but there might be no straws to grasp this time. "Ooh, ouch, something just bit me," said Prof. Church.

"What's it?" asked Jonas.

For what it's worth, this professor who has cheated death twice by a whisker has just been bitten by a snake, because a snake suddenly crawls out from under the professor and attempting to crawl out of the ditch. "Oh, it's a snake," said Prof. Church.

"Oh no, it's a black mamba," said Jonas. Unsurprisingly, while the snake tries to make an escape, Jonas rushed and killed the snake but exclaimed. "Oh my God, this isn't good at all," said Jonas.

Jonas's expression of fear did instil some fear in the professor, and while still motionless in the floor of the ditch, the professor interjected as he inquired to know what Jonas meant and asked if he's going to die. Jonas's disposition changed knowing that the snake in question is a black mamba and he needed to act quickly if this professor will survive this day. Jonas told the professor that with the black mamba's bite a man can die smiling because it's one of the world's fastest killing machines.

"Do something please, and I don't want to die! Eeh, hmm, ooh, my shoulder," said Prof. Church.

Sadly, the professor's shoulder hurts so badly, and he's beginning to scream on top of his lugs as Jonas attempts to drag him out of the ditch.

"You seem to have a hurt shoulder, but I'll need to tie your leg and suck out the snake's venom before it circulates all over your body," said Jonas.

Life's struggles and fantasy is all vanity after all, and it obviously exposes the futility of life because it didn't take long before the black mambas' venom got the best of the professor. The professor began speaking in a faint voice, because he was under intense pain resulting from the shoulder injury. Now that his second adventure in the grassland of Africa has gone up in smoke, the professor then apologised to Jonas for putting him through this needless stress, yet pleaded with the Jonas to do whatever he can to save him. The professor's new debacle is now making him look like a man whose left foot is suddenly looking like he's flat-footed.

Jonas quickly rummaged through his sack and brought out a tiny knife, he then used the knife to cut the spot of the bite, sucked out the venom as much as he could, and sadly, that didn't go far enough to stop the mamba's venom from taking over the professor. Immediately, Jonas had to decide whether to call his dad for help or to get Nora involved.

Nora on the other hand was in a retail supermarket doing shopping and requested the attention of an employee of the supermarket. "Excuse me, I need your attention please," said Nora.

Glenda Jordan, a store staff walks up to Nora with a smile "Hello good morning, what can I do for you?" she asked.

Your tomato sauce use to be on this shelf, I've been looking around and I can't find them," said Nora.

Glenda replied with an apology and told Nora they've just moved the tomato sauce to the second shelf on the third isle. Nora wasn't particularly impressed as she told the store staff that there should've been a notice or something to let customers know about the change. "That's why we're here to give assistance and make shopping experience fun for our customers, sorry for your troubles," said Glenda.

Nora chuckled "Cheeky you," she said.

Sadly, Jonas's phone call came in while Nora and Glenda were in a conversation. "Hello madam, this is Jonas," he said.

"Jonas! Why're you sounding like this, is anything the matter?" asked Nora.

"I won't work for your husband again after this, he has just been bitten by a mamba and he has broken his collar bone," said Jonas.

Unsurprisingly, the news came to Nora as a shock; she's now filled with emotion because the news left some eerie stillness in her. She stood statue-still and remained silent for a minute while still holding the phone to her ear as tears rolled down her cheeks.

"Hello madam, hello, can you hear me?" asked Jonas.

Glenda was surprised to see the cheerful customer she was just attending to suddenly all teary and then bursting into tears. She then quickly asked Nora if she's ok but didn't stop short of asking who it was on the phone, before asking what they said to her that got her shedding tears.

"What's happening to me? I hope I'm not losing my mind, Jonas where are you now," asked Nora.

"I told him, I told him, but he just won't listen to me," said Jonas.

Nora tried to stop Jonas from going on and on about how her husband doesn't listen as she tried to calm the situation. "Of course, you told me about him but where are you now, Jonas?" asked Nora.

"We're in the forest, and I just finished sucking out the venom from his leg, should I take him to the hospital?" asked Jonas.

While the conversation between Nora and Jonas was ongoing, Nora could hear someone groaning at the background, and then asked if that's her husband that's groaning. Obviously, Jonas didn't hesitate to confirm to her it was her husband that's groaning in pain. "Take him immediately to Doctor Shekuh and tell him everything, but be fast, and I'll give him a call right away," said Nora.

"Ok, I'll do that right away," said Jonas.

Glenda was still standing beside Nora as she spoke with Jonas even though she sobbed all through the time of the conversation. "Madam, are you ok? Come and have a seat for some time and calm down," said Glenda.

"I can't, it's my husband, he has an accident and I've to go, please return these things to the shelves," said Nora. She hands over the basket of groceries to Glenda and left as she sobbed continually.

Jonas rushed Professor Pratt Church to the Wonder World Clinics. Serendipitously, Tina Mbolelu visited her sick mum and was leaving the hospital when a taxi brought Professor Pratt Church who was already unconscious as a result of the snake bite.

Jonas alighted from the taxi and screamed "Nurse, please help me, help, he's dying," said Jonas.

Funnily, Tina Mbolelu who's on her way out of the premises rushed to the taxi to help from the sincerity of her heart, only to realise it's Professor Pratt Church. "Oh my God, that's Professor Pratt, what happened to him?" asked Tina. In the heat of the moment, Jonas's confusion got the best of him as he unwittingly told Tina everything without a flicker of recognition from their previous encounter. He told Tina Mbolelu that the professor fell into a ditch while being chased by a lion and ended up being bitten by a snake.

Nurse Theresa rushed out to give help to the patient that have just been rushed in only to realise it's the professor. "Err.., it's the professor," said Nurse Theresa. Sadly, the moment the nurse arrived the scene and realised it was the same professor, and then saw Jonas having a conversation with Tina, she immediately turned to Jonas and instructed Jonas not to speak any further with Tina that she's a journalist.

"What's it with you, nurse. Did I snoop through your files this time?" asked Tina.

"I don't want you causing us any trouble this time," said Nurse.

"But I've already gotten all the information for my headlines," said Tina.

"I hate you, because you're sleazy," said Nurse Theresa.

"I beg your pardon! Did you just call me sleazy?" asked Tina.

Tina was quite furious at Nurse Theresa for calling her sleazy, particularly when the headlines she seeks serendipitously fell in her lap without engaging in anything unethical. In the interest of peace, Tina had to calm things down, and the nurse then apologised to Tina but reminded her she's isn't wanted around anymore. "My mum is a patient in your hospital so you can't stop me from coming around," said Tina.

"Maybe we will soon discharge your mum from our clinic, so you won't have a reason to be here snooping around," said Nurse Theresa. The eeriness of Tina's serendipitous involvement in this professor's adventure makes her the professor's number one nemesis, and somehow their paths keep colliding even as she goes about minding her own business. This precipitated some concern in this nurse that's naturally a free-spirited person. The professor was rushed into the ward and Doctor Shekuch was on hand as he asked what happened to the patient.

"It's like he was bitten by a snake and possibly a shoulder injury," said Nurse Theresa.

But soon there was a flicker of recognition as the doctor realised the person just admitted to the hospital is the same Professor Pratt Church "Oh my God, how come it's the same professor, what's going on?" asked Dr. Shekuh.

"His wife said I should bring him to you. Has she called you?" asked Jonas.

Doctor Shekuh interjected and told Jonas that Nora didn't call him, yet surprised she would even consider asking Jonas to bring her husband to him because she wasn't even grateful for the help he gave her husband the last time. Interestingly, the wheels take time to turn but they do eventually turn, and the doctor basically exclaimed, asking Jonas how come Nora suddenly realised he could be of help.

Jonas had no dog in this fight but pleaded with the doctor to please do something, assuring him that Nora will call him to apologise for her mistake just as she apologised to him and his dad. It's glaringly obvious that Doctor Shekuh has a bone to pick with Nora after the quite belittling treatment he got from her.

"Ok, let me keep him alive first before we continue with what his wife did and didn't do," said Dr. Shekuh.

"What do we do first?" asked Nurse Theresa.

"Let's start treating the snake bite first, and then we follow up with a scan immediately to be sure there isn't any form of internal bleeding," said Dr. Shekuh.

"But he's unconscious," said Nurse Theresa.

"Yes, that's what a black mamba's bite can do; you die slowly without feeling any pain," said Dr. Shekuh.

Doctor Shekuh began treatment immediately, and sadly, Nora's attempt to call Doctor Shekuh immediately failed because she never bothered to get his phone number in their previous meeting, so she decided to go online to search for the wonder world clinic phone contact details. Nora was quite shaken by the news of her husband latest attack and after finding it difficult to reach Doctor Shekuh, she then turned to Professor Walker for help.

"Hello Walker, how're you doing?" asked Nora.

"I'm fine Nora, how're you and the kids doing, and has your husband called you since he returned to the wild?" asked Prof. Walker.

Nora didn't hesitate to hit the nail on the head and she told Professor Walker why she called, and began to sob as she told him her husband is unconscious and hospitalised again.

"What do you mean unconscious, and does it mean he hasn't fully recovered before running back to the wild?" asked Prof. Walker.

Nora narrated the sad story just a Jonas passed it to her, that her husband was chased by a Lion, and he fell into a ditch and then got bitten by a snake. Professor Walker was taken aback by the chain of events leading to the latest debacle the professor just suffered, and immediately asked Nora, how all this happened to him within one week of returning to the wild. Walker couldn't help himself to come to terms with this insanity as he unwittingly exclaimed that this madness needs to stop. Sadly, while their conversation was ongoing Professor Walker just saw the news of the latest attack suffered by Professor Pratt Church making the headlines.

"What! You mean the headlines?" asked Nora.

"It's already being reported in the news, turn on your television," said Nora.

Nora quickly turned on the television "Oh, it's true, you're right Walker," said Nora.

While still on phone, Professor Walker listened to the news for a while even as he held onto the phone and told Nora that comments and reactions about her husband are bad.

"I've to rush to Zimbabwe possibly tomorrow, and will you be able to go with me?" asked Nora.

"I'm meant to present a paper in a seminar tomorrow," said Prof. Walker.

Since Professor Walker won't be able to make it to Zimbabwe with Nora, she's now on her own, and she quickly asked the professor to help get Billy Alfred the embassy attaché who help out the other time to assist her.

"I'll try, but I don't think he'll want to help," said Prof. Walker.

"Why! My husband is an American citizen, why won't they help him?" asked Nora.

Professor Walker considered the public sentiment about Professor Church's action and advice her to go it alone because Americans now sees her husband as a man who purposefully put's himself in danger just to waste taxpayers' money.

"Ok, I'll have to leave for Zimbabwe tomorrow," said Nora.

"Ok, I'll give you a call to know how and where to come in," said Prof. Walker.

Immediately after his phone conversation with Nora, Professor Walker walked into the bedroom and his wife Gloria sensed something is amiss from his disposition. He hesitated but couldn't help himself as he stopped short of narrating the sad news about his friend's attack, but told Gloria it's Pratt, and he's all over the news again.

"What about him this time?" asked Gloria.

Sadly, Professor Walker had no choice but to narrate the sad attack as he told Gloria that Professor Pratt Church has been attacked again, and this time he was chased by a Lion, he fell into a ditch and ended up being bitten by a snake.

"I feel so much for Nora because this man is like a plague," said Gloria.

"I'm tired of getting involved in this, and I just don't know when it'll end," said Prof. Walker.

"Let's pray he makes it, since you said he's unconscious," said Gloria.

Nora called Doctor Shekuh, but this is sadly one of those awkward phone calls she had no choice but to make, not just because of her husband's debacle, but for the fact that her last encounter with Doctor Shekuh wasn't quite fitting for what could be described as cordial. Interestingly, the doctor has fish to fry with Nora.

"Hello doctor, it's me, Nora Church," she said.

"Mrs Church! I'm surprised to hear you asked Jonas to bring your husband to me," said Dr. Shekuh.

"Why're you surprised, aren't you a doctor?" asked Nora.

The doctor didn't hesitate to refresh Nora's memory about her accusation in the recent past, and asked why she would send her husband to a doctor whose work seem creepy to her. Sadly, Nora is now in a bind and her defence was quite weak but tried reminding the doctor she's aware they started on a wrong foot, but she never said his work is creepy. The doctor had to get so much off his chest as he insisted he and Nora didn't only start on a wrong foot but did end on a wrong foot and despite all he did for her and her husband, she still didn't see anything good about him.

"But I never said anything bad about you," said Nora.

"When we got to the United States you never said a thank you, you walked away as if I never existed, it's a shame and I'm disappointed in you," said Dr. Shekuh.

"I'm sorry for whatever I've done that got you this upset. Please let's just move past this," said Nora.

Doctor Shekuh was upfront as he told Nora he has moved past it already and won't use it against her now that she's boxed in a corner. Nora felt relieved and thanked the doctor, but didn't stop short of promising to find time to right every one of her wrongs.

"Your husband is stable, though he was convulsing at one point, but he's stable and his condition is still critical," said Dr. Shekuh.

Nora promised the doctor she'll be in Zimbabwe the next day and pleaded with him to please just continue doing his good work on her husband. She then asked the doctor to please tell Jonas she'll be on her way the next day.

"Ok, I'll do that," said Dr. Shekuh.

Joe just cancelled his visit to the library and returned home after a phone conversation with Eileen that their dad has been attacked. He met his mum seated in the living room with the phone by her side and didn't hesitate to ask if his dad has been attacked again.

"Yes, but who told you about it?" asked Nora.

"Eileen called me from school and said her friends told her about it, and that it's all over the news," said Joe.

"Yes, you can see for yourself, it's all over the news," said Nora. She immediately pointed to the television for Joe to see for himself.

"Mum, what do we do about this?" asked Joe.

Nora told Joe she's leaving for Zimbabwe the next day, and didn't stop short of narrating her conversation with Professor Walker that she had wanted to get the embassy involved but he suggested to her not to bother them because they might not help this time.

"Walker is right, and people will react negatively if the government continues to spend taxpayers' money on dad," said Joe.

"Most importantly when he deliberately put's himself in danger," said Nora.

"For me, I don't feel pity for dad anymore, I only feel for us," said Joe.

"How is your sister taking it?" asked Nora.

Joe subtly reminded his mum she's the only person that's heart-broken over his dad's recent attack. Joe made it plain to his mum that Eileen didn't really show so much emotion. Sadly, after the previous accident they all wept for their dad and what he did was to give them his middle finger and run straight back to the wild. "He's your dad, you must share in his pain, I know he has let the two of you down," said Nora.

Sadly, Joe thinks his dad has done them more harm than his mum could imagine, as he unblinkingly told his mum that his dad has done more than merely letting them down and doesn't deserve their tears. Nora is equally pained by her husband's twists and turns, yet she thinks taking her foot off the pedal too soon might darken the shades of grey.

"I'll be travelling tomorrow, and will you want to go with me," said Nora.

"No mum, I've got plans," said Joe.

Nora tried sweet talking Joe as she reminded Joe that he and Eileen were eager to go with her to Zimbabwe the other time, and now is the time.

"Yes, that was then, when we were emotionally attached to dad, but now we know better and I don't think Eileen would want to go either," said Joe.

Sadly, too much water has gone under the bridge and Nora is on her own this time and would have to go it all alone because the dice are now cast.

Nora couldn't help herself as tears rolled down her cheeks yet told Joe if he changes his mind concerning the trip, he should let her know. Nora is now in a bind, sadly her tantrums and fits of anger hasn't helped either and she's now torn between loyalty to marriage and rescuing a sinking ship that's most likely going to sink.

The evening of the next day, Nora arrived Zimbabwe and went straight to the Wonder World Clinics. She headed straight to the doctor's office immediately she finished concluding the usual formalities with the receptionist.

"Nora Church, you're welcome," said Dr. Shekuh.

"How's he?" asked Nora.

"He's stable and just regained consciousness about an hour ago," said Dr. Shekuh.

"Err.., has he been unconscious?" asked Nora.

Doctor Shekuh narrated the professor's medical condition to Nora, and that the professor has been convulsing but also told Nora he deliberately withheld other details during their phone conversation to avoid panic.

"Ok, can I see him?" asked Nora.

"Of course yes, and I know you've come to take him with you," said Dr. Shekuh. Unsurprisingly, Nora told the doctor she's taking her husband with her and wants to pay his medical bill.

"Ok, you can come with me," said Dr. Shekuh. They walked through the ward and ended up by the Professor's bedside.

"Nora, you came, good to see you," said Prof. Church.

Nora didn't fall for the professor's flattery words, because she didn't hesitate to give the professor a piece of her mind. Funnily, even as the professor was trying to be cheerful, Nora sternly told him that when this is over, she'll be asking for a divorce, so the professor will be free to feed himself to big cats. The professor considered Nora's threat of a divorce as a bit too harsh stressing that divorce isn't fitting for the occasion. Nora on the other hand made it plain and simple that she's trying to sever ties with her husband so no one will associate her with the professor's future misfortune.

"Nora, I know you're angry, and I'm just trying to experience the wild," said Prof. Church.

Nora couldn't stop the tears rolling down her cheeks even as she turned to Jonas and thanked him for everything he has done for her family. "You're welcome, madam," said Jonas.

"You've to stop crying, Nora, you need to be strong," said Dr. Shekuh.

Nora replied in a very faint voice as she told the doctor that her husband made her feel so empty, and he's just sapping the little strength left inside her. She then fixed her gaze on the doctor and asked. What's it her husband is looking for in the wild, she then muttered saying his miraculous escape from death is more the product of luck, than of good judgement.

"Actually, I was surprised, when Jonas rushed him here, and I had no choice but to keep him alive," said Dr. Shekuh.

Nora thanked the doctor, and told him he made her realise she didn't do well in their previous meeting, but this time she thanked the doctor for his previous help and for this time. Sadly, Joe and Eileen seem not to understand the game their mum is playing in this matter, as they are now convinced that their mum would continue to live in denial thinking she has it all under control.

"Ok, I'm glad we were able to stabilise him," said Dr. Shekuh.

"Are you taking him with you?" asked Jonas.

"Yes Jonas, I intend to take him with me, and can you help me recover his passport?" asked Nora.

"I'll do that but it's going to be tomorrow morning and I will possibly bring his bags along," said Jonas.

Nora pleaded with Jonas because time is now of the essence, and she wants her husband's stuff recovered first thing in the morning of the next day because they're leaving the next day. She then dipped her hand into her pause, and took out some money, and handed it to Jonas, then said this should take care of his troubles. Sadly, the doctor has more sad news for Nora.

"He has a broken collar bone and this could affect his posture, even after he has healed," said Dr. Shekuh. Nora grimaced as this new revelation was brought to her knowledge, and somehow this unpleasantness has taken a toll on Nora.

"You want to experience the wild, can you hear that? You might end up being bent over!" exclaimed Nora.

This professor who considers himself the Goldilocks of the African Grassland seemed to have gotten the short end of the stick from his wild adventure. Faced with the stark reality of a bent posture, the professor tried to make light of the obviously sad situation. "How bent do you think I might be, doctor?" asked Prof. Church.

"I don't know how bent you might be, but I know there's every possibility your posture will be affected," said Dr. Shekuh.

"I know I'll be fine, if it's just the collar bone you're talking about," assured Prof. Church.

The doctor made the situation grimmer as he made the professor aware that some other bones around his shoulder were damaged and a scan will reveal the level of damage suffered. Nora also needed an assurance from the doctor because she needs to be sure it's safe to fly her husband home in his present state. Thanks to the friendly ambience, the doctor was quite corporative with Nora this time as he assured Nora it'll be safe, and he will get her husband ready to make that possible.

The next morning while Nora and her husband were in the airport waiting for their boarding announcement, Eileen called to hear from her mum.

"Hello mum, where are you?" asked Eileen.

"We're at the airport, and our flight will depart in the next hour," said Nora.

"Why aren't you taking the first flight?" asked Eileen.

Nora told Eileen they were only able to retrieve his passport from the wild that morning before booking their flight. But Eileen proceeded to ask her mum if she's ok.

"Your dad is ok and he's here, do you want to speak with him?" asked Nora.

"I only asked if you're ok, and I never asked you if dad is ok, he put himself in that condition," said Eileen.

"Eileen, don't let your anger overtake your sense of reason," said Nora.

"Ok, see you when you return," said Eileen. Professor Church understood that Nora was on the phone with Eileen and immediately the conversation ended the professor asked Nora to know what Eileen said.

"Nothing, let's just go home, but when this is over we're going our separate ways," said Nora.

"I know you and the kids are out to punish me for pursuing my dream in the wild," said Prof. Church. Eileen on the other hand broke down in tears immediately she ended the conversation with her mum because she's never known to give the middle finger to her dad whom she loves so much and considers her best friend.

An hour later, their flight departed Zimbabwe and they arrived in the United States late at night and then called an ambulance that took them straight to the hospital. The professor was admitted to the same hospital he stayed during his previous ordeal.

Lindsay Black was on hand to attend to them as the doctor on duty. "How're you, Nora? I'm not surprised to see you because I heard about your husband in the news," said Dr. Black. "I know, and it's a shame we're making the headlines for silly reasons," said Nora.

Lindsay Black collected the file containing the treatment given to the professor by the Zimbabwean doctor for an initial assessment as to what treatment the doctor gave and where he stopped. "It's all in there, but the doctor said he has been treated for the snake bite," said Nora.

"From his file, he has some damaged bones around his shoulder. We'll do an X-ray immediately and carry out some blood tests before we decide on how to go," said Dr. Black.

Nora didn't hesitate to remind Doctor Black that her husband is in a serious pain, requesting that something should be done immediately to ease his pains. "We will give him something to ease the pain, and then wait for his test results to be ready," said Dr. Black.

Unsurprisingly, now that Nora is sure her husband is in safe hands, she needed a cup of coffee to help her relax her nerves, so she turned to Doctor Black. "I'm dying for a cup of coffee; just give me a minute, and I'll be back," said Nora.

"Take five minutes, Nora," said Dr. Black.

The morning of the next day Ryan Parks takes over from Doctor Black. "Nora Church, I'm Doctor Ryan Parks, and I'll be attending to your husband. "Good morning, doctor," said Prof. Church.

Nora seems to have bonded with Lindsay Black and didn't hesitate to ask where Lindsay Black went because she's the doctor attending to her husband.

"Lindsay is the doctor on night shift, and I'm the doctor on morning duty," said Dr. Parks.

"I didn't see you the other time my husband was here, are you a new doctor or what?" asked Nora.

Ryan Perks told Nora he was on holiday during her husband's previous visit to the hospital, but he heard about her husband's attack. Nora smiled as she tried making light of her line of questioning, and she then said she's just being curious. "From your husband's file, he's being treated for snake bite, which we intend to continue, and the scan results showed multiple fractures around his shoulder," said Dr. Parks.

Nora's nightmare is that her husband could end up with a bent posture and this new twist kept her thinking as she hopes Doctor Shekuh is wrong this time, and she anxiously asked Doctor Ryan if her husband's posture could be affected as the doctor in Zimbabwe projected.

"Yes, there's a likelihood his posture might be affected, let's see how it turns out to be," said Dr. Perks.

"How bad will this be, doctor?" asked Nora.

The doctor did all he could to assuage Nora of her fears as he urged her to be positive about this whole thing, and just hope for a good outcome. The doctor finished with Nora and then began administering treatment on the professor. The professor spent three months in the hospital because he was moved to the physiotherapy department where he spent quite a considerable time receiving treatment. It's now time for the professor to be discharged from hospital and while Nora and her children were at home seated at the table having breakfast, she urged them to come to the hospital with her.

Joe had a toast in one hand and a cup of tea on the other. "Why do we've to join you today, and what's special about today?" he asked.

"Your dad is being discharged from the hospital today, let's welcome him home," said Nora.

"Mum, you know I have to be in school, and you're suggesting I join you to the hospital?" asked Eileen.

"I've some catching up to do with my friends, and I'm sorry I can't join you," said Joe.

Nora felt quite alone, helpless and frustrated and asked Eileen and Joe if they both entered into a pact of some sort, not to visit your dad. Eileen unblinkingly retorted to her mum and reminded her not make them look like the guilty party and if for anything their dad is the guilty party here because he knowingly put himself in the hospital.

"Isn't it absurd that your dad has been in the hospital here in New York for the past three months and none of you cared to visit him?" asked Nora.

"You might say it's absurd, but I don't care what he thinks about us," said Eileen.

Nora urged her children to put this behind them and move on because resentment holds people back. Sadly, Eileen has been hurting inside, and she suddenly began to sob as she made it clear to her mum that her dad has moved on, it's them that needs help, and reminded her if she knew what their dad's actions has done to them. Joe made Nora's hope grimier as he said he doesn't have a single tear to shed for his dad and even if the news of his death comes right now, he won't feel for him.

"I know how hard this has been for us, yet we must find a way of moving past this," said Nora.

Joe became cheeky with his mum and Nora isn't one to get cheeky with, but Joe did anyway, as he said he has written his dad out of his mind the moment he returned to the wild after the first attack. He touched a nerve when he erroneously said he doesn't have any business with his dad, and that his friend just hinted him that he has written a eulogy in case his dad dies in the wild. Joe's rudeness has now gone off the rails, and his mum insists his bitter indignation towards his dad doesn't give him the right to get flat out rude about his dad in her face.

Joes' comment touched a nerve and it came at a time when Nora was in no mood for a joke from this clown of a son. "What do you mean, you've written a eulogy for your dad?" asked Nora.

"Mum, you don't have to be furious, it's dad that actually wants to kill himself," said Eileen. "Ok, this session is over," said Nora.

CHAPTER

NINE

The Zombie

By evening of that day, it's now time for Professor Church to return home. Doctor Maisie Kyle walked into the ward. "Professor, the nurse is preparing the paperwork for your discharge," said Nora.

Despite spending some considerable time in therapy, the professor's posture remains a concern that Nora needed to address, she then asked the doctor if there's a planned outpatient therapy to help with her husband's posture. "His posture isn't a good sight," said Nora. The doctor reminded Nora that she hinted her at the beginning of the physio that this was to be expected. "Does it mean once I am discharged, that's it?" asked Prof. Church.

"Yes, that's it, but we will give you some medication to help with the pain, and we'll recommend some exercises," said Dr. Kyle.

"How can my husband be out and about looking like this? His posture looks like a joke," said Nora.

Maisie Kyle tried to put Nora's worries to rest as she reminded her that this doesn't mean the end of the world for her husband, and that even though he's a bit bent, this doesn't stop the professor from enjoying a normal life. The news was a bit disappointing, and this left the professor making unsolicited excuses as he said he knew there are risks associated with the wild, but he didn't see this coming. "You're lucky to be alive, at least you escaped a Lion's jaw," said Nora.

Maisie Kyle sensed the need to urge the professor to please make sure he takes his medication as prescribed and if he feels unwell, he should come to the hospital immediately for a follow-up. "Ok doctor, we'll do as you've instructed" said Nora.

The doctor leaves, and funnily the couple couldn't help but return to their usual squabbles, as Nora took a swipe at her husband, saying his bent posture is a souvenir from the wild. The professor took the banter on the chin, and instead of reacting to his wife's cheeky comment, he asked about his children, and said they haven't visited since he was admitted. "The fact that they haven't come visiting says it all, and at least you know you aren't a good example of a caring father," said Nora.

The professor tried another line of excuse as he said he knew his children expected him to act differently but he equally expected them to understand him. Unsurprisingly, Nora didn't hesitate to correct her husband as she reminded the professor that he should seek to understand rather than to be understood.

The professor's excuses are being knocked down by his wife at every turn because she considers them lame, and he's now taking up the option of pleading with Nora and his children to under-stand with him in his present circumstance. Sadly, Nora pushed the goal post further as she moved the conversation away from the professor's immediate family to the wider public and asked her husband if he equally expects people to understand, now that his posture is nothing but a spectacle.

The professor smiled as he made light of Nora's reference to his posture and asked his wife if she's implying he now looks like a zombie. Nora scoffed and said she can hear the fat lady singing that her husband's adventure is over, yet he doesn't see it in that light.

"Oh, ask me about it, the combination of a posture like yours and scars all over your body ultimately make you a zombie," Nora retorted.

"I hope the kids are prepared to receive a zombie into the house?" the professor asked jocularly.

"Stop making this as a joke! You've made a mockery out of us and brought so much shame on us," said Nora. Sadly, Nora began to sob again, sending her husband in a guilt trip, and her husband looked away in guilt yet has no regret for pursuing his dream in the wild.

Professor Church is now sober, and his only way of showing remorse is by saying he know his life has been characterised by progress and regress during this period of his expedition in the wild. "Your family has been under attack by the press because of your crazy expedition, go through media reports and see the barrage of negative reporting against your family," said Nora.

The professor chuckled at Nora's unnecessary focus on what the press had to say and didn't hesitate to tell Nora the media can continue their spurious remarks about him, and he isn't perturbed about that. He was however thankful to Nora for going through thick and thin with him but held onto his passion for the wild because he isn't much of a liar and not a drifter either.

"You've put your family through so much trauma, your actions are tantamount to wickedness," said Nora.

Moments later the nurse stepped into the ward to finish the process of the professor's discharge, and moments after the nurse left them to themselves, they quickly returned to their bickering.

The professor felt frustrated and plagued by Nora's constant nagging as he passively tried reminding her that all she does is to exploit every opportunity to discredit his interest in the wild. Nora smiled for the first time that day as she put the conversation back into the right perspective and reminded her husband that the crux of the matter is about him being an advocate rather than being a clown.

"Why this tittering! And when did you become a woman with a short fuse?" asked Prof. Church.

"What suggests I have a short fuse?" asked Nora.

The professor was quite upfront in his accusation yet seems to forget that his constant pushing of his wife's button will eventually turn her into a person with a short fuse. He rhetorically put Nora in the spotlight, as he reminded her that her demand for divorce, her constant nagging and continuous sobbing, and a myriad of others too numerous to mention are indications of her fuse being shortened.

"You're completely delusional and selfish," said Nora.

"I'm not selfish, but sometimes I've lost my cool when it relates to the wild," said Prof. Church.

Even as she packs up their bags in readiness to return home, their squabble didn't abate, as Nora continue to hold her husband's feet to the fire. She insisted that these repeated attacks have exposed his sheer witlessness on the most rudimentary of matters as it relates to the wild.

Professor Church has been stuck at home since his discharge from the hospital and the ambience at home has been quite humid and sadly his isolation within his home remained because of the unspoken animosity between him and his family. The professor's worries aren't just limited to his household but his inability to integrate back to the society as the scars and his current posture automatically makes him an outcast. It's now a week after the professor's discharge from the hospital and in one of the evenings, the professor asked his son Joe to assist him with some of the recommended exercises which is part of his therapy. Sadly, Joe walked past his dad, and told him sorry he can't be of any help to him and urged him to get the Rhinos and Hippos to help him out. As expected, Nora lost it because Joe's flagrant use of words got her hopping mad with her son, and this disrespect for his dad might mean he's obviously getting the short end of the stick from his mum who now finds him insufferable.

"Joe, I forbid you to say things like that, you should be able to help your dad out," said Nora.

"Dad cares about those animals more than us, we're worth nothing to him, he should get them to spend time with him," said Joe.

Unsurprisingly, Joe remained stubborn as he seems to be taking the mickey out of his dad, and it seems the professor has had enough of this insolence as he growled at Joe, warning him not to walk out on him because it's rude. Sadly, just as Eileen, Joe was hurting inside, and these tantrums are his only way of expressing his inner hurts. The tantrums from friends is now getting to Joe, and his inability to manage his friends banter meant he's now lashing out at his sick dad. The professor looked on in anger, and the expression in his face looks like he's about to knocking his son's lights out, yet he constrained himself. Eileen decided to speak up in defence of her brother, and asked her dad if he thinks he can just come here, use them and dump them like he did the other time.

"What are you talking about?" asked Nora.

"Dad is just here to use us, when he's back on his feet, he'll return to the wild," said Eileen. Arguably, Nora's ability to tame her children's protest seems to have lost steam, and Joe suddenly walked back into the conversation, and told his dad he owes him nothing.

"Where's all this scorn coming from! And what have I done to deserve this bitterness?" asked Prof. Church.

Joe tried to make his dad understand the enormity of his actions by referring him to the headlines for him see for himself what the press has said about them, and maybe he then will understand how much he has hurt them. "Sorry to disappoint you, dad, you can't have your cake and eat it," said Eileen.

Nora quickly tried to put an end to the biter conversation, as she told her children this session is over and she doesn't want to hear anymore about this.

After month of prolong isolation Professor Church felt the best he could do to get his life back is returning to the world that understands him, a world he knows best, and that means returning to the wild, so he gave Jonas a phone call.

"Hello Jonas, how're you?" asked Prof. Church.

"I'm fine. Professor, is that you?" asked Jonas.

"Of course, Jonas, it's me. It's been quite a while and how is everybody, your dad, your mum, all of them?" asked Prof. Church.

"They're all doing great, and I hope your wife is doing good as well?" asked Jonas.

After exchanging pleasantries and the usual catching up that happens between friends who have lost touch for a while, the professor went straight to the point and hit the nail on the head, as he told Jonas he's coming over to Zimbabwe.

"To do what, if I may ask?" asked Jonas.

The professor told Jonas he will be in Zimbabwe in two weeks time, and he's returning to the wild because he no longer has a place in regular society. Sadly for the professor, Jonas seems to have had enough of the professor, and he isn't playing a part in it anymore. He quickly interjected and advised the professor that returning to the wild isn't a good idea. After all, he just narrowly cheated death for the second time. The conversation took a funny twist as the professor saw an opportunity for jokes and reminded Jonas that the fact that he's able to cheat death twice means dying in the wild isn't for him, he then became jocular and said he intends to continue pursuing his dream because he's now convinced that there isn't any certain inevitability that his adventure in the grassland of Africa will have a fatal end.

"But I don't think I'll want to work with you anymore," said Jonas.

"I know you haven't been properly rewarded, and I'll make it up to you this time," said Prof. Church.

"Sorry to disappoint you, no amount of money will make me part of your spectacle," said Jonas.

"What are you insinuating?" asked Prof. Church.

"Forget about me, and forget about the wild," advised Jonas.

Professor Church was irked by Jonas's bluntness and this got the professor kicking off, and he didn't hesitate to put Jonas in his place by reminding Jonas it isn't up to him to tell him about what to forget. He sternly reminded Jonas that if he can't make himself useful, then he will get somebody else.

Jonas immediately began talking tough, as he asked the professor to look for somebody else and let him be, Jonas then ended the phone the call.

Immediately after his conversation with the professor, Jonas dialled Nora who was in the bedroom to intimate her of the professor's motive. "Hello madam, this is Jonas," he said.

"Err.., Jonas, good to hear from you. Sorry, I haven't called you to say a proper thank you," said Nora.

"No problem, madam, your husband just called me now and he said he's coming over," said Jonas.

Jonas's comments struck a chord in Nora, and it was as if she was hit by a ton of bricks, and she's automatically thrown into confusion as it now dawns on her that her family is practically going to disintegrate. She quickly asked Jonas, "coming over to where? I don't understand what you mean," asked Nora.

"Your husband said he's returning to the wild and I just told him I'm no longer working for him," said Jonas. Nora's disposition changed immediately, and she queried further. "What! You mean my husband wants to return to the wild?" asked Nora.

"Yes madam, I've told him I'm not interested, and he said he'll get somebody else to work with him," said Jonas.

Nora quickly concluded the conversation with Jonas and thanked him for intimating her about her husband's next move. She then without hesitation got up from bed and left the bedroom and walked straight to meet her husband in his study area. She immediately asked him if he just called Jonas.

"Have you been eavesdropping on my conversation?" asked Prof. Church.

"I don't care what you think; Jonas just called me now to tell me of your silly conversation," she said.

"Oh, you now have an alliance with Jonas, and why do you have to do that?" asked Prof. Church.

With her disposition like that of a poisoned dog, Nora immediately returned to her usual nagging self as she told her husband that it's now obvious that Joe and Eileen are right about him. She looked straight at her husband and asked if this is what she gets for all her troubles, rescuing him from the African grassland and nursing him back to health.

Professor Church stood up to show vigour as a way to prove he's fine and back to health but didn't stop short of putting the conversation in the right perspective as he told his wife he's now back on his feet just that he looked cutely different because of the scars.

"Oh, the look of a zombie as you descried your look earlier?" asked Nora.

Unsurprisingly, the professor hit the nail on the head as he told Nora he doesn't think he belongs to the civilised society anymore, and his new look further justifies the need for him to return to the wild. This always-looking scholarly professor has now completely turned rustic and his cuteness has gone with the wind. "Your curiosity will be satiated when this trip of yours ends in derision," said Nora.

"I don't know you to be a prophet of doom," said Prof. Church.

Nora's anger seems to be building up inside of her as the professor continues his attempts to justify his moves. She became teary and asked why he's doing this, and if he truly cares about her and her children.

"Why would you say a thing like that? I care about them, but lately, the wild has taken priority," said Prof. Church.

"Then the wildlife comes first before your kids?" asked Nora.

The professor began pleading like a baby asking for a candy bar, as he pleaded with Nora to let him return to the wild and continue with his dream in the wild because he just can't sit at home looking droopy and flabby. Nora has a perfect response to this bleak situation as she suddenly became very courteous, and all smiles. She then told her husband she will speak to her lawyers to serve him the divorce papers so he can sign them before running back to the wild.

"But I'm still in love with you, and why would you want to do that?" asked Prof. Church.

"At least people won't judge me if I look away when you suffer the next attack," said Nora.

"Let's not emphasize on the negatives, please," said Prof. Church.

Nora continued her previous line of conversation of wanting to get a divorce, as she insisted that they both go their separate ways so he can bear the cost of his foolishness without dragging her along. Her subtle request for divorce is a new addition to the mix as she now shifted the goal post further, and she has now decided that the sticking plaster approach of making the problem go away by going to Africa to rescue her husband hasn't worked.

Professor Church is now faced with a subtle threat, one which Nora might likely act upon. He's now in a bind and pleaded with Nora to please rethink her threat and not allow her impulse to take the best of her.

Nora didn't sleep all through that night as she tries to set her priorities right and protect her sanity but decided to intimate her husband's closest friend of her decision to quit her marriage. Nora felt it's best to make it a face to face conversation, and decided to visit Professor Stone Walker. She arrived at Professor Walker's home and walked straight to the door but stopped momentarily and stood for a while, wiped her face and then knocked the door. "Is anybody home, hello, is anybody in the house?" asked Nora.

Professor Walker opened the door. "Yes, there's someone in the house because we knew you were coming," he said. Nora laughed. "Hello Walker," said Nora.

"Hello Nora, you're welcome, please come inside," said Prof. Walker.

"Where's everybody?" Nora asked jocularly.

"Gloria just rushed out to get groceries while the kids are still in school," said Prof. Walker.

Nora sat down as she makes herself comfortable, and asked Professor Walker to get her a glass of water. A minute later, he got her a glass of water, and asked Nora if she's ok, then asked about her husband who has turned into a strange character of late.

"From my countenance, you'll know everything isn't ok, because he's at it again," said Nora.

"Your husband! Is he planning on returning to the wild?" asked Prof. Walker.

Nora didn't hesitate to let Walker know that her husband is actually returning to the wild, but also laid it bare to him that the moment she leaves his house she going to speak to her lawyer because she's getting a divorce.

"Why is he doing this? But Nora, that shouldn't be the best way to handle this," said Prof. Walker.

"What other way is there, I want to cut the strings tying me to him. So, if anything happens to him, nobody will look my direction," said Nora.

Professor Walker turned to Nora who seem distracted and asked her to look at him to get her attention, and he then asked Nora if she still loves her husband. He urged Nora to consider other options but divorce, as a way around this.

"Yes, of course, I love my husband but I'm tired of this, and I don't have any strength left for this," she replied.

The thought of a divorce got Professor Walker all riled up as he began finding a way to save his friend's marriage and didn't hesitate to let Nora know that divorce isn't the answer. Professor Walker brought in a logic that would make Nora reconsider her move as he told her if she divorces her husband, it means she has given him the impetus to run back into the wild and remain there.

"He can do whatever he wants after the divorce, I wouldn't really care," said Nora.

After spending some time trying to reason a way of dealing with Professor Church's next move into the wild, Professor Walker suddenly thought to himself that since all that matters to Professor Church is being around wildlife, what if they arrange for him to work in the zoo here in New York.

"Oh, that isn't a bad idea and I never thought of that before, are you sure he'll go with this suggestion?" asked Nora.

Professor Walker foresees a situation where his friend could get carried away if left alone, and run into the big cat's cage. He then suggested that they arrange for him to be with Zebras, giraffes and the elephants but not the big cats.

"Oh, you just addressed another fear that came to my mind," said Nora.

"Yes of course, with zebra and giraffe even if he gets carried away and enters their cage, he might still be safe," said Nora.

Gloria walked into the house while Nora and her husband were busy discussing a way around Professor Church's' current debacle. "Oh Nora, you're here already," said Gloria.

"Of course, Gloria, Walker told me you went to shop for some groceries," said Nora.

"Yes, how're you and the children, what about your husband?" asked Gloria.

Nora quickly dispensed of all the pleasantries and went straight to the point and told Gloria her children are fine but her husband is preparing to run off to the wild again, and that's what she's discussing with Walker.

Gloria thinks Professor Church's case is more of a psychiatric case as she reiterated her earlier comment, insisting that Professor Pratt Church is now a social menace and his obsession for the wild isn't just within the context of animal rights, but an untamed passion for wildlife. Gloria didn't hesitate to remind Nora that she'll frown at any recourse to her usual ways of handling this issue.

"You're right, Gloria. That was why I suggested getting a divorce as the only way out," said Nora.

Funnily, divorce isn't the kind of solution Gloria is suggesting, all she wanted is for Nora think of addressing the problem with outside help. Unsurprisingly, Nora seems lost because she has no idea about what Gloria is suggesting she do to break this cycle of twists and turns that's causing her heartbreak. Gloria thinks Nora can continue in this approach until the cows come home, stressing that unless she does things differently this cycle will continue.

"I expect you to get on your knees and pray for your family, seek divine intervention," said Gloria.

"My family don't go to church, and I know your husband doesn't go to church either, but do you go to church?" asked Gloria.

"I go to church, Nora. Don't mind Walker with his political correctness, we wives pray more than priests to keep our husbands and kids safe," said Gloria.

"Oh my God, but most professors I know aren't Christians," said Nora.

Gloria introduced faith into the mix and told Nora that most Professors would say they don't go to church, but they enjoy the cover of a praying wife who's always on their knees praying for them.

"I didn't know you go to church, Gloria, but I thought you're just some kind passive Christian," said Nora.

"I've never missed church, I'm on my knees every day praying for the safety of my husband and children, and one thing most mothers in America do is pray," said Gloria.

"I can't remember praying, what do I say when I come before God in prayer?" asked Nora.

"Just go before him and open your mouth, just say whatever you want him to do for you, he hears," said Gloria.

Nora took Gloria's advice on board as she pursues the plan she just hatched with Professor Walker to get her husband a place in the New York zoo, at least, to prevent him from running off to the grassland of Africa.

CHAPTER

TEN

The lecturer, the zoo keeper

Professor Stone Walker and Nora's first point of call is the New York Zoo as they meet with Morgan Benson, the manager in charge of the zoo to seek his help with Professor Church. Funnily, the moment Morgan Benson sets his eyes on Nora there was a flicker of recognition. "Hello, Nora Church, you're welcome to my office?" said Morgan. He then turned to Professor Walker and welcomed him as well.

Nora was surprised at how Morgan Benson knew her name and didn't hesitate to ask how he knew her name because she never met him before. Interestingly, Morgan told Nora he attended most of her husband's seminars on animal rights, and he does see her with him most of the times he attended. Sadly, Morgan didn't stop short of reminding Nora that her husband's present fame now makes every American know more about him and his family.

"What do you mean by his present fame?" she curiously asked.

Unsurprisingly, Morgan didn't chew his words before spitting them out as he decided to hit the nail on the head and told Nora that the idea of living in the wild and always being attacked makes those who believes in her husband to have a rethink.

Nora by her nature is highly irritable, and particularly not overly fond of people who are muggy to her face, and derogatory comments like this one will only add insult to her injury as she immediately became furious. Funnily, Nora got so wrapped up dealing with careless comments forgetting she came to seek favours from the same person, and she didn't hesitate to join issues by accusing Morgan of being among those saying vile things about her family.

Professor Walker taps Nora to calm her down and quickly introduce himself as Professor Stone Walker, and then told Morgan they need his help.

"What help do you seek, Professor?" asked Morgan.

Professor Walker told Morgan that Professor Pratt Church is his friend and about to return to the wild, but they want him to give Professor Church a job to stop him from returning to the wild.

"Hell no! I can't do that; do you want him to kill himself here and people will crucify me for employing a mentally disturbed person?" said Morgan. Sadly, things quickly went sour as Nora took exception with Morgan's poor choice of word in his qualification of the professor in the presence of his wife.

"What an insult! And did you just call my husband mentally disturbed?" asked Nora.

"Mrs Church, what do you think people think of him?" asked Morgan.

Nora knew quite well what people think and she will remain in denial until the cows come home, but she told Morgan she doesn't care about what people think of her husband and Morgan doesn't have to say it to her face. Unsurprisingly, Morgan apologised for not choosing his words carefully but insists he believes Nora understands what he meant.

"Please do us this favour, Benson. If this man was your mentor at one time, then contribute to his restoration," said Prof. Walker.

"This is a bitter pill you're asking to swallow, and how do you suggest I go about this?" asked Morgan.

Professor Walker pleaded with Morgan to make sure Professor Church has nothing to do with the big cats, and rather his role should be limited to the zebras, giraffes and elephants. At least his safety will be assured.

Morgan was touched and felt the need to help, but stressed he's doing this for the professor and not for her, saying she's too explosive. Nora felt relieved, but then apologised saying she's sorry, if he thinks she exploded on him.

Now that the working in the zoo thing has worked out, Nora then suggested to Professor Walker that working in the zoo alone might create a whiplash effect on her husband and suggested he gets his lecturing job back to prevent burnout. Nora and Professor Walker brainstormed and came up with the idea to visit the vice chancellor's office to give steam to the idea.

Professor Scowl welcomed Nora into her office but was lost as to the purpose of the visit, and the first thing that comes to mind was that something is wrong with his former employee. "Nora Church, how're you doing, and is Pratt ok?" asked Prof Scowl.

"Professor, you know already that Pratt Church isn't ok and that's why we're here," said Prof. Walker.

"What's it about him? This University doesn't have funds to donate to assist a man running around in the mist of wildlife," said Prof Scowl.

Professor Walker quickly interjected and told Professor Scowl they didn't visit him for the purposes of fund raising. Professor Walker chuckled, then continued and said the purpose of their visit is to prevent Pratt from returning to the wild.

"How do I fit into your plan? Because I've had enough of him," said Prof. Scowl.

"We just secured a part time job for him at the zoo, where he can have a feel of the wildlife and still be with his family," said Prof. Walker.

Professor Scowl was quite pleased to hear of this development because he considers this a sensible way of keeping Professor Church on a tight leash and out of harm's way. He congratulated Nora for the success and asked them to get on with it but he doesn't think they needed him to get that going.

"We want you to offer him a job in the university, to help him return to his old lifestyle," said Nora.

"What? That won't be possible, his resignation has been processed and he has already claimed his entitlement," said Prof. Scowl.

Professor Walker interjected again and pleaded with Professor Scowl to please give Professor Church a part time job, maybe a two days a week lecturing job, at least his lecturing skills and experience aren't in doubt. This is a big ask for Professor Scowl who also had a lot to get off his chest concerning Professor Church as he told Nora he considered Pratt a man that's quite assuming, and has attained certain level of intelligence and altruism, but he's surprised at how he blatantly burnt his own bridges.

"Professor, we're here on a salvage mission, please, just do what you can to help," said Prof Walker.

Serendipitously, Professor Scowl told Nora that the University currently needs a part time lecturer at the moment, but he doesn't think Pratt is the right person for the job. Nora saw an opportunity to exploit, and now increased her plea for help as she told professor Scowl, she's only trying to get her family together.

It's now obvious to the Vice Chancellor that the much talked about wild adventure of Professor Church is nothing but a sting in the tail. Professor Scowl remained silent for a while as he considers the implication of having Professor Pratt back without tying himself in knots, and after a while, he promised to help, then cautioned that if Pratt comes up with any drama he would have to let him go.

"Ok, Professor, thank you," said Prof Walker.

"Professor, this means a lot to me, thank you very much," said Nora.

The Vice Chancellor sensed this mission is more about damage control but needed them to clarify how they intend to go about this.

"Is Pratt aware of this, does he know you're here?" asked Prof Scowl.

"No, he doesn't, we intend to put him in the picture when all is set," said Prof Walker.

Professor Scowl told Nora he would like to see Professor Church before this week is out to discuss his employment further. Now that a lot has been put in place to prevent Pratt Church from returning to the wild, it's now time to sell the idea to him. Nora and Professor Stone Walker then sat him down to talk things through. Unsurprisingly, Professor Pratt sensed Walker is here to stop him from going to Africa since this visit is coming on the heels of his latest disagreement with his wife over his plans to return to the wild. Professor Church who has remained the underdog in all of this decided to remain calm and tried making the conversation seamless with his friend to see where he's headed, to avoid tying himself in knots too soon. "Hello Walker, it's been a while, how're Gloria and the kids?" asked Prof. Church.

"We're fine, and how're you doing? I'm made to believe you're already feeling better," said Walker.

Professor Church tried making light of the situation with banter as he told Professor Walker he's now feeling better but with a bent posture. "Tell me about it, people are aware that you had an accident that affected your posture and that's why you look the way you do," said Prof. Walker.

Professor Pratt Church saw this line of conversation as an opportunity to state his case and told Professor Walker that this accident coupled with the scars from these attacks gives him the perfect look for a man who should be in the wild. Professor Walker looked on as his fellow professor stated his case, like him or loath him, he's a man with a ravishing appetite for the freedom the wild offers.

Nora quickly interjected and said she has suggested a skin graft, to help with those scars, but her husband was too busy running around in the wild. Just as the man with the magic wand, Professor Walker went on to hit the nail on the head and authoritatively told Professor Church he isn't going back to the wild any time soon.

"Why? That decision is for me to make, not yours, Walker," said Prof. Church.

Professor Walker felt there isn't any need to belabour this matter further and without hesitation he handed Professor Church the employment letters from the zoo and the university. "We've secured employment for you at the zoo, where you'll enjoy some closeness with wildlife," said Prof. Walker.

Sadly, Professor Church's dream is about the freedom of roaming the wild in the mist of wildlife roaming freely in their natural habitat. Freedom is a priced commodity in the eyes of this professor, and the wild is just the right place to act it out in full glare. He blatantly told Professor Walker that the experience in the wild and that of the zoo aren't the same and being held back will give poachers the opportunity to have a free reign in the forest.

Nora finds her husband's excuses as a misnomer and didn't hesitate to slap it down the sucker pit. She quickly reminded her husband he never lasted more than a day in the wild before being rushed home and asked him how many poachers he has been able to stop.

She felt that by now her husband must be reeling from the trauma of the leopards attack, and even the venom of the black mamba, yet she's surprised at his unwavering pursuit of his dream in the grassland of Africa.

"We went to a great deal of trouble to get you these offers, take it for the sake of your wife and children," said Nora. Interestingly, Professor Church's hardened position begins to thaw as he gave thought to the offer placed before him. Meanwhile, while this conversation persists, Eileen stood in the shadow hoping that these offers will pacify her dad to stay with them.

"The zoo thing is how many days a week?" asked Prof. Church.

"You'll work three days a week and lecture two days a week, then spend the rest of your week with your family," said Prof. Walker.

The offer of hanging around in the corridors of the zoo when compared with the extensive freedom of co-habiting alongside wildlife in their natural habitat isn't anything but fraud. For all it's worth, a bird at hand is worth two in the bush, and in fairness, this professor hasn't lasted more than a day in the wild.

"Ok, I'll give it a try, provided I've an opportunity for some quality time with the wildlife in the zoo," said Prof. Church.

Eileen rushed into the living room. "Dad, will you accept the offer?" she asked.

"Yes, for your sake, for your brother's sake and for your mum's sake," said Prof. Church.

Eileen felt so excited and quickly laid all animosities towards her old man aside, she then thanked her dad for considering the offer, and sadly, Joe wasn't at home when the offer was presented to his dad, because he doesn't think the offers are convincing enough to make his dad change the course of his adventure.

"You'll need to meet with Prof Scowl within the week for briefing," said Prof. Walker.

"Walker, thank you," said Prof. Church.

Days later, Nora accompanied her husband to the Vice Chancellor's office to conclude conversation around his part-time lecturing job offer. Funnily, it's been quite a while since the pair saw each other, and their last meeting was the day of Professor Church's resignation before kicking off his wildlife adventure.

"How're you, Pratt! It's been a while and why do you look like that?" asked Prof. Scowl.

"I know my new look will surprises you," said Prof. Church.

"I'm just taken aback, you look bent and with too many scars, making you to look scary, sort of," said Prof. Scowl.

Professor Church was upfront with the fact that he knew the Vice Chancellor never expected his scars to be this much, but this is now his new reality. Professor Scowl suddenly began having doubts as to the suitability of having Professor Church in the classroom as he told him he looks too scary and it won't look good enough having him in the lecture room. He's now rethinking the decision to employ Professor Church. Sadly, Professor Church argued that his looks have nothing to do with the message he'll deliver to the students.

"Your looks could be a distraction for the students, and why don't you go for a skin graft?" asked Prof. Scowl.

Nora quickly interjected to salvage the situation and told Professor Scowl they've arranged for a skin graft procedure, but that'll be in three months' time.

"I would've suggested he enters the lecture room after the skin graft procedure," said Prof. Scowl.

"Professor, you know why we're doing this, I don't want him returning to the wild, just let him resume and the skin graft procedure will follow," assured Nora.

Professor Church finds Nora's characterization of him to be belittling and gave a subtle word of caution and asked her to stop describing him as somebody staging a theatrical show. Pratt Church isn't some guy looking all scruffy in the street. He was a professor that commands the respect of his peers. Though, his present state makes him laughable, yet he once admonished his Vice Chancellor demanding he show him some respect because he soon will be referring to him as his guest. Sadly, the table didn't really turn as he'd hopped because he's now thankfully accepting whatever crumbs that falls off the hands of this Vice Chancellor whom he once loathed and finds insufferable.

"Ok Pratt, you'll resume next week, but I encourage you to go for a skin graft," said Prof. Scowl.

"Thank you, professor. I'm truly grateful," said Nora.

A week later, it's now time for Professor Pratt Church to return to the classroom, it felt a bit strange retuning to the classroom after a while but the university environment is one he's used to and can thrive in.

Prof. Church: Good morning class.

The professor walked into the class looking bent and scary as he stood in the front of the class like somebody who has come to stage a pantomime. Immediately the professor walked into the classroom the students burst into laughter, because that was the first time many of them had set eyes on the professor since he resigned.

Prof. Church: Good morning class, why don't you stop the noise?

The laughter continued until the professor became frustrated and left.

Two days later, Professor Pratt Church returned for his second lecture, this time the professor's looks isn't news to the students any more, the students laughed for a moment but quickly became calm enough to have their lecture.

Professor Church later did a skin graft to help with the scars, but his posture remains bent, he remains a part time lecturer and still works with the zoo where he enjoys some closeness with the animals and also spends time with his family.